SHADOWS OF THE FORGOTTEN

THE SHADOWS SERIES BOOK 1

John D. Clay

John D. Clay Books

Shadows of the Forgotten
© 2025 by John D. Clay
All rights reserved.

Cover and Interior Design © 2025 by John D. Clay Books
Cover Image © 2025 by John D. Clay Books
Interior Layout © 2025 by John D. Clay Books

Published by John D. Clay Books
ISBN: 979-8-9924541-0-9 (tr. pbk.)
Printed in the United States of America

First Trade Paperback Edition

For more information, visit:
www. johndclay.com

To Linda C.,

For your unwavering support and endless inspiration.

John D. Clay

Contents

Before the shadows

The city hummed with life. Its skyline gleamed under the warm embrace of the sun, a sprawling expanse of silver and glass stretching endlessly into the sky.

Streets bustled with people, their laughter blending with the rhythmic sounds of distant trains and the hum of electric cars. Children's voices echoed in the parks, where towering trees stood as guardians of a world brimming with possibility.

Allen loved these streets. He would stroll through the vibrant markets on his way to work, surrounded by the scent of freshly brewed coffee and the comforting smells of baking bread and sizzling street food.

People nodded and said hello—neighbors, coworkers, and even strangers, all familiar faces in a community where everyone knew each other. It was a world where smiles came easily, and the only shadows cast were those of the trees in the park.

He had a routine back then. Morning runs along the riverbanks, his sneakers crunching against gravel as he chased the rising sun. Evenings spent at the local bar with friends, their conversations filled with dreams, plans, and debates about the future.

And then there was the woman—her name hovered at the edge of memory like a song almost forgotten. She had a laugh that could light up the darkest corners of his world, and he would've done anything to protect her.

The city, his city, was alive, free, and full of promise.

But freedom has a way of being taken for granted.

The signs were subtle at first—a campaign promising security, a new initiative touting "progress and stability." Techno-Synth had been a name whispered in boardrooms, celebrated for its groundbreaking innovations. People welcomed the company's vision, blind to the darkness gathering on the horizon. Even Allen, sharp as he was, couldn't see it coming. Not then.

As the sun dipped below the skyline, casting orange and blue across the sky, Allen would often pause to admire the view from his apartment window. He never imagined it would one day be different—that the laughter, the trust, and the life that defined it would be smothered beneath cold, mechanical precision.

These were the good times.

And they were about to end.

Chapter 1

The first sensation that struck Allen was the cold pavement against his cheek, like a hand trying to drag him into the abyss. He jolted awake, his muscular frame tensing as a sharp, pulsating headache throbbed behind his eyes. He struggled to sit up, groaning in pain and confusion.

"What the...where am I?" he muttered, cradling his head in his hands. The sound of his own voice seemed alien to him, swallowed by an eerie silence that enveloped the surroundings.

Allen's piercing blue eyes darted around, taking in the desolation before him. The cracked street beneath him stretched out like a spider's web, reaching towards the towering ruins of skyscrapers that loomed oppressively over the abandoned street. Their once-gleaming surfaces were now scarred and ravaged, their broken windows staring back at him like the hollow eyes of the dead.

A faded digital billboard caught his eye, its neon lights flickering weakly above a collapsed building. The remnants of a once-glorious message were barely legible: "Unity and Order for All—Techno-Synth, Your Future." Below it, a defiant streak of graffiti had been hastily scrawled: "Lies." Allen frowned. The message stirred something unsettling in his memory, but the connection slipped away like sand through his fingers.

Something's not right, he thought, his brow furrowing and his lips pressing into a thin line. He racked his brain for answers, but the intense headache clouded his thoughts, leaving only fragments of memories and a gnawing sense of dread.

As he surveyed the ruins, Allen noticed the streets were littered with the skeletal remains of vehicles, their corroded frames a grim testament to a world that once thrived. Neglected storefronts stood eerily silent, surrounded by debris that was once merchandise, now just scattered remnants. Through the jagged gaps where doors once stood, he saw a chaotic jumble of overturned shelves and dust-covered counters, a silent scene of a world left behind.

The echo of Allen's heavy breathing was the only sound punctuating the oppressive silence, a stark reminder of his solitude in this dystopian cityscape. He tried to recall what this place had once been, but the familiar landmarks were twisted and distorted beyond recognition, leaving him feeling utterly lost.

"Think, damn it!" he hissed to himself, frustration boiling within him. "How did I get here?"

But the answers remained elusive, disappearing as quickly as they came. He knew one thing for certain: he couldn't stay here, exposed and vulnerable. He needed to find shelter and gather his thoughts. Clenching his jaw, he pushed himself to his feet, swaying momentarily as the world spun around him.

As Allen steadied himself, a faint sound echoed in the distance—a voice, distorted and warped, broadcast from some hidden speaker. "Techno-Synth: Keeping You Safe, always." He narrowed his eyes. The words felt like more than just noise. There was an emptiness in them, like a machine pretending to care.

Had this been normal once? Had people believed this propaganda? A fragment of a memory tugged at him, but it was lost in the haze of his mind. Despite the disorientation and his pounding headache, Allen's determination began to emerge, fueled by an unwavering commitment to uncover the truth. He knew that somewhere in this desolate city lay the answers he sought – and he would do whatever it took to find them.

Alright, he thought, readying himself for the journey ahead. *Time to get moving.*

With cautious, deliberate movements, he began to navigate the urban wasteland, each step taking him further into the heart of darkness. And as the shadows closed in around him, a single thought echoed through his mind:

"Who am I?"

The wind whistled through the exposed steel frames of the skyscrapers, sending a shiver down his spine as he scanned his surroundings. The desolation was unnerving, but he couldn't shake the feeling that he was being watched. He had to find shelter – and fast.

"Okay, focus," he muttered to himself, eyes darting from one shadowy crevice to another, searching for any signs of danger. As if coming from the depths of his blank mind, suddenly he thought to himself. *This is just like a tactical exercise. Assess the situation, identify potential threats, and adapt.*

As his eyes swept the area again, they caught sight of an alleyway nestled between two crumbling buildings. It appeared to be a perfect hiding spot – dark and secluded yet offering a clear view of the street if someone or something were to approach. With each cautious step towards the alleyway, Allen's muscles tensed, ready to spring into action at the slightest hint of movement or danger. His military training was kicking in, allowing him to move with a silent grace that seemed impossible with his imposing frame.

Stay focused, he reminded himself, his thoughts racing almost as quickly as his heartbeat.

Finally reaching the entrance to the alleyway, he paused for a moment, listening intently for any sound that might betray a hidden threat. Hearing nothing but the distant howl of the wind, he allowed himself a small sigh of relief before slipping into the shadows.

As Allen crouched in the darkness, his mind began to race once more, grappling with the countless questions that plagued him. *Who was he? How did he end up in this forsaken place?* And most importantly, *how could he escape the ever-present feeling of being lost?*

But despite his best efforts, the answers remained tantalizingly out of reach, hidden behind the veil of amnesia that shrouded his mind. And as the shadows deepened around him, he couldn't help but wonder if he would ever unravel the mystery of his past.

Well, only one way to find out, he thought, determination flaring in his eyes. *Got to keep moving and stay alive.*

A sudden, sharp cracking sound shattered the silence, and Allen instinctively dropped to his belly and pressed his body against the ground. His hands were steady despite the adrenaline surging through his veins—a testament to his training—with every sense heightened to its peak performance.

He homed in on the sound, trying to distinguish whether it was a threat or just the city's bones settling more into decay. He stayed still, almost blending into the shadows, his breathing slow and controlled. Beneath him, half-covered in rubble, lay a shattered digital poster. Its fractured surface flickered weakly, showing glimpses of an old newscast. The words flashed by— "Heroes of the State," "Commander Blake's Valor"—before the screen faded to black. The mention of Blake stirred something deep within him, a name that tugged at the edge of his awareness. But as quickly as it came, the thought evaporated, leaving him to focus on the now.

Time seemed to stretch; minutes felt like hours as he waited for another sign. Finally, after an agonizing wait, there was nothing but the whispering wind once again. "False alarm," he muttered under his breath with a mixture of relief and irritation at his jumpiness. But in this new world, paranoia was becoming a survival skill—one that he was rapidly honing.

Rising to a crouch, Allen advanced further out of his shelter into the alley. It twisted and turned like a serpent, leading him deeper into the unknown. As he moved, ghostly images flickered in his mind—a woman's face, a flash of a symbol that made his heart race with an undefined emotion—but they were suddenly gone again, leaving him with more questions than before.

As he struggled to calm his racing thoughts, he scanned the area, alert for any signs of danger. It was then that he noticed it – the gleaming eye of a surveillance camera mounted on a nearby lamppost, its lens sweeping the area methodically.

His heart skipped a beat, and he instinctively ducked behind a pile of debris, peering out with caution. The omnipresent eyes of a corporation that seemingly controlled every inch of the city scanned the area with precision.

Allen knew he needed to disable it. Doing so would give him a temporary blind spot under Techno-Synth's watchful eye and maybe even provide a clue to what they were up to in this wasteland.

"Time to go dark." he said to himself.

He knew the camera's blind spots all too well; the knowledge seemed ingrained in his muscles, an echo of a past that was both familiar and foreign. He waited for the camera to make its mechanical sweep away from him before he moved again, slipping through the blind spot with a predator's precision.

He timed his approach perfectly, climbing quickly, he yanked his tattered jacket over the lens just as it panned in his direction. With the camera temporarily blinded, he took the opportunity to dismantle it, careful not to trigger any silent alarms that might have been set up as a countermeasure.

Allen fiddled with the camera's innards. *Every system has its back doors, its weaknesses,* he thought as he worked. His hands moved with the confidence of someone who had done this countless times before, despite the lingering fog in his memory.

With a final twist, the camera gave a soft whir and went dead, its red recording light winking out like a snuffed flame. For the first time since awakening in this urban tomb, Allen felt a quiver of triumph.

He slid down against the wall to sit on the sidewalk, taking a moment to catch his breath and let the wave of relief wash over him. He couldn't afford to be careless; there would certainly be more cameras, more sensors to evade. But for now, he was invisible to any prying eyes.

The break was short-lived; he knew he couldn't linger in the open for long. He scanned the area once more, searching for any other electronic eyes that might compromise his newfound anonymity. Finding none, he pushed himself to his feet, his mind already strategizing the next move.

He navigated the labyrinth of streets with a cautious agility, every so often pausing to listen or peer around corners. It was during one of these pauses that he leaned back against the cool concrete of a wall, feeling the rough texture against his skin.

Allen's eyes caught the remnants of a painted symbol on the crumbling wall—a crescent moon crossed by a bolt of lightning. It was almost invisible, but he remembered it from somewhere. It was a signal, a marker used by the resistance in the days

before everything had collapsed. The "Voice of the Forgotten."
They had broadcast stories of Techno-Synth's victims, stirring
rebellion in the shadows. Was that still happening now,
somewhere within these ruins?

Closing his eyes, he focused on steadying his breath, finding
solace in the rhythm of inhaling and exhaling. In these small
moments of stillness, he could almost forget the chaos that had
become his reality.

Suddenly, his lungs hitched in his throat as the distant hum of
a drone reverberated through the air. Panic set in — every
muscle tensed, his heart pounding like a drum.

"Shit," Allen whispered, looking about frantically for a hiding
place. The mechanical buzz grew louder, closer, threatening to
expose him. He couldn't afford to be caught, not when there
was still so much to figure out.

An abandoned building loomed nearby, its windows
shattered, and the facade cracked. Allen rushed towards it, the
adrenaline coursing through his veins lending speed to his
powerful stride. His pulse roared in his ears, drowning out the
ever-persistent hum of the approaching drone.

"Please, let there be a safe spot in there," he silently pleaded,
pushing the heavy door open with a creak that seemed
amplified by the dead silence.

Inside, the darkness surrounded him, shielding him from the
outside world. As his eyes adjusted, he spotted a dark room off
to one side — a sanctuary from the relentless pursuit of the
drone. With a sigh of relief, he slipped into the space, his chest
heaving as he fought to catch his breath.

"Close call," he murmured, running a hand through his
tangled dark hair. The pounding in his chest slowed, but the fear
still lingered, a constant companion in this dangerous world.

Can't let my guard down again, he thought, his eyes narrowing with determination. *That's how they get you.*

He listened intently, straining to hear any sign of the drone's departure. As the hum of the drone finally faded into the distance, Allen allowed himself a moment of relief, the weight of his situation settling into his tired bones. He knew there would be no solace until the truth was uncovered. His headache still pounding, he closed his eyes and again practiced his breathing.

When he opened his eyes, they were sharp and clear, reflecting a resolve as unyielding as the broken city around him. Out of the corner of his eye, a glint of light in some debris caught his attention. He quickly turned to get eyes on it. He lost sight of it, then moving his head to the side a little bit he caught it again.

Walking over to the pile hiding the mysterious item, he dug a little bit, pulling out a small digital device—a relic from before Techno-Synth solidified its grip on the world. With a few taps on its cracked screen, he tried to access any local networks that might still be operational, any sliver of information that could give him an edge.

The screen flickered but eventually displayed a series of weak signals—remnants of a once vast and interconnected web. Allen's fingers danced across the surface as he worked to bypass security protocols that had likely not been updated in years.

A map began to materialize onscreen, its lines and contours distorted by time and neglect. He was about to dismiss it when a blink of light caught his attention—a signal transmitting in a pattern that spoke of intention rather than random static. It was a beacon, a call.

Allen's pulse quickened. This could be the break he needed, perhaps a remnant of some underground communication network or even another survivor trying to reach out. The signal's origin was buried in layers of encryption, an old technique, but one Allen recognized. It was familiar—too familiar. Techno-Synth had used a similar tactic, cloaking misinformation campaigns as truth. A trap? Maybe. Or perhaps a remnant of those fighting back, someone using the shadows to spread their own message, just as the rebels had done before the fall.

With practiced precision, he initiated a trace on the signal, staying prepared to sever the connection at any hint of foul play. As the layers of encryption fell away under his persistent probing, a message began to form on the device's screen:

"Rally Point Delta at dawn. Be vigilant."

The words were cryptic yet promising. Rally Point Delta—he vaguely recalled references to such places from his fragmented memories, hidden locations where those opposed to the tyrannical government could meet and share resources.

He glanced up at the sky through the skeletal frames of the building, calculating how much time he had before dawn. Not enough to waste idly; he knew he had to move if he was going to make it. Allen pocketed the device and set out once again, his purpose renewed and his determination rising. With each step towards Rally Point Delta, he could feel the weight of his unknown past and the importance of his near future pressing upon him like the pollution-laden air he breathed.

The city's dead arteries spread out before him, a twisted maze of streets and avenues that once teemed with life. Allen navigated them with a grim familiarity, avoiding the unstable structures and the occasional remnants of Techno-Synth's vicious automatons—silent now, but a stark reminder of the regime's ever-present threat.

The night deepened around him, a blanket of darkness pierced only by the occasional flicker of broken streetlights and hourly broadcasts echoing through hidden speakers and small orb shaped propaganda drones flying high above, the orbs projected holographic messages onto the sides of buildings, some reading "Unity. Safety. Order." And "Together we stand. Trust Techno-Synth.". Allen's senses were fully alert, attuned to the slightest sound or shift in the dark.

As he neared what he presumed to be Rally Point Delta's coordinates, a sense of trepidation gripped him. He slowed his pace, each footstep deliberate and silent. This part of the city seemed different, more intact than the ruins he'd traversed earlier. It was as if this area had been spared the brunt of whatever calamity had befallen the rest.

Chapter 2

A soft glow on the horizon signaled the approach of dawn. Allen stood motionless at the edge of Rally Point Delta, his eyes scanning the gathering below through a crack in the crumbling wall that concealed him. His tall, muscular frame was coiled tight, every sense attuned to the subtlest of shifts in the air, all while his gaze remained fixed on the figures moving stealthily in the dim morning glow.

The meeting, a hushed congregation of weary resistance fighters, had drawn him here. His breath misted softly in the chill air, vanishing as quickly as it appeared, much like the fragments of memories that teased the periphery of his consciousness.

Without warning, the stillness beside him fractured. "Put your hands up!" a voice cut through the quiet, "You're not as invisible as you think," the voice snapped again.

Mia Turner materialized from the shadows aiming her gun, her presence sudden and surprising. The stark morning light played across her angular features, bringing into view the intensity that always lurked within her keen eyes. She scanned Allen with a look that mingled challenge with recognition.

Allen's hands rose slowly and deliberately, as if conceding to gravity's pull. He locked eyes with Mia, his expression unreadable yet undeniably tranquil amidst the threat of her firearm. "I didn't come here for trouble," he said, his voice calm and even.

Mia's grip on the gun didn't waver, but there was a flash of curiosity behind her guarded demeanor. "What did you come for then?" she demanded, her tone sharp and precise.

"A common cause," Allen replied, tilting his head slightly towards the assembly below. "The same shadows that hide you, hide me. But I suppose introductions are overdue—I'm…" Allen paused for a moment, "well I don't actually know who I am."

Her expression remained skeptical, but Mia lowered her weapon a fraction, inching towards cautious acceptance. Suddenly feeling like she might recognize the man, she said, with reserve.

"You don't have a name?"

"I'm not exactly sure to be honest," Allen replied, while staring down the barrel of the automatic rifle holding him at bay. "I woke up yesterday in the middle of this hell hole, and I have no memories, and I have no idea who I am."

Leaning in for a closer look, Mia began to realize that she might be holding a real legend at gunpoint. Her mind raced, trying to figure out how it could possibly be him in the flesh, alive and breathing. Could it be possible he survived?

Mia's head snapped to the north, her eyes narrowing. The silence of the morning shattered by a distant but unmistakable whine—a sound that made Allen's blood run cold. In one fluid motion, she was at his side, her hand gripping his arm with a strength that did not match her frame.

"Drone," she hissed, the word slicing through the still air like a blade.

Allen tensed, instinctively reaching for the weapon he no longer carried. His eyes followed hers, and there it was—an ominous speck in the distance, growing rapidly larger as it approached. The silhouette was all too familiar: a dragon drone, its sensors sweeping for signs of life, for any hint of rebellion against the iron fist of Techno-Synth.

"Come on! We've got to move, now!" Mia's command left no argument, her body already in motion. She had already mapped their escape in her mind, every step and turn calibrated with the precision of a chess grandmaster contemplating the endgame.

With a reluctance born of years spent standing his ground, Allen allowed himself to be pulled from his vantage point. They darted between the shadows of the skeletal buildings, silent except for the soft fall of their boots on the rubble-strewn pavement.

Mia led with an urgency that burned in her dark green eyes, though her breaths came even and measured. Her knowledge of the city's ruins was intimate, a lover's caress guiding them through the twisted arteries of a once-pulsing metropolis.

"Left—now!" Her voice was a whip crack, and Allen obeyed without thought, ducking into the gaping maw of a collapsed storefront. The drone's incessant hum grew louder, a harbinger of destruction so close now that each beat of its rotors sent ripples through the dust at their feet.

"Down." Mia's whisper was a ghost as she swept aside a tattered curtain of vines, revealing a narrow crevice between the fallen debris. They slipped through just as the drone rounded the corner, its shadow passing over the space they had occupied moments before.

They crouched in silence, the drone's searchlight probing the darkness mere inches from their sanctuary. Allen felt the thrum of its engines vibrating through the ground at his feet, the chilling reminder of what awaited them should they be discovered.

But Mia was a ghost in this graveyard of civilization, her presence frozen in time as she held her breath, waiting for the mechanical predator to pass. It did eventually, the sound of its departure a fading buzz.

In the quiet that followed, Allen looked at Mia, her features etched with the grim determination of their predicament. Her quick thinking had saved them both, and as the adrenaline of the moment faded, a newfound respect settled within him. *Who is this girl?* he thought to himself.

"Okay, let's move," Mia whispered, emerging from the dark like a wraith. Her eyes held the fire of resistance. And Allen followed, knowing that in this desolate landscape, trust was not freely given—it was earned.

They traversed the city's streets with a synchronicity born of necessity. Not a word passed between them; the situation demanded silence. But in this speechless exchange, a mutual understanding was cemented—one that acknowledged the gravity of their combined purpose. Mia navigated them through the ruins, her body language articulating directions more clearly than any spoken command.

Allen kept pace, a step behind and slightly to her right, covering angles she couldn't. Though this dance of survival was new to him, his body remembered the steps, a muscle memory that hinted at a history of combat. Something within him responded to Mia's confidence with recognition. It was as if they had fought side by side in another life, one that his fractured memory could not recall.

Eventually, they arrived at an unassuming steel door nestled within the rubble, almost invisible to the untrained eye. Mia paused, glancing back at Allen with a stare that was equal parts warning and reassurance. She pressed her hand against a cold, biometric scanner—contraband tech that had survived the fall. The door clicked open with a sigh, showing its age and disuse.

Inside, the space was surprisingly intact; a bunker of sorts, shrouded in darkness except for the faint blue glow of emergency lights that lined the floor. They descended stairs worn by the passage of desperate feet, delving deeper into what remained of the old world's bones.

The bunker expanded into a wider chamber, where hushed voices and the clinking of metal on metal suggested life persistently enduring against all odds. This was where the heart of the resistance beat strongest, a clandestine symphony of rebellion conducted beneath the tyrant's feet.

Mia gestured to Allen to wait by a rusted pillar as she navigated toward a group of people huddled over maps and screens aglow with data streams. She exchanged short nods and quiet words with several individuals before returning to his side.

"This is it," she said softly, her voice carrying a sense of solemnity. "The hub of our operations. There are only 5 of us calling this place home now, but you'll be safe here."

Allen surveyed the space, taking in the rebel bunker with a mix of awe and uncertainty. The walls, lined with mismatched screens and archaic tech, spoke volumes about the ingenuity and resourcefulness of those who defied Techno-Synth.

He stepped closer to Mia, lowering his voice to match hers. "How do you manage to stay hidden?" he asked, his curiosity piqued by the seeming impossibility of their existence beneath the ever-watchful eyes of their enemy.

Mia's lips curved into a wry smile, tinged with the hint of secrets she was not yet willing to share. "Let's just say we're good at being ghosts. It helps when you know your opponent's blind spots."

A sudden pang of familiarity hit Allen as he watched Mia interact with her team. There was chemistry here—a shared purpose that transcended individual fears and aspirations. In this darkened cavern of hope, he found himself yearning to be a part of something again, to fight for a future he couldn't remember but somehow deeply desired.

Before he could ponder further, Mia spoke. "This is Anne," she said, motioning toward a woman with steel-gray hair who looked up from her console with intelligent eyes that blinked with recognition upon seeing Allen. "She's our comms expert. And that's Sam—he's good with drones and surveillance."

Sam, a skinny man with restless hands, gave a short nod before returning to his work, disassembling what appeared to be a downed drone like the one they had just evaded. The table was littered with scavenged parts—gears, wires, and chips—a chaotic yet purposeful disarray.

Allen felt some deja vu as he observed the scattered technology, like echoes of knowledge he once possessed but could no longer grasp. He watched Sam's fingers move with precision, dismantling the Techno-Synth drone.

Suddenly Anne was standing next to him, "Good to see you made it out alive Mercer." The sound of that name sent a shock through Allen's bones. "Who?" he replied blankly.

"Mercer" Anne quipped. "The Allen Mercer! you are a legend sir, everyone thought you were dead though, so I'm glad to see you made it out alive."

"Wait," Allen pondered, the name ringing in his ears, "Allen Mercer," he repeated the name aloud and then it struck him. "Holy shit...That's Me!" grabbing Anne's shoulders with both hands, a smile plastered across his face. "Thank you, Anne, thank you so much, you just helped me remember my name."

Anne's eyes widened at the sudden contact, but the corners of her mouth twitched upwards in understanding. The revelation had ignited something in Allen, a spark that danced across his features. For the first time since he had stumbled into the ruins, a fragment of his identity had been reclaimed.

"You're welcome," Anne said softly, gently extracting herself from his grasp. "But keep it down, will you? We can't afford to attract any unwanted attention, even down here."

Allen released her, the gravity of their situation settling back onto his shoulders. But the weight felt different now—less like a burden and more like a purpose. He looked around at each member of the small group, his eyes finally resting on Mia.

"You knew," he stated, not as an accusation but as an acknowledgment.

Mia held his look steadily. "I had my suspicions," she admitted. "There were rumors about a man with your... capabilities. Someone who was a thorn in Techno-Synth's side before most of us even realized how deep the thorns were planted."

A mixture of confusion and clarity swirled within Allen. "But why didn't you tell me?"

"It wasn't my place to," Mia replied, her voice firm yet not unkind. "And honestly, I needed to be sure you were who we thought you were, not just another memory-wiped pawn the corporation sent to infiltrate us. We can't be too careful these days."

Allen nodded in understanding. Trust was a commodity more valuable than any currency in this shattered world, and he was grateful for whatever sliver he had been granted. The fractured shards of his past were slowly piecing together, and with each revelation came a renewed sense of determination.

"Alright," Allen said, squaring his shoulders as if shedding the remnants of his confusion. "So how do I help? What's the plan?"

"That," Mia said, her eyes brightening with an intensity that seemed to set the dim bunker alight, "is what we need to figure out. Their grip is tightening. They're upgrading their surveillance tech, drones are becoming harder to dodge, and we've lost too many already."

Sam looked up from his workbench, chiming in with a tone tinged by grim acceptance. "We hit them where it hurts whenever we can," he suggested. "Their data centers, their communication hubs and the like, if you disrupt the flow of information then you in turn, disrupt control."

Anne, standing nearby, crossed her arms and leaned in. "That's where the Shadow Web comes in," she said. "It's an underground network that evades their surveillance. We've set up servers hidden in the ruins, linked by encrypted signals. We communicate through pirate radios and the hidden servers— things Techno-Synth can't easily track." Anne added, "The Whisper Networks are even more low-tech. Information is passed in person, coded in messages, graffiti, or even through old-fashioned notes. No electronics, no traceable signals—just people passing the word, quietly. It's risky, but it's how we stay ahead."

Mia nodded thoughtfully before turning back to Allen. "And having someone with your... particular history," she said, eyeing him in a new light, "could provide us with an advantage we've never had before." She paused, considering her words carefully. "If you're willing to tap into that history, to use whatever memories and skills you can dredge up against them, then we might stand a chance."

Allen's mind raced. "Okay...but what exactly is this 'particular history?'" he said hoping she would share something about his past.

Mia hesitated for a moment, scanning the faces of their small band of rebels for signs of objection. Finding none, she pulled up a chair next to Allen and gestured for him to sit.

"You were a high-ranking security officer for Techno-Synth," she began, her voice barely above a whisper. "But you were different—rumor has it that you questioned their methods, their morality. You had access to some of their most sensitive operations before... before something changed."

Allen felt his pulse quicken with each word; some memories flashed in his mind. He remembered tight corridors, cold screens, and orders that didn't sit right. A gnawing feeling that clawed at the back of his brain.

"And then you vanished," Mia continued. "Some say it was a botched operation; others think you tried to expose them and got caught. What's clear is that you know their systems, their protocols. If anyone can break through their defenses, it's you."

A torrent of emotions washed over Allen as he processed Mia's revelation. He was both an amnesiac and a turncoat, a man whose hands were likely stained with actions he could no longer recall.

"But I don't remember any of that Mia?" Allen questioned.

Mia wasn't finished. "There's more," she said quietly. "You didn't just disappear into thin air. There was a raid—one that Techno-Synth executed with frightening precision. And on that day, we lost not just a potential ally, but you left behind secrets that could have ended this war."

Allen's breath caught in his throat. He tried to imagine the situation she described, tried to visualize himself as the man she sketched out—a walking enigma clad in corporate armor, privy to their darkest deeds. The thought of what secrets his mind might hold, now locked behind a door he couldn't open, was maddening.

"Mia, I..." he began, but words failed him.

"Look," Mia said gently. "No one's blaming you for what happened per se—it's not your fault that your memories are gone. But if there's even a chance you could remember something—anything—that can help us dismantle them from the inside out... we have to take it."

Allen stared at the faces around him—faces filled with hope and desperation—and felt an unwavering resolve solidify within him. He didn't know if he could become the man they needed him to be, but he had to try.

"I'll do it," he declared, voice steady despite the turmoil inside him. "I'll do whatever it takes to recover my memories and get back at whoever did this to the world."

Mia's expression softened, seeing the resolve in Allen's eyes. "We will, Allen. But we need to be smart about this. We need more information, and I know just the person who can help us. We will head out first thing in the morning, now go get some rest, you'll need it."

Chapter 3

Allen hoisted the worn rucksack over his shoulder, its straps frayed from years of use. The weight of it was a reassuring burden; within lay the survival essentials: water filtration tablets, protein bars that tasted like chalk, and a compact toolkit that Mia had insisted they bring.

Putting his hand on his hip and checking his newly replenished holster, He surveyed the dimly lit cavern one last time, the walls echoing with the whispers of the underground rebel base.

"Ready?" Mia's voice cut through the stillness; her silhouette framed by the sturdy door that marked their exit.

"Let's do it," he replied, his voice solid despite the uncertainty clawing at his insides.

They moved through the abandoned service tunnels with purpose, the rhythmic clank of their boots against the concrete made an ominous drumbeat. Allen's fingers brushed through his short dark hair, a sign of apprehension he could never quite shake off. They said nothing, each lost in the gravity of what lay ahead. The Outlands were a lawless expanse where only the resilient—or the mad—dared to tread.

Emerging through one last heavy door, closer to the city's edge, they still had quite a way to go. The scent of decay filled the air, a tangible reminder of the world that lay in ruins before them. Allen's eyes scanned the horizon, where skeletal buildings clawed at the ashen sky, their dark forms once again hulking reminders of a civilization that had thrived here. Mia gestured towards a map, the screen on her portable device flickering with a pale glow, showing routes and markers that only those initiated into the rebellion's cause would comprehend.

"Routes have been updated," she said in a low tone, her eyes not leaving the screen. "Techno-Synth patrols have increased. We'll need to reroute through sector seven."

Allen nodded silently; his intent stare fixed on the maze-like pathways ahead. Sector seven was notorious for its unpredictability—a labyrinth of ruins that many had entered but few had left. But they had little choice. The direct paths were suicide with drones sweeping relentlessly.

As they entered the sector's outskirts, they encountered remnants of life before the fall—an old playground with rusted swings creaking in the wind, a shattered doll with unseeing eyes staring from beneath a pile of rubble. The silence was oppressive, the only sounds were their footsteps and the distant buzz of drones like angry hornets searching for prey.

They ducked into an alleyway as a drone buzzed by overhead. Suddenly, out of nowhere, a Techno-Synth soldier and his k9 on patrol appeared rounding the corner. Allen and Mia were caught somewhat off guard.

Allen's instincts kicked in, he drew his side arm without hesitation and shot a single round straight through the soldier's cheek. Having no hand to hold it back and being well trained, the dog leapt into action, grabbing Allen's arm and preventing him from firing another shot.

"Oh Fuck!" Mia shouted as she pulled her gun, putting the dog down with a quick shot. "You ok Allen?".

"Yeah, I'm good" He replied.

Allen shook off the numbing pain radiating from his arm, the dog's iron grip having drawn blood through his jacket. His heart hammered against his ribs, the adrenaline singing in his veins urging him to move. Mia's sharp features were set in a grim line as she swiftly scavenged a data pad from the fallen soldier's belt.

"We need to go. Now," she urged, pocketing the device. "Those shots will have every drone swarming here within minutes."

The urgency in her voice spurred him into action despite the throbbing in his arm. They hastened away from the scene, darting through the maze of rubble with practiced stealth. Shadows played tricks on their eyes, every piece of twisted metal and broken stone seemed like it could be another enemy lying in ambush.

As they navigated further into sector seven, the atmosphere of destruction weighed heavily on them. Once grand edifices now stood as mere shells of their former glory, the hollow wind moaning through their exposed frameworks as if lamenting the past.

Allen glanced at Mia, her eyes were focused ahead, scanning for signs of trouble. In that moment he recognized not only her strength but also the burden she bore; this rebellion was more than a fight for her, it was personal.

The distant whir of the approaching drones grew louder, a reminder that time was their enemy. Allen's arm ached, but he pushed through the pain, his determination refusing to let him falter. They ducked into a decrepit building with walls covered in graffiti—the symbols of the rebellion.

"This place," Mia whispered, glancing around the crumbling walls, "It's where the Founders of the resistance were executed. Techno-Synth wanted to erase them from history, but we keep their legacy alive." She reached into her pack, pulling out a small, outdated communication device. "This is Echoes of Freedom," she said, showing the device. "It's an underground broadcast that airs stories of people who've fought back, who've resisted Techno-Synth's lies. The Founders started it. Now, it's all we have left of their voice." Allen stared at the device, its screen flickering softly in the dim light. "It's dangerous to listen to," Mia continued. "But sometimes, just hearing those stories—it gives people hope."

Allen felt a chill that had nothing to do with the cold. He stared at the walls, now understanding the significance of the hastily drawn symbols. Blood had been spilled here for the same cause they were fighting for.

"They must have been really great people." Allen added.

"Absolutely," Mia replied, "we would all be speaking "Techno-Synth" right now if it wasn't for them, they gave us a chance." She turned toward the area where everything had taken place that fateful day, with a big sigh she bowed her head in a quick moment of silence. Allen joined her.

Now with the drones gone and feeling safer, they resumed their trek through sector seven, avoiding open spaces and using the shadows as their ally. The map on Mia's device was a beacon in the darkness, guiding them through the maze of destruction.

Suddenly, Mia grabbed Allen's arm and pulled him to a stop— a signal so urgent he instantly dropped to one knee, scanning their surroundings. Up ahead, barely visible through a crack in a dilapidated wall, were more Techno-Synth soldiers; this time it was not just a solo patrol but a whole squad, accompanied by an armored hovercraft that silently glided over the rubble. Its searchlights swept back and forth like predatory eyes seeking out the smallest hint of defiance. They couldn't afford a head-on confrontation.

Allen's gaze shifted to the left, catching sight of a flickering console, still attached to the wall. The screen displayed a distorted image, the words barely visible: *"Unity and Order for All—Techno-Synth, Your Future."* His stomach twisted as the message repeated. Even broken and abandoned, Techno-Synth's propaganda lingered like a ghost, a constant reminder of the control they claimed over everything. He glanced at Mia, who shook her head in silent disgust. They exchanged a look that conveyed volumes.

Silently, they began retracing their steps, taking a longer, less hazardous route that took them through collapsed buildings and over precarious terrain. The ever-present whir of drones seemed to stalk them, a mechanical predator on the hunt.

As they maneuvered through the ruins, Allen's mind raced. The data pad Mia had taken from the soldier could contain valuable intelligence—patrol patterns, supply routes, maybe even communications protocols. If they could make it to the Outlanders base without being captured or killed, it could possibly help turn the tides in their favor.

They reached an area that had once been a residential block, now nothing more than a graveyard of concrete and steel. After diligently working their way through the neighborhood they could begin to see some distance between them and the city.

As the edge of the Outlands began to materialize, the harsh urban decay gave way to a more rugged, untamed landscape. Allen and Mia navigated through this transition with caution, aware of the dangers that the lawless lands held, but also hopeful for the sanctuary it promised.

The silence was interrupted abruptly as a rustling sound erupted from the thick underbrush to their right. With a sudden burst of movement, a large rabbit darted out from the bushes. Its rapid, bouncing escape sent a scattering of leaves into the air, its unexpected appearance both startling and comical.

Relief washed over Allen as he straightened up, a chuckle escaping him despite the residual adrenaline. He nudged Mia lightly with his shoulder, teasing, "Damn! You were so scared."

Mia, who hadn't flinched at the rabbit's sudden appearance, quickly responded with her own shove to Allen's shoulder. "I saw you shaking at the sight of that deadly beast," she retorted, her voice laced with amusement.

Their laughter echoed in the cool evening air, a brief respite from the tension that had built up during their long trek. The momentary fright from the rabbit had dissolved into a shared moment of levity, lightening the mood as they continued their journey into the Outlands.

The landscape around them grew wilder, with thick underbrush and towering trees that blocked out much of the sky. As they navigated through this rugged terrain, the natural world seemed to watch them with quiet curiosity. The path became more challenging, with roots snaking across the ground and rocks jutting out, eager to trip the unwary traveler.

As they walked, Allen found himself glancing at Mia, taking in her confident stride and the way she moved with such familiarity in this untamed environment. It was clear she had made this journey many times before. Her familiarity with the landscape, coupled with her quick reaction to the rabbit, reminded him of the countless stories she must hold—stories of survival and resistance.

"Mia," Allen started, breaking the silence that had fallen between them since their laughter had subsided. "How often have you traveled these parts?"

Mia looked over, her eyes reflecting a mix of thoughts. "Quite a few times. It's necessary to connect different parts of the resistance, and sometimes, to escape Techno-Synth's many patrols."

Allen nodded, processing her words. The concept of widespread resistance still felt a bit foreign to him, his memories of such alliances fragmented at best. "And the people we're about to meet... What are they like?"

"They're like us," Mia replied. "Fighters, survivors. Some of them have been here since the beginning of the resistance. They've lost homes, families and more... but not their hope. You'll fit right in."

Allen wasn't sure about fitting in, but he appreciated her confidence in him. The path they were on now started to decline, leading them deeper into a valley surrounded by dense foliage. As they descended, the sound of distant voices began to carry over the wind, a sign that they were approaching their first destination.

Finally, after navigating into a densely wooded area, they came upon a clearing where a small camp was nestled against the backdrop of steep hills. Makeshift tents and shelters were scattered around, each constructed with whatever materials were at hand. It was a far cry from the structured military bases Allen faintly remembered, yet there was a sense of order and purpose in the layout.

People milled about, some tending to a central fire, others checking equipment or talking quietly in groups. As Mia and Allen approached, the activity within the camp paused, curious eyes turning their way.

Mia raised her hand in greeting, a smile breaking across her face.

"Friends!" she called out, her voice carrying across the clearing. "This is Allen, the one I've told you about!"

A murmur ran through the crowd, and one by one, people began to approach, their expressions ranging from cautious interest to open curiosity. A man, broad-shouldered and with a scar running down one cheek, stepped forward, extending his hand to Allen.

"Name's Roth," he said, his grip firm. "Heard a lot about you. Welcome to the Outlands."

Allen shook his hand, feeling the sincerity in Roth's welcome. "Thank you," he managed, his voice steady despite the whirl of emotions. "It's good to be here."

Mia introduced Allen to a few other key figures within the camp, each of them nodding with a mixture of curiosity and respect. The story of his mysterious past and his sudden reappearance had preceded him, creating a buzz of whispered speculation among the group.

As night fully settled over the camp, Allen found himself seated around a fire with Mia and several other rebels, the light from the flickering flames dancing on their faces. They shared stories of their skirmishes with the enemy, their losses, and their small victories.

Allen listened, absorbing every word, every laugh. It was here, among these outcasts and rebels, that he began to feel a part of something larger than himself—a movement for change.

As the flames flickered, Roth leaned back against a log, his eyes distant. "You know, I wasn't always with the Outlanders," he began, voice low. "I used to run solo, scavenging, surviving... until I met the Founders." His gaze swept across the fire, landing on Allen. "They found me when I was nothing but a broken man, angry at the world. But they saw something in me, something I hadn't seen in myself for a long time."

"They recruited you?" Allen asked, intrigued.

Roth nodded, his hand brushing the scar on his cheek. "Yeah. They didn't just recruit me—they saved me. Showed me what it really meant to fight, not just to survive, but to resist." He paused, letting the weight of his words settle. "They believed in something bigger than themselves, and I couldn't walk away from that."

Mia scooted closer to him, her presence a comforting constant. As the fire crackled, she leaned over, her voice soft. "See? I told you. You belong here."

Allen looked at her, then back at the flames, their light reflecting in his eyes. "Maybe I do," he admitted, allowing himself to feel the warmth of the fire and the community. In a rare moment since waking up on that desolate street, he felt a glint of hope, a sense of purpose.

As the embers died down and the rebels retired to their tents, Mia and Allen remained, lost in conversation under the starlit sky. "We'll need to move at first light," Mia said, her voice low. "There are patrols to avoid, and we need to reach the main base by noon tomorrow."

Allen nodded, feeling more resolved than he had in days. "I'll be ready," he affirmed, the weight of his lost memories still pressing on him but now tempered by a renewed sense of purpose.

The sun was a white scar in the gray canvas of the sky when Allen and Mia broke camp. With the makeshift outlander camp now behind them, they trudged through the desolate expanse of the Outlands, the weight of their packs a constant reminder of the journey ahead.

"Keep your eyes sharp," Mia said, looking back at the horizon where the ruins of the old world clawed at the heavens like skeletal fingers.

Allen nodded, his hand instinctively reaching for the hilt of the knife strapped to his thigh. The Outlands were notorious for their unpredictability; desperation turned even the most docile into predators.

It wasn't long before the stillness shattered.

"Hold it right there?" The voice was like gravel thrown against metal, harsh and uninviting.

Two figures emerged from the trees, their faces obscured by cloths wrapped around their heads, leaving only their wary eyes visible. Allen and Mia froze, slowly raising their hands, looking down the barrels of the two guns that held them at bay.

"We're not looking for any trouble," Allen called out to the men, his voice steady despite the adrenaline coursing through his veins. "We're just passing through."

"Perfect, now get down on your knees" One of the figures chuckled, a sound devoid of humor. "Now empty your packs and don't try anything stupid." The man stepping closer to Mia and pressing his gun against her temple.

Realizing they were in no position to negotiate; they both slung their packs from their shoulders to the ground. The man pressed his gun even harder into Mia's head making sure she and Allen didn't even consider make any aggressive movements.

Suddenly two shots rang out in quick succession. Both the men dropped and crumpled up like wet rags. "You guys okay?" a voice yelled from inside the tree line. Allen and Mia both snapped their heads in the direction of the familiar voice.

Roth and two other Outlanders emerged, the barrel of his rifle still smoking. "Bet you're glad to see us?" Roth said with an almost humorous tone. "These two assholes have been causing a lot of trouble on this route lately, robbing people, so I figured we better tail you guys for a bit and make sure they didn't get the drop on you."

Mia stood up taking a deep breath. "God damn right we're glad to see you Roth, but we had it under control."

Roth raised an eyebrow at Mia's comment, a smirk tugging at the corner of his mouth. "Sure you did," he said dryly, his look shifting to Allen as he offered a hand to help him up. "No harm in having a little backup, though."

Allen accepted the hand and rose to his feet, clapping Roth on the shoulder in silent gratitude. He was beginning to understand that in this new world, trust had to be earned quickly, and actions spoke louder than words.

Roth gave Allen a friendly nod, holstering his rifle as the other Outlanders began to check the fallen assailants for any salvageable supplies. "Well, I guess you two should get going now. Daylight is burning."

"Thank you Roth." Mia said gratuitously, as she gave him a strong hug and a pat on the back. Knowing she had probably just avoided being killed thanks to his helping hand. "Stay safe out there," Roth replied, releasing Mia and turning his head to the horizon. "Remember, Techno-Synth patrols could be anywhere. Don't let your guard down."

Allen watched as Mia shouldered her rucksack again, her movements efficient and precise. The close call had shaken them, but it also reinforced the sense of urgency that drove them forward.

With a final nod to Roth and his companions, Allen and Mia set off once more across the rugged terrain, their steps synchronized. The silence of the Outlands enveloped them again, but now with an awareness that they were not alone.

As they walked, Allen found himself glancing at Mia again. Her beauty, coupled with her ability to handle seemingly any situation, struck something inside him. He couldn't figure it out yet, but he knew he was lucky to have crossed paths with her.

Hours later, as the sun began its descent, barely casting shadows through the thick forest cover, they arrived at the main Outlanders base. It was a fortress of salvaged materials, imposing and resilient—a testament to human tenacity.

"Welcome," a deep voice boomed from the gate.

There stood Knox, the Outlanders leader, larger than life. His presence was a beacon, commanding and solid. The rebels who flanked him looked to him with reverence, the air around him charged with respect and purpose.

"Hi Knox, great to see you," Mia smiled as she greeted him with a big hug.

"Knox," Allen said, extending his hand. "Nice to meet you."

Eyeing Allen from top to bottom, Knox gave a curious response "So, you're the legendary Allen Mercer. We thought you were dead."

Allen met his gaze, sensing the respect and underlying tension. "So I've been told." Allen replied. Knox finally accepted his handshake.

The rebel leader's grip was firm, his piercing look assessing them both. "Mia, Allen. I've been briefed by Anne and Sam. Come, let's walk. There are things you need to see."

They followed Knox through the compound, each structure and face telling a story of the rebellion. They passed workshops where weapons were forged from scrap, medical tents where healers worked miracles with limited supplies, and training grounds where young recruits were molded into warriors.

"Everyone here has lost something to Techno-Synth," Knox explained, his voice somber. "But in loss, we found unity."

He stopped before a large communal fire where a group of rebels shared meager rations. Their laughter, tinged with defiance, pierced the ever-present gloom.

"Meet Lena," Knox gestured toward a woman with eyes as sharp as the blade she cleaned. "She is our lead tactician."

Lena nodded, her look appraising. "I've heard of your skills," she said to Allen, a challenge and an invitation all at once.

"And this is Jonas," Knox continued, introducing a wiry man with hands stained from explosives. "He knows every inch of the Outlands."

Jonas offered a grin that hid his dangerous expertise. "And I hear you're not too bad with tech," he said to Mia.

"Well, I hope to live up to the reputation," Mia replied, the corner of her mouth twitching in a semblance of a smile.

As night fell and the fire crackled, the outlanders gathered close, their faces illuminated by the dance of flames. In their eyes, Allen saw reflections of his own resolve, the same mixture of hope and fear, courage and doubt.

"Tonight, we share our stories, our burdens," Knox announced, his voice resonant. "Tomorrow, we fight not just for survival, but for freedom."

In the glowing light, Allen felt the weight of his past and the pull of the future. Here, amidst the fractured remnants of society, he found a new sense of belonging. And as the fire cast its glow on the assembly of outlanders, he knew this was where his true fight began.

Chapter 4

The fire crackled, its hungry flames licking at the underbelly of a charcoal sky. Around its warmth, the rebels' faces flickered between illumination and shadow, each line and scar etched with stories of survival. Allen sat close to Mia, his back straight as if still on parade, the heat pressing against his arms.

"Remember the bread lines?" Mia's voice pierced the hush that had settled over them, her tone carrying an edge of dark amusement. "Standing in line for hours just for a loaf that tasted like sawdust."

A few chuckles rose from the group, stirring the silence. Allen watched as the firelight danced in Mia's eyes, her sharp features softened by the shared memories of hardship. He could almost forget the weight of the world beyond the fire's reach.

"Those bread lines would stretch for blocks," Mia muttered, her voice tinged with frustration. "That's Techno-Synth's 'Unity and Order' for you. That's how they started to take control of everything, even down to the food supply, rationing it to keep people dependent on them. The campaign promised a future of stability, but it was just a way to keep everyone in line—hungry, desperate, and willing to follow their rules in exchange for a loaf of bread." She shook her head.

"They call it order. I call it control."

"Or when the blackout hit Mid Sector," another rebel piped up, "and everyone thought it was the start of the Rapture or something."

Mia chuckled softly, but her eyes darkened. "That's exactly how they wanted us to feel—lost and terrified. They used the rolling blackouts as part of their 'Keeping You Safe, always' campaign. Cut off power, throw people into chaos, then swoop in claiming they're the only ones who can protect us. It wasn't about safety—it was about more and more control. They keep us scared so we rely on them." Mia said with a shake of her head, the corners of her mouth twitching upwards. "God, we were such idiots,"

Allen allowed himself a rare smile, his eyes shifting across the fire to Knox. The old soldier sat with his legs crossed, one hand resting on a knee, the other cradling his chin thoughtfully. Even seated, he seemed to tower over them all, a monolith carved from the very bedrock of their resistance.

"Those were difficult days to say the least," Knox said, his deep voice resonating with experience. His eyes, dark and steady, met Allen's. "But they forged us. Tempered our spirits. We learned who we were when stripped of comfort and certainty."

The rebels nodded; their expressions somber once more. Allen felt the truth in Knox's words; they resonated within him, somewhere deep, where the fires of his own resolve burned low and constant.

"Mercer," Knox addressed him directly now, his stare unwavering. "Your path has been... unique. But it leads here, to us. To this moment."

Allen held Knox's glare, the blue of his eyes hardening like ice. The older man's presence was undeniable, a force as natural and as commanding as the elements themselves.

"Unique," Allen echoed, his voice showing no hint of emotion.

"Indeed," Knox said with a nod, acknowledging the vast, unspoken history that lingered between them. "We all carry our pasts. They shape us but do not define our future. What matters is what we do next, how we use our experiences to fight back."

Allen felt the eyes of the others upon him, a collective weight of expectation and camaraderie. The fire popped and hissed, throwing embers into the night like fleeting stars, and for a moment, amidst the gloom of a world undone, there was a glimmer of something else—a spark of defiance, a flare of hope.

"Knox," Allen began, curiosity threading his voice. "You talk about shaping the future—how do you stay so sure in all of this chaos?"

"Assurance?" Knox cut in, a confident gleam in his eyes. "We make our own assurance, Allen. With every act of defiance, with every blow we strike against Techno-Synth."

The rebels around them nodded in silent agreement, their faces illuminated by the sporadic bursts of light from the fire. Knox leaned forward, the orange glow reflecting in his eyes as he addressed Allen's unvoiced concerns.

"Techno-Synth is not simply an oppressive regime; it is the embodiment of control, the antithesis of freedom." Knox's hands gestured as if carving the very air with his conviction. "Their networks enslave minds, their drones patrol our skies, and their lies weave a narrative that shackles the soul. They've razed our cities, poisoned our lands, and turned brother against brother."

Allen found himself captivated, the fire reflecting in Knox's eyes as he spoke. The certainty in his words, the unshakable belief—Allen felt himself pulled into it, no longer resistant, but intrigued. He studied Knox's face, searching not for deceit, but for the source of this unwavering belief.

"You've survived the worst of them," Allen said. "What drives you to keep fighting, to keep pushing?"

Knox's expression softened slightly, as if recognizing the spark in Allen's voice. "In the face of tyranny, we evolve, Allen, and sometimes... we have to become the very thing we fear to defeat it."

As Knox spoke, the fire seemed to burn brighter, lending a fervor to the encampment. The others were rapt, hanging onto each word as though it were a lifeline in these desperate times.

"They have robbed us of our past and seek to steal our future," Knox said. "But we are the resistance. The ember that refuses to be snuffed out. We need minds like yours, Allen."

Allen felt something shift within himself—a loosening of the guarded walls he had built, a growing connection to the words Knox spoke. Knox's eyes held him, demanding that Allen confront the truth. There was no deceit, only the raw, visceral essence of their fight.

Knox's voice dropped to a near whisper. "We don't fight for violence's sake. We fight to rebuild, to take back what they've stolen. And we need every soul who yearns for that world to stand with us."

The fire crackled, punctuating the stillness that followed. Allen's eyes lingered on Knox, the flickers of doubt waning as the older man's resolve shone through, a beacon in the night that called to the fighter within him.

The fire crackled between them, casting shadows that flickered like the uncertainties in Allen's mind. But those doubts were slowly fading, replaced by the same unyielding resolve he saw in Knox.

Allen crouched closer to the fire, watching the embers dance in the night. Knox's words had become more than just a speech—they were a lifeline, pulling Allen out of his internal storm.

"I've been in fights before," Allen said, his brow furrowed. "But there's something about this one... something pulling me in, like there's a part of me that knows this fight is where I'm meant to be, even if I don't fully understand why yet."

Knox chuckled, his arms folding as he leaned forward. "You've got the instincts, Allen. The fire is already in you. Now it's time to join the fight."

Allen's eyes rose to meet Knox's. For the first time, he didn't question the man's purpose—he wanted to understand it, to embrace it.

"Come," Knox said, rising to his feet. "Let me show you."

They moved away from the fire, stepping into the chill of the night where the darkness was a shroud cloaking their movements. Knox led Allen through a series of combat drills, his instructions crisp and decisive. Even in the moonlight's pale wash, the older man's rugged features were set in a mask of concentration, every motion deliberate and efficient.

"Balance is key," Knox instructed as he demonstrated a low sweep, designed to unseat an opponent. "It's not just physical—it's mental. You must anticipate and adapt."

Allen followed suit, mirroring the movements. His body was a coiled spring, each action precise, yet there was a fluidity to Knox's technique that eluded him.

"Good," Knox said, nodding slightly as Allen completed the maneuver. "Now faster, sharper. Like the strike of a viper."

This time Allen executed the move with such precision and power it sent Knox tumbling to the ground. The crowd that was left watching from around the fire gave a collective gasp. Shocked by what he had just done, Allen quickly extended his hand out to help Knox to his feet. "Shit, are you okay Knox?"

"Yeah Allen, I'm good." Knox said, groaning as Allen pulled him to his feet. "That was perfectly executed, seems like that part of your memory didn't get lost," he chuckled, brushing the dirt off his side.

"Enough for today," Knox declared, his voice softer now, tempered by the bond of shared exertion. "We will build upon this tomorrow."

Allen nodded, feeling the thrum of his pulse slow, the echo of his military training settling into his bones. It was more than the honing of skill; it was the forging of trust. And as the remnants of his past rang in his head, Allen realized that amidst the desolation, he had found a guide in Knox—a beacon in the treacherous path that lay ahead.

As the first shine of dawn cast a pale glow over the base's command center, leaders began to gather inside as Knox unfurled a tattered map across a large table. The room was awash in shadows, with consoles and equipment reduced to mere silhouettes against the dim light filtering through the dust-covered windows.

"Strategy," Knox began, his voice low and steady, "is the lifeblood of our resistance." He pointed to various sectors on the map, his finger tracing the arteries that connected the desolate wastelands with the heart of Techno-Synth's dominion. "Every move we make must be measured; every attack synchronized."

Allen leaned forward, his eyes narrowing as he absorbed the topography laid out before him. The blue of his eyes reflected a mind already at work, calculating and considering each word that Knox uttered. "And what about their defenses?" Allen asked, pointing to a heavily marked zone swarming with digital annotations.

"Ah yes," Knox replied with a nod of recognition toward Allen's inquiry. "Their fortifications are formidable, but not insurmountable." He tapped the map where green zones indicated rebel hideouts. "We have allies waiting in silence, ready to cut through the chaos when the moment arises."

Allen's hand hovered over the map, his fingers brushing the edges of the zones as if physically testing the boundaries. His past, littered with tactical maneuvers and the stark rigidity of military doctrine, shifted, allowing room for the guerrilla warfare that had become the rebellion's heartbeat to rise within him.

"We could disrupt supply lines here," Allen suggested, tapping a critical juncture that would leave a key Techno-Synth outpost vulnerable. "Force them to redirect resources and expose their flank."

Knox's eyebrows lifted, a silent concession to the astuteness of Allen's insight. "Indeed, we can, good eyes Allen," he concurred. "It's not always about the frontal assault; it's about dismantling the beast, piece by piece." His weathered face cracked into a rare smile. "Your head's in the game, Mercer. Good."

Humor flickered momentarily in the exchange; a shared camaraderie born from the grim dance of war. But the levity was brief, swept away as quickly as it had come by the gravity of their undertaking.

"Coordination will be our edge," Knox continued, shifting gears back to the gravity of their discussion. He slid markers across the map, simulating a sequence of attacks. "Synchronized strikes, communication lines secured, and fallback points predetermined."

Allen watched, his mind racing ahead of Knox's explanations, envisioning the rebels moving like ghosts through the ruins, striking with precision before vanishing into the void. The dance of insurgency came alive inside him, a pulsating rhythm that resonated with his own instincts for survival.

"We'll need to hack into their communication network," Mia interjected, pointing to a cluster of digital towers on the map. "If we can sow misinformation and confusion within their ranks, we can buy precious time for our ground forces."

Knox flashed Mia an appreciative glance, recognizing the critical role her skills played in their intricate dance of rebellion. "Can it be done without tipping them off?" he asked.

Mia's lips curved in a smirk that made her confidence infectious. "They won't know what hit them until it's too late," she assured them both.

Inspired by Mia's idea, Jonas moved his finger in a circle around an area close to the towers adding, "We could potentially take out some of the cameras in this area too, I could place a couple of surprises for any patrols that might respond to the area."

Knox's eyes gleamed at the notion, acknowledging the layers of strategy now unfolding like a grandmaster's chessboard. "Surprises?" he echoed, the hint of a growl in his voice that couldn't hide his intrigue.

"Yeah," Jonas said, his hand still circling the sector on the map, "I've been working on some makeshift EMPs. They won't knock out anything big, but they'll fry any surveillance equipment they have in the area. It'll be blind chaos for a bit."

Knox considered Jonas' suggestion, his eyes tracing the proposed perimeter on the map. "I like the way you think," he said after a moment of thought. "But we need to be prepared for quick extraction. Techno-Synth patrols are no joke; they come down hard and fast."

Jonas nodded, already calculating risk versus reward in his head. "I'll set up remote access," he replied confidently. "We hit them with a series of distractions, draw them out, then vanish before they can mobilize a counter-response."

The table was silent for a moment as each person contemplated the parts they would play in the intricate ballet of guerrilla warfare. The stakes were high, and every move had to be executed flawlessly.

"We'll need to run drills," Allen stated. "Ensure everyone knows their role inside and out." His voice carried the authority of someone who had been hardened by countless life-or-death decisions. "Any hesitation could mean death—or worse, capture."

Knox gave an approving nod at Allen's foresight. "Agreed. We can't afford any loose ends or uncertainties. Precision is our greatest ally." He stood up, his frame towering over the map in a silent vow to every soul that depended on their leadership. "Starting immediately, we drill until every rebel can navigate the plan blindfolded."

Allen rose alongside Knox, feeling the weight of responsibility settle upon his shoulders. The room's atmosphere thickened with determination—a collective resolve punctuating the air like static before a storm.

As they dispersed to prepare for the coming trials, Mia pulled Allen aside, her sharp stare probing beneath his stoic exterior. "Are you sure you're ready for something like this," she said, her words edged with equal parts warning and respect. "This fight... it's not just about tactics and formations, lives will be on the line. Remember that."

Her reminder was a pinprick to Allen's burgeoning sense of purpose, widening his perspective beyond the scope of combat and strategy. She was right; beyond each maneuver and tactic lay lives entangled in the crosshairs of a greater war—a human element that couldn't be quantified on any map or battle plan.

"I will make sure I do everything I can to prepare for this Mia," Allen said with confidence, "my mind is still foggy, but I know deep inside of me that this is where I'm supposed to be."

Mia held his intent look for a moment longer, perhaps searching for the conviction behind his words, then nodded slowly. "I believe you," she said, her voice carrying a quiet strength. "Just... be careful, Allen. We can't afford to lose you." With a curt nod, she turned and walked away.

Allen watched her go, feeling the weight of her words settle over him like a cloak. He knew he had to get combat ready as quickly as possible and that the training would not be easy.

Chapter 5

Allen's breath came in measured gasps as he launched himself over a waist-high barrier, the rough texture of the recycled metal grazing his palms. The obstacle course spread before him was an unforgiving labyrinth of scrap and ruin, each station a testament to the world that had fallen and the resilience of those determined to rise from its ashes.

The sun scorched down on the wreckage, casting stark shadows that seemed to mock his every step. Sweat mingled with the grime on his skin, creating streaks of determination that lined his face. Allen's muscles burned with effort, yet he moved with a fluidity born from countless hours of rigorous training, his body a well-honed instrument of both strength and agility.

He scaled a wall of mismatched bricks, remnants of buildings that once scraped the sky, now repurposed for the rebellion's gauntlet. At the top, he paused just long enough to survey the next challenge—a precarious balance beam stretched over a pit filled with debris—before descending with practiced precision.

His feet found the narrow strip of steel, and he willed them to steady as he began to cross. Each step was a calculated risk, his eyes fixed on the end that seemed to sway with the heat haze rising from below. Allen's mind raced, calculating weight distribution and compensating for the subtle give in the metal beneath his boots.

Midway across, a sudden shift sent a spike of adrenaline through his veins. The beam groaned, tilting precariously. Allen's heart hammered against his ribcage, the thought of failure looming as he fought for balance. His arms flailed, seeking equilibrium.

"Come on, Mercer." His own voice broke the spell of uncertainty, gritty and low. He couldn't afford hesitation—not here, not now. With a deep breath, Allen stilled the tremor of trepidation and resumed his trek.

One step. Then another. His focus narrowed to the singular objective: reach the other side. The world fell away until there was nothing but the beam, the heat, and the rhythm of his breath.

Finally, his boot connected with solid ground, and he allowed himself a fleeting grin of triumph. It was a small victory, but it propelled him forward, fueling his resolve as he tackled the remaining hurdles—an uphill climb, a dive through a narrow tunnel, and a sprint toward the finish line where Mia and Knox waited, their expressions a blend of scrutiny and expectation.

"Push through, Allen," Mia called out, her voice a beacon amidst the clatter of his exertions.

He crossed the finish, the finality of his stride punctuating the air. Chest heaving, Allen doubled over, hands on his knees, allowing himself this moment of respite. He had conquered the course, but more importantly, he had conquered the creeping tendrils of doubt that sought to ensnare him.

"Nice work," Knox said, clapping him on the shoulder with a gruff nod of approval. The praise was sparse, but in the sparsity lay its sincerity.

"Thanks," Allen managed between breaths, straightening up. The pride in their eyes was unmistakable, mirroring his own sense of accomplishment.

Knox lingered as the dust settled around Allen, his keen eyes tracing the lines of exhaustion etched into the younger man's face. "Your mind is your ally, Allen," he began, his voice carrying the weight of years spent outmaneuvering a world that had turned against them. "Instincts honed by training are sharper than any blade. Remember that."

Allen nodded, his eyes locking onto Knox's with an intensity that almost hid his fatigue. He took a deep breath, feeling the truth in Knox's words settle within him like pieces of a puzzle snapping into place.

"Let's see those instincts in action," Knox said, gesturing toward the training mat where several fighters awaited—a gauntlet of flesh and bone.

The air in the combat zone hummed with anticipation. Allen stepped onto the mat, muscles tensing, a primal part of him responding to the challenge. The opponents circled, their movements predatory, yet Allen's stance remained unwavering—a fortress amidst a circling storm.

The first came at him with a feint, a blur of motion meant to deceive. Allen's breath came in controlled bursts as he pivoted, the soles of his boots grinding against the dust-coated floor. A fist whistled past his ear, close enough that he felt the disturbance in the air. With the fluid grace of a falcon in a dive, he ducked and weaved through the flurry of blows, his own hands snapping out like coiled springs to deliver calculated counter punches.

The second opponent lunged, seeking to capitalize on perceived vulnerability, but Allen was already pivoting, his heel connecting with a satisfying thud against the aggressor's midsection.

Sweat beaded on his brow, but Allen's focus never wavered, each breath a silent rhythm punctuating the dance of combat. He was a tempest, each move flowing into the next—a testament to the potential Mia and Knox saw in him.

A third opponent, larger than the others, advanced with a barrage of strikes. Allen's back hit the edge of the mat, but there was no panic in his eyes. He quickly rolled left and popped back up to his feet. He absorbed a blow to the face, used the momentum to spin away, and then surged forward, his fist driving through the space between them to find its mark.

The flurry of movement slowed, and one by one, the opponents found themselves dropping, lying scattered like fallen leaves around Allen's feet. Chest heaving, he stood victorious yet unassuming, the very image of resilience and strength born from relentless purpose.

From the shadows of the periphery, Mia watched, her keen stare dissecting every shift of Allen's form. Beside her, Knox stood, his posture a bulwark against the uncertainty of their future.

"His progress is remarkable," Mia said, "He's adapting faster than any recruit I've seen."

Knox gave a noncommittal grunt, his weathered face carved from stone. "He's got talent, no denying that. But raw skill isn't enough. Not in the world we're up against."

A ghost of a smile played on Mia's lips, though it never reached her eyes. "I believe in his potential. He's more than just a former Techno-Synth officer. You've seen it, the way he plans, executes... leads."

"Belief can be a dangerous thing," Knox replied, his voice the rumble of distant thunder. "It blinds you to flaws. And in our line of work, flaws get people killed."

Mia's retort was as sharp as a blade. "And doubt can paralyze. If we don't trust in our own, who will?"

Their exchange was cut short as Allen executed a deft maneuver, disarming his next opponent with a twist and an application of leverage that sent the man slamming to the mat. Knox nodded, a silent acknowledgment of the display of finesse.

"Keep an eye on him," he told Mia, his words carrying the weight of command softened by the underlying note of respect. "He could be the edge we need, or the blade that cuts us."

"Trust me, Knox," Mia answered, her promise as binding as any oath. "I'll make sure he's ready."

In the center of the ring, Allen exhaled slowly, resetting his stance as he prepared for another bout. He could feel the weight of their eyes upon him, the hope and skepticism mingling like smoke in the air.

Blood dripped from the corner of Allen's mouth as he squared off against the next challenger, a wiry figure whose sinewy muscles hinted at a coiled ferocity. The rebel—a ghost from the ranks—moved with a grace that hid his lethal intent. Allen's breath steadied; this was no ordinary spar.

The opponent struck, a blur of motion that whispered death. Allen sidestepped, his training kicking into overdrive. But this ghost was extremely fast, each attack confusing and impossible to predict. Allen's eyes darted around, trying to decipher the moves of his opponent but struggling to keep up with their lightning-fast speed. As he focused on defense, his thoughts were consumed with finding a way to outsmart the relentless onslaught.

A fist grazed his jaw, a reminder that even shadows could leave bruises. Allen faltered, backpedaling, feeling the edge of the combat zone beneath his heels. His adversary advanced relentlessly.

He pivoted, dodging a jab designed to end the match, and shifted his weight. Lunging with a burst of clarity, his final counter punch was not just a strike but a declaration, a roar of defiance that echoed through the gym as his opponent crumbled to the mat.

The crowd of rebels that had gathered to watch the intense exchange started cheering and clapping. Allen extended a hand to help him up, a warrior's respect bridging the gap between victory and camaraderie. "Nice fighting!" he said as he helped the rebel to his feet.

"You too sir, it was a pleasure to step in the ring with such a legend." The rebel said with resounding respect. As if summoned by those words, Mia stepped onto the mat, her presence slicing through the air like a blade. "Time for the real test," she said, her tone light but eyes sharp.

"Come with me Allen. Let's move to the simulator," she added, pointing to a makeshift building nearby. As they made their way to the building Mia gave Allen a shove on the shoulder. "Great fighting Allen," she said with a smile on her face. "I knew you still had it in you."

"Thanks Mia," Allen replied, looking at the expression on her face. "It felt good too" he said, not being able to hold back his own smile. Mia pulled the door open, and they entered the building.

The room hummed with the low, steady thrum of machinery as Allen stepped into the simulation chamber, a stark contrast to the sparring ring. He cinched the neural interface snugly around his forehead, its cold touch a familiar brace against the onslaught of virtual chaos he was about to enter. With a subtle nod to the operator, the world blinked out of existence.

Instantaneously, Allen found himself in the midst of a war-ravaged cityscape, the sky choked with ash and the ground littered with the bones of fallen buildings. The stench of burnt metal filled his nostrils—a sensory illusion so convincing he almost believed it real. His breath came out in visible puffs, though the air in the chamber remained temperate. Virtual soldiers materialized around him, their weapons raised, their expressions blank slates programmed for battle.

Allen's mind whirred into high gear, synapses firing like the guns of his enemies. There was no room for hesitation; every decision had to be made in the span of a heartbeat. He sprinted forward, ducking into the shell of a scorched vehicle, the simulated rounds peppering the carcass in a deadly rhythm.

"East flank, two tangos advancing!" he barked into the comms, his voice slicing through the din of digital warfare. The words were barely out before his body responded, twisting to evade a sniper's laser-sight, a red dot that danced mockingly across the cracked pavement.

"Copy that," came Mia's voice, calm amidst the chaos. She slipped into the virtual fray beside him, her avatar's movements as fluid and precise as her own. Together, they communicated with swift hand signals and clipped phrases, a language born out of necessity and trust.

"EMP in three... two..." Allen counted, holding up his fingers as he and Mia took cover. A shockwave of electromagnetic pulse tore through the battlefield, enemy drones dropping from the sky like metal rain. Mia's timing was impeccable, the detonation synced to the millisecond.

"Move!" she shouted, her voice tinged with exhilaration that echoed Allen's own. They surged forward, their avatars' feet pounding over the rubble-strewn landscape. Allen could feel the phantom resistance underfoot, the give of gravel and the treacherous slide of debris, as if his very nerves were entangled with the simulation.

Their communication was seamless, a dance of tactical precision. Allen took point, clearing a path with calculated bursts of fire while Mia flanked, her avatar laying down a barrage of covering shots. Each move was an answer to the other's, a silent dialogue punctuated by the roar of virtual gunfire.

"Left side, heavy armor!" Allen warned, sighting the hulking silhouette of an enemy mech suit lumbering through the haze.

"Got it—going high," Mia responded without missing a beat. Her avatar vaulted atop a crumbling wall, fingers flying over the controls on her wrist console. Moments later, the mech's systems glitched, its movements stuttering as she hacked into its core.

Allen didn't wait for it to recover. He charged, exploiting the opening Mia created, and planted a series of charges along the mech's legs. "Clear!" he called, and together they retreated to a safe distance as the charges detonated, reducing the once-daunting foe to a heap of twisted metal.

As the last echoes of the explosion faded, the simulation wound down, the cityscape dissolving into the sterile reality of the chamber. Allen peeled off the interface, a bead of sweat tracing a path down his temple despite the coolness of the room.

"Good run," Mia said, her eyes meeting his with that spark of camaraderie that had grown between them. It was a look that acknowledged their growing bond as comrades in arms.

"Couldn't have done it without you," Allen replied, the corner of his mouth lifting in the shadow of a smile. It was a rare moment of calm in a world that offered little room for such luxuries.

They stepped out of the chamber, side by side, ready to face whatever reality had to throw at them next. In the coming days the small team continued to rehearse the mission through simulated attacks on the target warehouse.

A few days before the scheduled attack, Knox instructed everyone that they would move the team to the underground rebel bunker in the city. Anne, Sam and others were already briefed on the mission. They had also been rehearsing their technical support roles for the mission and would be ready when the team arrived.

Chapter 6

On the night of the mission, the rebel bunker was quiet and dark with anticipation, the only illumination coming from the array of screens casting a cold glow on Mia's focused face. Knox stood before the assembled team; his imposing silhouette outlined by the dim light.

"Listen up," Knox's voice cut through the silence, deep and resonant. "Tonight, we hit Techno-Synth where it hurts. Our target is their newest cache of tech. We get in, we get out, no alarms. Stealth and precision are your gospel tonight."

He paced slowly, eyes sharp as flint, scanning each member of the team. "Mia, Anne and Sam you're first up. We need eyes blind, and systems crippled. Can you deliver?"

"Always do," Mia replied, her voice cool and steady, as she cracked her knuckles in anticipation. Her fingers hovered over the keyboard, ready to dance across the keys like a pianist poised for a complex concerto.

"Jonas, once we're inside, you ready the charges. Timing is critical; synchronize with Mia's signal." Knox continued, assigning tasks with surgical precision. Each rebel nodded in turn, their expressions taut with focus.

"Everyone else, you know your roles. Stick to the shadows, keep your comms clear unless it's mission critical."

As Knox's briefing melted into the darkness of the room, Mia turned her attention to the screens before her. They displayed a labyrinthine network of data streams and security protocols—a digital fortress guarding Techno-Synth's secrets. Her gaze narrowed; this was her battlefield.

"Let's move out, we will radio when we are in position Mia," Knox said, as he swung his arm in a sweeping arc, prompting the group to start the mission. They made their way through the corridors and out into the darkness of the broken city.

Allen's boots crunched softly on the broken pavement as he led the way. The night air was still, heavy with the scent of moisture and rust, a reminder of the decay that had consumed the city. In the sky above them, multiple propaganda drones clustered together, projecting a humungous holographic screen over the city. Audio for the video began to echo below through the city's hidden speaker network.

"Heroes of the State," the screen declared in bold, flashing letters. The image flickered for a moment before solidifying into the stern face of Commander Blake, his features chiseled and heroic, highlighted by the artificial glow. Behind him, scenes of carefully crafted triumph played out—Blake standing over conquered enemies, leading Techno-Synth forces into battle, his arm raised as if he were the savior of a dying world.

The screen shifted to a montage of Blake's so-called victories—crumbling rebel strongholds, civilians being "rescued" by Techno-Synth soldiers, all with the same message blaring beneath: "Loyalty, Strength, and Unity. Follow your Heroes of the State."

Allen looked up at the display above. Seeing Blakes face. He clenched his jaw, feeling a wave of anger rise within him. Blake was no hero. He knew the truth was buried beneath layers of lies, hidden behind that polished image of strength and loyalty.

This extra noise and distraction allowed the small team to make their way through the debris-strewn streets quickly, their presence swallowed by the shadows that clung to the ruins of what once was.

The warehouse loomed ahead—an imposing edifice of concrete and steel, untouched by time and conflict. As they approached, Allen raised a clenched fist, halting the group with practiced ease. He exchanged a glance with Jonas—a silent understanding passing between them.

Allen turned his earpiece to a low whisper. "Mia, we're in position. How are we looking?"

"Looking good," she replied. "Knox you in position?" she asked over the comms.

"Ready," Knox's voice crackled through Mia's radio. "Start when you're ready Mia, everyone standby for the go signal," he commanded.

"Copy," Mia radioed back.

She initiated a series of keystrokes, a symphony of commands executing with rapid-fire succession. Lines of code cascaded down her screen, reflecting in her piercing eyes as she worked to infiltrate the system. A smirk touched her lips as she encountered the familiar resistance of firewalls, slicing through them with practiced ease.

"Surveillance is going dark in three... two... one" Mia's voice was calm, besides the adrenaline coursing through her veins. The screens flashed, then went black one by one as she systematically disabled the cameras. "You're clear to move."

The warehouse's external floodlights flickered and died, plunging the perimeter into darkness. She was an artist in her own right—the strokes of her keys painting over security measures with masterful grace.

"Copy that," came Knox's response, his voice crackling through the comms unit. In the void left by the vanquished security feeds, Mia could almost hear the soft footfalls of the team as they moved unseen toward the enemy's stronghold.

"Creating your blind spots now," she murmured, diverting patrols away from the team's path. "North side is clear. West junction—wait for my mark..."

On screen, digital guards shifted routes, unwittingly aiding the rebels in their silent advance. Mia's hands flew with relentless purpose, each stroke ensuring her family of fighters remained ghosts among the machines.

"Mark," she whispered, and the rebels slipped through another snare set by Techno-Synth.

With Knox leading the charge and Mia orchestrating the surveillance blackout, the rebels approached the entrance of the warehouse, undetected yet not unchallenged. The night air was thick with tension, punctuated by the scattered hums and clicks of deactivated technology.

Knox crouched low in the shadow of an abandoned container, his grizzled face a mask of keen focus. Beside him, Jonas held a small EMP device like a grenade, his finger caressing the activation strip. The night was eerily still, save for the distant thrum of the city beyond the Techno-Synth compound.

"Ready with the distraction," Jonas murmured, the hint of mischief in his voice stark against the gravity of their task.

"Wait for my signal," Knox replied, eyes fixed on the dimly lit warehouse entrance where two guards stood, unaware of the storm brewing in the darkness.

Allen watched the scene from the opposite angle, Lena at his side, her fingers deftly dancing over a portable console. Her brow furrowed in concentration as she worked to unravel the intricate web of laser grids barring their main entry point. Allen admired her quiet intensity, the way her mind dissected problems like complex puzzles only she could solve.

"Almost there," Lena whispered, the blue glow of the screen casting spectral highlights across her features. "Just need a few more seconds."

"Take your time," Allen said, patience laced with urgency. "We can't afford any mistakes."

Knox's hand rose, then fell in a swift motion. Jonas pressed the EMP device, and it hummed to life before he lobbed it toward the warehouse door. The tiny orb spun through the air, releasing a pulse of electric current that made the nearby lights flutter and dim.

In the resulting confusion, Knox moved with silent precision, closing the distance between himself and the guards. His hands were swift and sure, disarming one guard with a fluid motion while wrapping an arm around the other's neck, pulling him into the shadows.

The takedown was a quiet ballet of violence; no shouts rang out, no alarms blared. With the guards neutralized, Knox signaled the all-clear, his eyes sweeping the area for any sign of disturbance. There was none.

"Grids are down," Lena announced, her voice a triumphant whisper. Allen peered at the now-invisible lasers, trusting Lena's expertise completely.

"Good job," he said, clapping a reassuring hand on her shoulder. Together, they stepped through the unguarded threshold, the cool air of the warehouse swallowing them whole.

"Let's move," Knox ordered, gesturing for the team to proceed with caution. Each step was measured, each breath controlled—a symphony of resistance orchestrated by a shared desire to reclaim their identities, to dismantle the very entity that had sought to erase them.

Allen led the advance, the weight of responsibility heavy on his shoulders, yet lightened by the trust he placed in his comrades—trust forged in the crucible of rebellion and sharpened by the edge of survival. In this dance of shadows and silence, they were more than rebels; they were harbingers of the dawn that would soon break over their dystopian world.

They navigated the labyrinth of corridors with a silent language of hand signals and terse nods. Allen's tactical vest brushed against the cold metallic walls; its pockets filled with the tools of their insurrection. Knox, Lena, Jonas and the team were several paces behind, mirroring Allen's movements with skillful precision.

"Left at the next junction," Mia murmured into her comm unit, the screen's glow casting her face in sharp relief. Allen adjusted his course, trusting Mia's guidance as she mapped out their digital trajectory through the belly of the beast.

"Stop," she whispered suddenly. "Guard patrol ahead—four hostiles, armed."

Allen signaled Knox to approach, the older man moving up with practiced stealth. They shared a brief look before fanning out, taking position on either side of the corridor. The patrolling guards approached, their chatter an unintelligible hum punctuated by the occasional clank of weaponry.

"Three... two... one..." Mia counted down, and the world narrowed to the pulse of adrenaline coursing through Allen's veins.

The firefight erupted in a controlled burst of chaos. Allen's weapon whispered death as it spat out silent rounds, precision over spray-and-pray. Across from him, Knox was an immovable force, every shot finding its mark with lethal efficiency. Their movements were a grim dance, synchronized to the soundless symphony of rebellion.

In moments, it was over—the guards crumpled to the floor without a chance to raise the alarm. Allen scanned the area; eyes alert for any sign they'd been detected. But the corridors remained silent, except for the distant hum of machinery.

"Status?" he asked, his voice low.

"Clear," Knox confirmed, checking the bodies with a clinical detachment born from years of conflict.

"Keep moving," Mia instructed, already tapping away at her computer to cover their tracks. "You're not far now."

Allen nodded, the ghosts of past decisions whispering in his ear. He shook them off; this was not the time for doubt. With each step forward, he wove another thread into the tapestry of their resistance—a pattern of identity reclaimed, and freedom fought for.

"Next corridor then right," Mia said. Her voice, usually so direct, held the faintest tremor of excitement. They were close now, close to striking a blow against the monolithic entity that had sought to stifle their very beings.

"Let's go," Allen said, determination steeling his features.

Allen paused at the imposing metal door that barred their path, its surface cold and unyielding to the touch. The maze of corridors had led them here, to a threshold beyond which lay the heart of Techno-Synth's technological trove. His fingers itched for action, but he stilled them, waiting for the signal.

"Standby," Mia's voice crackled in his earpiece, a beacon in the sterile silence. In the dim glow of his wrist-mounted display, Allen saw her avatar working furiously, lines of code cascading like a digital waterfall.

"Door's opening in 3... 2..." Mia counted down, her tone a mixture of anticipation and calm professionalism. With a hushed click, the locks disengaged, as silent as the grave. A faint smile touched Allen's lips—not from humor, but respect for Mia's deft touch.

"Good work," he murmured, pushing the door open. It swung silently on well-oiled hinges, revealing the shadowed expanse of the target area. Rows upon rows of shelves towered above them, housing the spoils of Techno-Synth's relentless ambition.

"Focus," Allen whispered, more to himself than to Lena who stood beside him. Together they stepped into the vault, the air thick with the scent of lubricant and cold metal.

Lena moved ahead, her compact frame weaving between the aisles, eyes scanning for the prize. Allen followed close behind, every sense alert. The weight of responsibility pressed on his shoulders—a burden made lighter by the presence of his team.

"Here," Lena beckoned, her voice barely above a whisper. She pointed to a case sealed within a glass enclosure. Inside, the technology gleamed with an otherworldly aura, its surface etched with circuits that promised untold capabilities.

"Careful," Allen instructed, as Lena deployed a set of specialized tools. They worked in tandem, her hands steady as a surgeon's while Allen stood guard, his weapon ready. The enclosure gave way with a soft sigh, revealing its contents to their eager grasp.

"Container," he said tersely, and Lena produced a padded case from her backpack. Delicately, as though handling the most fragile of relics, they transferred the device into its new cradle. Once secured, Lena looked up at Allen, a twinkle of triumph in her eyes.

"Escape route is still clear," Mia's assurance came through the comms, a lifeline in the darkness. "But move quickly."

"Understood," Allen replied, feeling the pulse of victory thrumming in his veins. They retraced their steps, the container a symbol of hope against the oppressive shadow of Techno-Synth. Every quiet footfall was a step towards reclaiming their stolen identities, a march in the anthem of resistance.

"Almost there," Mia urged them on, her presence a constant guide in the labyrinth they navigated.

With the precious cargo in tow, Allen felt the edges of a grim smile play upon his lips. This was more than mere theft; it was an act of defiance. And with each act, they stitched together the fabric of a future free from tyranny.

Allen's muscles tensed at the sudden chirp of an alarm, a sound that cut through the silence like a blade. He didn't need to look up to know they had company; the sudden whir and hum of rotors told him everything. A security drone — sleek, merciless, and utterly unexpected — hovered above them, its red optic sensors locking onto their position.

"Knox, we've got eyes in the sky!" he barked into the comms, his voice a low growl of urgency. "Lena, keep that tech safe!"

"Roger that!" Knox's response was almost immediate, his voice steady despite the quickening drumbeat of peril.

In seconds, the once-quiet warehouse erupted into chaos. The drone's alarm pierced the air, relentless, threatening to summon a storm of reinforcements upon them. Allen's mind raced even as his body remained poised, a predator ready to strike. He knew that if they were going to get out without a fight against overwhelming odds, this flying harbinger had to be silenced — and fast.

"Sam, we need you!" he ordered over the comms, his eyes fixed on the mechanical monstrosity above. "Quickly please."

Sam quickly jumped into action from his console in the underground bunker. He immediately started to work his magic, "On it sir" he replied to Allen.

The drone's movements became erratic under Sam's hacking assault, its alarm cutting in and out as it struggled against his invisible grip. Allen seized the opportunity, aiming his weapon with deadly precision. A single shot, a whir of disrupted circuits — and then silence as the drone crashed to the ground with a finality that echoed through the warehouse.

"Path's clear," Sam confirmed, his voice crackling with static but victorious nonetheless.

"Move out!" Allen ordered, his senses on high alert for any further surprises. Lena clutched the case tighter to her chest, her resolve unspoken but resolute as she darted behind him. Together they dashed through the maze of shelves, their movements quick and silent — like shadows fleeing from the encroaching dawn.

Knox and Jonas fell into step beside them as the team made for the exit, their pace swift and silent once more. The stolen technology was secure, the drone incapacitated, and their path clear, but the echo of the alarm still rang in their ears, a reminder of the fragility of their victory.

"Nice work," Knox grunted, a nod of respect directed at Allen and the team.

"Thanks to you too," Allen replied, knowing full well that the day's success was born of unity.

The darkness of the warehouse swallowed their hurried steps, but the ghost of an alarm still whispered through the chaos they'd left behind. Allen led with a predator's grace, his frame a shadow among shadows, while the others trailed like waves in his wake. The team moved as one entity, exploiting the temporary blindness of a surveillance system that Mia had crippled with her digital prowess.

"Left here," she murmured over the comms, her voice the thread guiding them through the labyrinthine corridors.

As they reached the entrance, where the cold light from outside cast long, distorted shapes across the floor. It was a scene drained of color, except for the occasional flicker of warning lights that still sputtered, confused by Jonas's sabotage.

"Almost there," Knox whispered, his hand instinctively resting on the hilt of his weapon.

Abruptly, figures materialized at the exit—dark silhouettes bristling with weaponry, a barrier of flesh and steel. The guards, unexpected and unwelcome, were the embodiment of a corporation's will to crush any defiance.

"Contact!" Lena hissed—a single word igniting the fuse of confrontation.

Without hesitation, Allen's voice cut through the static of surprise, commanding yet calm. "Engage!"

His body moved with mechanical precision; the result of training that had been drilled into him until it became second nature. Each motion was a testament to his resolve, an unspoken oath to defy the very institution he once served.

Bullets sang their deadly lullaby, stitching the air with trails of lethal intent. Allen dodged, rolled, and returned fire, the rhythm of combat a savage dance he'd mastered long ago. Beside him, his comrades matched his ferocity, their shots punctuated by the sharp barks of gunfire, a chorus of resistance.

"Covering left flank!" Lena shouted, her voice a blade cutting through the din.

"Suppressing fire!" Knox added, his form a bastion amidst the storm of bullets.

Allen found himself shoulder to shoulder with Lena for a moment, their eyes locking in silent acknowledgment of the trust they'd built—a bond forged in the crucible of rebellion. A stray bullet whizzed dangerously close, a metallic bee with a sting that could kill, but Allen's reflexes prevailed, and he pushed her out of harm's way.

"Keep moving!" he barked to the team, his voice a thunderclap over the chaos.

Together, they pressed forward, an unstoppable force born from shared purpose and sheer tenacity. Each rebel knew the stakes, each heartbeat a drumbeat of defiance against the oppressive rhythm of tyranny.

As the last guard fell, a hush descended, the echoes of battle fading into a grim silence. They stood at the precipice of survival and doom, their breaths mingling with the dust of a world that had forgotten what it meant to be alive.

"Clear!" Knox called out, his tone a rugged whisper in the aftermath.

As they exited and sprinted through the ravaged streets, the thrum of their boots against the broken concrete a frenzied rhythm in the stillness that followed the chaos. Allen led the charge, his muscles protesting and his head slightly aching, reminiscent of the first few days after waking up this new world.

The desolate cityscape, a once-thriving metropolis, loomed around them—a mausoleum of humanity's lost splendor. Skeletal buildings pierced the sky, their windows like unblinking eyes, witnesses to the resistance's fleeting victory. Lena kept pace with Allen, her eyes darting to each shadow that could hide danger, her fingers twitching, ready for another dance with death.

"Almost there," Knox grunted from behind, his voice a gravelly assurance that spurred them onward.

The team worked their way through the next few city blocks, dodging cameras and rerouting around a patrol. Allen led them down a series of alleyways connected by tight turns and cluttered paths leading out to a courtyard. They moved through the open area, every rebel sensing the vulnerability of having no cover.

At last, the hidden entrance to their base materialized before them—a nondescript door tucked away in the skeleton of a fallen skyscraper. Allen entered the code with fingers that were steady, despite the adrenaline that coursed through him. The door slid open with a hush, as if respecting the sanctity of what lay beyond.

Inside, the dim lighting embraced them like an old friend, and the familiar hum of their sanctuary wrapped around their senses. The rebels dispersed, each to their own corner of solace within the warren of rooms carved out from the ruins. The technology was placed in the center of their command room, a beacon of potential amidst the maps and plans that wallpapered the walls.

"Look at this," Lena murmured, her hands already caressing the tech with the tenderness of a lover, "We'll have Techno-Synth reeling from this."

"Let them reel," Allen said, his voice hoarse but steady, "We'll be ready."

Mia locked eyes with him, a silent vow passing between them. They had done more than hit Techno-Synth where it hurt—they had proven that the behemoth could bleed.

71

"Good work today, everyone," Knox's voice cut through the murmur of conversations, "But let's not forget the road ahead."

The rebels gathered, their faces etched with exhaustion and triumph. There was laughter, brief and bright, a counterpoint to the somber reflection that settled over them like ash. They spoke of the way they all worked together in such harmony, and how well they would do in the future.

As the meeting disbanded, Allen found himself standing by the window, looking out at the city that bore the scars of their struggle. Somewhere out there, Techno-Synth was already adapting, preparing. But so were they. He felt the weight of leadership heavy on his shoulders, yet there was a clarity in his purpose that made the burden bearable.

"Hey," Mia approached, her hand resting lightly on his arm, grounding him, "You did good. We all did."

Allen turned to her, the ghost of a smile teasing the corners of his lips, "Together," he affirmed.

"Always," she replied, and in that word, there was a promise, an oath that bound them all to a future they dared to shape with their own hands.

The next morning Allen woke to the noisy hustle and bustle of the rebel bunker. Mia and Jonah were already hunched over the new tech they had scored in the previous day's raid, cords were plugged into the device running up to handheld computers they both held as they tried to crack the encrypted barriers that Techno-Synth had woven into the fabric of their software. Allen watched for a moment; admiration mixed with a sense of urgency. The success of the previous day was only a steppingstone, and time was a luxury they couldn't afford.

"Any luck?" he asked, his voice breaking the hum of concentration.

Mia glanced up at him, her eyes narrowed in focus. "It's sophisticated," she admitted, "but not impenetrable. We're getting there."

Jonah gave a grunt of agreement, his fingers flying over the keys with a speed that belied his bulky frame.

Allen nodded and left them to their work, stepping over to where Knox was huddled with Lena and a few other rebels, poring over maps and photographs so worn that the edges threatened to crumble at a touch.

"We hit them hard yesterday," Knox was saying, his finger tracing a line across a satellite image of what used to be downtown. "But we can't give them time to recover. We strike again, soon."

There was an edge of steel in his voice that matched the look in his eyes. Knox had seen too much to believe in resting too long.

"What's the target?" Lena asked, her eyes keen.

"This communication hub here," Knox replied without hesitation, pointing to a spot marked on the map. "If we can figure out how to implement this new tech into our plan, we could really do some damage."

Mia joined the group. "We have gained access into the mainframe of the device, but we cannot quite figure out how to put it to use yet." she said, with a look of partial defeat on her face. Just then Jonah pipped in from across the room.

"We can see that it will help us gain access to top level plans and communications from the enemy, but some of the firewalls are on a higher level then we have seen in any of their tech as of yet." Jonah put his head back down to focus on his computer screen as he continued typing and trying to make ground.

"I hate to even bring it up, but we may need some help from the FreeTechs to really put this tech to use and get the full potential out of it. They have some abilities that we don't when it comes to this type of stuff." Mia added.

"You really want to trust Cipher with this? and give her access to our new advantage? Knox questioned Mia's idea with a stern voice.

"Of course not Knox, but what choice do we have at this point?" Mia retorted. "The last thing I would ever want to do is include her in our operations, at the same time though...we may have bitten off a little more than we can chew with this one."

Allen felt the weight of the decision settle over the room. He knew Mia's suggestion was a gamble, one that could play right into Techno-Synth's hands if Cipher or any of the FreeTechs betrayed them. Yet it was a risk that might very well shift the tides in their favor—a chance to crack open Techno-Synth's secrets like a nut waiting to be broken.

"We need to consider all our options," Allen finally said, breaking the tense silence. "If Cipher can give us an edge, then it's worth reaching out. We just need to ensure we're not walking into a trap."

Knox grunted, his expression contemplative as he measured Allen's words against his own misgivings. "We have to stay one step ahead," he conceded, "and sometimes that means dancing with devils."

Mia nodded; her eyes locked with Allen's. There was an unsaid understanding between them—their mission transcended personal feelings; they were warriors first and foremost.

Knox took a deep breath and turned to Jonah. "Prepare a secure line of communication with Cipher. We'll set up a meeting on neutral ground."

Jonah gave a curt nod and returned to his workstation; his hands already busy at work.

The rest of the day was spent planning. Knox led the way as they waited for a response from the FreeTechs.

Chapter 7

After several days waiting for the FreeTechs reply, Jonah got a message ping on the secure line. "Okay, just got a response from Cipher, let's open it and see what it says."

Jonah's fingers trembled slightly as he tapped the decryption sequence into the device. The assembled rebels huddled around him; their haggard faces illuminated by the faint blue glow of the screen. The air was thick with expectation, each breath held as if it could sway Cipher's decision. Seconds stretched into an eternity until the message unraveled onto the screen:

"Jonah and Resistance Allies,

The FreeTechs have deliberated. Your cause aligns with ours. We meet at dawn, four days hence. Coordinates and plan to follow.

- Cipher"

A collective sigh rippled through the group, followed by murmurs of relief and cautious optimism. Jonah looked up from the message, finding new strength in his comrades' eyes.

"We have her support," he announced, a rare smile breaking the tension in his features. "Cipher's in."

He didn't need to elaborate; Cipher's reputation preceded her, an invisible threat that had haunted Techno-Synth's most secure vaults and systems. With her on their side, they had a real chance.

"Start preparations," Knox commanded. "We have four days to get ready for what might be our worst decision or the best choice we've ever made."

Later that day a second message pinged through the secure line. Cipher wanted to meet at the rebel bunker. The message read:

"Jonah,

The FreeTechs will come to you. Your bunker is secure and familiar ground for your team. It's time we see the faces behind the cause – and assess whether the alliance is as solid as your encrypted channels. Be prepared to discuss strategy, resources, and your commitment to the endgame. We do not enter this lightly.

- Cipher"

As Jonah read the message aloud, an undercurrent of tension resurfaced amongst the team. Cipher was taking a risk meeting them in their own territory—a sign of trust, or perhaps a test. The rebels exchanged wary glances; Cipher's scrutiny would be rigorous and unapologetic.

"Enhance security protocols," Knox commanded. "I want eyes on every possible approach to this bunker. If we're going to host Cipher and her FreeTechs, we need to show strength, but also that we're not a threat."

Over the next few days, preparations were made with meticulous care. Backups for the backups were created, escape routes mapped out, equipment checked and double-checked. No detail was too small for consideration.

On the fourth dawn, as faint light crested the horizon of the desolate cityscape, a silent phalanx of figures approached the bunker. They moved with precision, their forms cloaked in tech-enhanced gear that glimmered on the security cameras watching them.

Inside the air in the command center was electric with tension, a tangible undercurrent that seemed to hum along with the flickering lights overhead. Knox's fingers drummed a staccato rhythm against the metal table, his dark eyes locked onto Mia's with an intensity that could cut through armor.

"Forming an alliance with the FreeTechs is like making a deal with the devil," he said, his voice low and laced with caution. "We can't trust them—Cipher especially. She's too secretive, too... unpredictable."

Mia leaned forward, her shoulders casting a shadow over the map strewn with markers and lines. "Unpredictable or not, they have resources we lack," she countered, her green eyes steady and resolute. "And Cipher... she's got a mind for this sort of warfare. We need that on our side."

Knox scoffed. "Strategic minds are only an asset when they're pointed at the enemy, not when you're worried they might pivot towards you at the slightest provocation."

Before Mia could respond, the doors to the command center burst open with a pneumatic hiss that silenced the room. All heads turned as Eliza Cormac—Cipher—made her entrance, the embodiment of controlled purpose. Her attire was a patchwork of functional fabrics and technology, a wearable arsenal that spoke of countless battles waged in the digital realm.

The murmurs that had filled the space moments before fell away, replaced by a collective breath held tight in anticipation. Cipher moved with the grace of a panther stalking its prey, her gaze sweeping over the gathered resistance members before settling on Mia and Knox.

"Debating my trustworthiness, are we?" she asked. The question wasn't defensive; it carried the weight of someone accustomed to being doubted, yet undeterred. Her voice resonated with a clarity that demanded attention, each syllable measured and precise.

Mia stood up straighter, her analytical nature assessing the enigmatic figure before her. Despite any reservations, she couldn't ignore the respect Cipher commanded—a respect born of skill and a shared desire to dismantle the oppressive regime that was Techno-Synth.

"Trust has to be earned, Cipher," Mia replied, matching the other woman's stare without flinching. "And we've seen too many double-crosses to hand it out freely."

Cipher tilted her head, a ghost of a smile playing on her lips— a rare display of amusement in their grim reality. "Then let's talk business, shall we? Actions speak louder than words, after all."

The room seemed to exhale then, the tension breaking like a wave as Cipher stepped forward to join them at the table. Mia glanced at Allen, her expression softening just slightly—an acknowledgement of the gravity of their situation and the decisions that lay ahead. Together, they faced a turning point, one that could mean the difference between victory and annihilation.

Cipher unfurled a series of translucent data screens in the air before them, a holographic display of maps and schematics that illustrated her plan with an eerie glow. Her fingers danced across the virtual interface, pulling up images of corporate complexes, security grids, and potential points of infiltration.

"This Techno-Synth communication hub," Cipher began, her voice steady and controlled, "is the linchpin of their control. My proposal is simple in theory but complex in execution." She highlighted a central building pulsing red on the map. "We strike here, simultaneously, with precision that can only come from coordination between the FreeTechs and your resistance."

Mia leaned closer, her sharp eyes scanning the layers of information, noting choke points and defensive positions. Allen folded his arms, his brow furrowed, as if he were trying to read between the lines of code and strategy.

"Your plan hinges on synchronicity," Mia pointed out, skepticism lacing her tone. "But your methods, Cipher... they're untested with our people. We've always valued stealth over force."

"Stealth will get you to the door," Cipher countered, her gaze locking onto Mia's, "but it won't get you through it. Not with what they have guarding their secrets."

"Aggressive tactics could lead to unnecessary casualties," Allen chimed in, his concern mirrored in the faces of other resistance members who whispered amongst themselves. "And we live in the shadows for a reason. Your proposal would put us right in their spotlight."

Cipher's lips twitched. It was clear she had anticipated this pushback. "Sometimes the brightest light casts the darkest shadow, Allen. They won't expect an assault of this magnitude. They're prepared for skulkers and spies, not a hammer at their door."

The room was filled with a heavy silence, the air thick with doubt and the weight of impending decisions. Cipher stood still, a statue of resolve among the sea of hesitation, her proposal a beacon of controversial hope.

"Your secrecy has kept you safe thus far, I won't argue with that," she continued, her voice like a knife—sharp, but elegant. "But safety hasn't brought you any closer to freedom. To win this war, we need to evolve. Together."

Mia exchanged a look with Allen and then Knox, her mind racing with calculations and outcomes. The risks of Cipher's plan gnawed at her, but so did the stagnation of their current plight. To change the game, they might have to roll the dice with the devil they didn't know. Mia stepped away from the table, her hand gesturing for Knox and Allen to join her.

"An alliance could give us the edge we need," Mia murmured, more to herself than anyone else. The words felt foreign on her tongue, admitting the possibility that they couldn't win this fight alone. Her gaze flickered between Allen and Knox, seeking either confirmation or contradiction.

Allen's eyes met hers, and in them, she saw the reflection of her own doubts. But there was something else too—a glimmer of resolve. "We've always known we're outgunned," he said quietly. "The FreeTechs have resources we can only dream of."

"Resources that come at a price," Knox countered, his voice deep and steady. "What about our independence? Our values?"

"Sometimes," Allen replied, the weight of leadership lining his words, "we must adapt to survive. Cipher's plan has merit. It's... audacious."

Mia's lips quirked in an almost-smile, the briefest lapse in her armored facade. Audacious indeed. She turned her attention back to the digital layout of Techno-Synth's stronghold—a fortress of metal and malice.

"Let's make our position in all of this very clear with them," she said finally, stopping her pacing to look at each member of the resistance gathered around. "Outline what this alliance would mean for us. We'll need full transparency—no secrets, no hidden agendas."

"Agreed," Allen said, moving to stand shoulder to shoulder with her. He projected a sense of solidarity that rippled through the room, steadying the nerves of those who wavered.

They gathered around the holographic display that hovered above the table, the ghostly images of buildings and schematics providing a haunting backdrop to their negotiations. Cipher, ever the enigma, watched them, her presence an unspoken challenge to rise to the occasion.

"Resource sharing is non-negotiable," Mia stated, her tactical mind already mapping out the logistics. "We need access to your tech—weapons, shielding, whatever you can spare."

"Coordination is key," Knox added. "Joint operations will require precise timing and communication. No rogue elements."

Cipher nodded in approval. "You'll find the FreeTechs are more than capable allies. Our expertise in cyber warfare can complement your field tactics."

"Your plan is solid, Cipher," Mia began, her voice cutting through the hushed murmurs of the gathered resistance members. "But let's talk about the elephant in the room— transparency. We operate with open books here, and we expect the same from our allies."

Cipher's eyes, sharp as a blade, met Mia's squarely. "Transparency cuts both ways," she responded coolly. "The FreeTechs have our own methods of maintaining security. You're asking us to lay bare our networks, our safehouses."

"Without trust, this alliance is just empty words," Knox interjected, his eyes glancing between the two women. "We need assurances."

A collective breath seemed to be held among the resistant fighters, their stoic faces betraying the weight of the moment. They were a patchwork of survivors—mechanics, teachers, former corporate drones—all united under the banner of rebellion.

"Trust is earned in battle," Cipher conceded, "but I'll provide schematics of our tech. No secrets. In return, you'll do the same."

"Fair enough," Mia replied, though her gut tightened like wire. The very air felt charged, heavy with the gravity of their decision. "Then let's start with cracking this baby open," she said, pointing to the recently stolen, tarp covered tech hidden in the corner.

"Jonah and I have been trying to get through the last few firewalls, but it has proven to be much more sophisticated than anything we have seen so far." Mia added, as she walked over and pulled the cover off.

Cipher's eyes lit up upon seeing what the rebels had acquired. "Oh my god! What a great find, that's the new AI core prototype. It's like stumbling upon a dragon's egg. If we can harness this, the power shift could be monumental."

Cipher approached the device, her hands hovering over it reverently. Mia watched, wary of the awe the tech elicited from her, but also infected by its potential.

"We have heard some chatter about this through some backchannels, but we don't know exactly what it's used for...However, rumor on the street is that it has neural capabilities." Cipher continued. "It's a game changer to say the least."

"We've only scratched the surface," Mia continued. "But if your people can break through its defenses, we might just have a chance at cracking Techno-Synth wide open from the inside out."

Cipher nodded; her expression serious. "My team will gladly get started on it. With this, we'll not only break their defenses— we can turn their own weapon against them."

Mia felt a flicker of excitement stir within her usual calm. The thought of turning Techno-Synth's technology against them was exactly the kind of poetic justice she yearned for.

"All right then," Allen said, stepping forward to place a hand on the AI core. "It's settled. We work together, with full disclosure and shared resources. And our first order of business is making this thing sing our tune."

The group murmured their assent, a mix of trepidation and determination settling into their bones. Cipher glanced around at them all, her face unsettled yet somehow open in this moment of unity. "Then let's begin," she declared, her voice carrying a new kind of harmony—one born of aligned purpose.

One by one, the rebels moved to their stations, an improvised war room coming to life around the AI core. Mia sat at her console, fingers dancing across keys as she coordinated with Cipher's team through secure channels.

Knox stood by, a silent sentinel, eyes flickering between the unfolding collaboration and the door—as if expecting betrayal to walk through at any moment. Allen, meanwhile, had taken up a position at the main display, his strategic mind plotting courses and contingencies.

The next hours passed in a frenzied blur of data streams and encrypted communication. Cipher worked with a near-mystical focus, her expertise merging seamlessly with Mia's analytical prowess. Together, they peeled back layers of code like the skin of an onion, each tier more complex than the last.

"What about Techno-Synth's response?" Allen broke in after a particularly tense silence, his voice snapping them back to the gravity of what they were attempting. "They'll know something's up once we start prodding around in their systems."

Cipher didn't pause in her work. "We've planned for that," she replied smoothly. "Disinformation campaigns are already underway. By the time they notice the anomaly, we'll have planted enough seeds."

Moving to the table in the center of the room, Cipher stood, her presence like a storm on the horizon, dark and promising. "Let's begin planning the coordinated strike. Time isn't a luxury we possess," she stated, her voice carrying the crackle of command.

The underground war room now bore witness to an unprecedented alliance. Maps unfurled across tables, digital screens flickering to life with schematics only Cipher could have procured. Mia leaned over a blueprint of Techno-Synth's mainframe, her fingers tracing the labyrinthine network where she'd dance her hacker's waltz.

"Here," Cipher pointed to a node in the network, "is their Achilles' heel. If we synchronize our attacks—electronic and physical—we can cripple their operations."

"Assuming we get past their defenses," Knox countered, his eyes not leaving the screen, "which are notoriously lethal."

"Which is why my team will handle the infiltration," Cipher replied, the ghost of a smirk tugging at her lips. "We specialize in 'notoriously lethal.'"

Allen surveyed the terrain model of Techno-Synth's compound, its walls seemingly impenetrable fortresses rising from the wasteland. "And we'll need to time our ground assault perfectly. Any delay could be catastrophic."

"Then we don't delay," Cipher said simply, as if punctuality were all that stood between them and victory.

The hours bled away as they plotted, the room alive with the fervor of whispered debates and the scratch of pens marking targets. Despite the gravity of their task, laughter occasionally punctuated the air, a reminder that even in the darkest times, humanity's spirit could not be entirely quenched.

"Remember, we have one shot at this," Mia insisted, meeting each pair of eyes in turn. "One chance to make them bleed as we have."

"Or we bleed out trying," someone muttered, but it wasn't fear that laced the words—it was resolve.

"We stand united," Allen proclaimed, his tone leaving no room for doubt, "or we fall divided."

"United," the room echoed back, and with that single word, the rebels and the FreeTechs, once separate threads, now woven into a tapestry of defiance, were ready to unravel the tyranny of Techno-Synth stitch by bloody stitch.

Chapter 8

With battle plans drawn and teams trained, the new alliance was ready to start their assault on the communication hub. The rebel forces would control the ground operations while the FreeTechs controlled surveillance systems, patrolling drones and any entry points that needed to be hacked.

Although they hadn't been able to crack the AI core in time for the mission, they collectively agreed to proceed with the mission due to the stringent timelines they were up against.

"Go on my signal," Ciphers voice crackled through the comms units.

Allen crouched behind the crumbled facade of an old financial building, the skeletal remains of a once-bustling city center now serving as their staging ground. His piercing blue eyes flicked to each member of his ragtag team, their faces smudged with dirt, determination etched into every line.

They were a mix of hardened rebel soldiers and idealistic FreeTech fighters, bound together by a shared hatred for Techno-Synth and what it had become—a monolithic power dictating the lives of every soul left on this desolate earth. Allen's hand rested on the grip of his weapon, a comforting weight against his thigh.

He nodded at Cipher's signal through the comms. "On my mark," he whispered, even though their earpieces were encrypted. Old habits die hard, especially those born from paranoia and the need for silence in enemy territory.

Evelyn Carter was among them, her blue eyes mirroring his own in readiness. She was one of the FreeTechs more recent recruits, a formidable presence whose skills had quickly earned her a spot on Allen's team. However, Allen felt something was off in her presence and it festered in his mind, casting a shadow of suspicion that he couldn't quite shake off.

With the signal given, the team surged forward, a sudden explosion rocked the ground ahead, and instinctively he dropped to one knee, shielded by a slab of concrete that once was part of an ornate facade. The rebels exchanged glances, confirming that it wasn't their doing—the mission had just become a lot more complicated.

Cipher's voice cut through again, tense but controlled. "We've got incoming TechDrones. They're scrambling defenses."

The sounds of combat erupted almost immediately, a cacophony of gunfire and shouted commands. They were met with unexpected resistance; Techno-Synth's sentries were ready for the attack, but how?

Amidst the fray, a sharp pang of betrayal struck Allen. *Had someone tipped them off? Was there a mole amongst the ranks of this new alliance?* he thought to himself.

Chaos unfolded, with members of the resistance scattering for shelter amongst flying bullets and debris. Allen's gaze locked onto Evelyn's, and for a moment there was a silent plea that passed between them—a search for understanding that was swallowed by the roar of battle.

"What the fuck just happened?" Mia's voice came over the comms.

"Not sure, but we are taking heavy fire. It's almost as if they knew we were coming." Allen replied into his earpiece.

Suddenly the main entrance to the facility opened and more Techno-Synth soldiers and a few mech units emerged. *They definitely knew we were coming*, Allen thought as his mind raced for answers.

Allen instinctively motioned for his team to fan out, finding cover behind the fractured landscape of the city. His training kicked in, and even as the bitter taste of betrayal lingered on his tongue, he shouted commands to regroup and adapt their strategy.

"Cipher, I need eyes in the sky! Mia, work on re-routing their comms. We need confusion on their side," Allen barked into his earpiece, his voice calm yet urgent.

As a small squad of rebels moved to a new position they were struck with a flurry of gunfire, each of them dropping like flies.

Allen's heart sank; these were his people, his responsibility. Every loss was a personal blow, one he felt in the marrow of his bones. The smell of charred concrete and the taste of dust in the air became suddenly poignant reminders of the fragility of their cause.

He scanned the area, trying to pinpoint the source of the gunfire. He needed a way to turn the tides, something to give his team an edge. Mia's voice crackled back over the comms, her tone fierce with concentration.

"I've got something, rerouting their defense protocols now."

The mech units hesitated, their movements becoming erratic as Mia's digital sorcery took effect. The window of opportunity was small, but it was all Allen needed.

"Abort mission!" he roared into the comms. "Now!"

As the team started their retreat four drones swooped in from above, firing with precision and killing 5 more rebels and 3 FreeTech soldiers.

Allen's muscles coiled as he witnessed the carnage, each fallen comrade like a punch to his gut. But this was not the time for grief; this was a time for survival and vengeance. He snapped his attention back to the task at hand, his mind racing with tactical calculations.

He gestured wildly, directing the remaining members of his team toward a network of partially collapsed tunnels they'd mapped out before the mission—a contingency plan that suddenly felt all too optimistic.

"The tunnels!" he yelled over the roar of battle. "Move!"

Evelyn was close by, her rifle cracking in the cold air as she provided covering fire for the retreating rebels. Allen couldn't help but notice how her movements were precise, almost too perfect amidst the chaos. She caught his glance and nodded sharply, an unspoken acknowledgment before she ducked and sprinted toward the tunnel entrance.

As they regrouped beneath the city's scarred surface, Allen felt the weight of leadership pressing down on him like the tons of rubble that entombed them. The dim lighting danced across his team's faces, revealing a mixture of fear, anger, and confusion.

"We were set up," Mia's voice was a low growl on the radio, her fingers still dancing over her makeshift keyboard as she sought to provide some advantage—any advantage—in their new predicament.

"Someone fed them our plans."

Allen's jaw tightened. The sense of betrayal was a visceral knot in his stomach, and there was only one person who hadn't been with them from the start. He turned to Evelyn, the woman whose loyalty he had questioned from the beginning. The look in his eyes was an accusation that didn't need to be spoken aloud.

Her face was impassive, but there was a flicker, a brief glint of something indefinable in her eyes that betrayed her calm exterior. "It wasn't me," she said flatly, her voice cutting through the thick tension. "Think about it, Allen. If I had tipped them off, would I be down here?"

There was logic to her words, cold and hard as the walls surrounding them, but Allen wasn't ready to cast aside his doubts yet.

"We'll deal with this later," he decided after a moment, his voice firm as he addressed the group. "Right now, we need to focus on getting out of here alive and figuring out our next move."

The tunnels seemed to stretch endlessly into darkness, their only guide being the soft glow from the screens of portable devices mounted on their wrists. They moved quickly and quietly through the dank underground pathways, the distant echoes of the battle above fading into a haunting rhythm that pulsed with their footsteps. Allen kept pace at the front, his mind whirling with thoughts of the trap they'd narrowly escaped and the unseen enemy that had anticipated their arrival.

After finally reaching the concealed door to the rebel bunker, Allen quickly typed in the code and the door slid open. Everyone rushed in, a collective sigh of relief echoed down the entry tunnel. "Okay everyone, let's keep moving and reconvene in the command center." Allen ordered.

As they moved through the dimly lit corridors of the bunker, Allen's eyes never strayed far from Evelyn. Her presence was like a constant itch he couldn't scratch, casting doubt over every decision he made.

Normally being back in the bunker after a mission put the rebels at ease, but tonight, it felt different—tainted by the filth of treachery.

As the team members peeled off their gear and tended to their wounds, Allen's mind raced. Whoever had leaked their plans had intimate knowledge of their operations. He knew he had to address the elephant in the room before fear and suspicion tore his team apart.

He took a deep breath and turned to address those gathered in the command center. Every pair of eyes that met his held a glimmer of the same question: Who was the traitor among them?

"Listen up," Allen began, his voice steady despite the turmoil churning inside him. "We've been compromised from within. That much is clear. Our enemy knew too much and anticipated our moves way too accurately."

Whispers broke out like ripples across a pond as rebels exchanged wary looks.

"But fear and suspicion will only serve to further divide us," he continued, silencing the murmurs. "We survive by trust and unity. Now more than ever."

Allen's eyes swept over the assembled rebels, most of whom he had fought alongside on his first mission with the rebels. They were a family, bound by shared loss and a common enemy. However, within that family now lurked a potential viper, and Allen knew the danger of letting paranoia fester unchecked.

"We can't afford to turn on each other," he added firmly. "But we won't ignore this threat either. Cipher—Eliza," he corrected, using her real name to underscore the gravity of the situation, "I need you to run diagnostics on our internal comms. Check for any kind of breach or unusual activity."

Cipher nodded curtly, her eyes already alight with the challenge as she retreated to her workstation, fingers poised like a pianist ready to begin a symphony of code.

Mia crossed her arms, the lines on her face deepening with concern. "We need to consider that it might not just be our comms. It could be personal tech, or worse—someone we trust."

The suggestion hung heavily in the air as everyone considered the possibility. Allen's mind flashed through the time he had shared with the rebels so far, including personal conversations, and shared moments, searching for a sign he might have missed.

Evelyn remained silent, her posture rigid with an unreadable expression. Her eyes briefly locked with Allen's before she shifted her attention to the rest of the group. It was clear she understood the gravity of suspicion resting on her shoulders, yet she seemed to stand taller under its weight, unflinching and resolute.

"We tighten security," Allen concluded. "Nobody goes anywhere alone from now on. We watch each other's backs even closer. And until we figure this out, everyone's a suspect."

There was a collective nod of agreement around the room, though it was accompanied by an almost invisible shiver that ran through them—the realization that their sanctuary had been breached.

The meeting adjourned with a new sense of urgency, but no clear path forward. They were rebels trapped not only by the city's crumbling walls but also by the creeping shadows of distrust among them.

As they dispersed, Allen pulled Mia aside. Her eyes met his with a mixture of strength and vulnerability that always caught him off guard.

"Keep an eye on Evelyn," he said quietly. "Without making it obvious."

Mia nodded without saying a word, but her look told him everything he needed to know—she was on edge, just as much as he was.

He made his way to Cipher's workstation, where she was already deep into scanning their systems for any trace of sabotage.

"Anything?" he asked, his voice tinged with both hope and anger.

"Nothing yet Allen, but if I find out this was one of my people, justice will be swift, and I hope the same goes for you if you find out it was one of yours." Cipher replied, her voice stern and resolute.

"It will," Allen assured, though the thought of executing justice upon one of his own felt like swallowing shards of glass. "Keep me posted."

Leaving Cipher to her work, Allen moved through the bunker's nerve center, passing rebels hunched over screens and maps, their faces illuminated by the soft glow of electronic displays. The usual buzz of activity was subdued by the weight of suspicion that hung in the air like a toxic mist.

He joined Knox and Mia at a secluded corner of the command center, watching as Knox meticulously cleaned his weapon, a habit born out of necessity and nervous energy. Mia's eyes moved from the gun to Allen, her expression grave.

"I can't believe this happened," Knox growled. "We have to find who the traitor is and fast, if it's one of ours I will personally hand down justice."

"Knox, we need to be careful," Allen cautioned, placing a hand on his friend's shoulder to temper his resolve. "We can't afford to let anger cloud our judgment. Whoever did this is cunning and patient. We'll need to be the same."

Knox looked up, his eyes hard as the steel of his weapon, but he nodded in understanding. Mia leaned in closer, lowering her voice so only they could hear.

"We're not just fighting Techno-Synth anymore," she said quietly. "We're fighting fear and mistrust within our own ranks. This could tear us apart before the enemy even gets a chance."

"I know," Allen replied, meeting Mia's gaze with a steely determination. "Which is why we need to be smarter than them. We need to outthink and outmaneuver whoever is doing this."

Mia nodded, her expression hardening as she considered their next move. Knox finished with his weapon and stood up, snapping it back into place on his belt with a click that reverberated through the tense silence.

Cipher suddenly appeared standing next to them. "Guys, I think I have something." she said in a whisper. "Come with me."

Following her back to her workstation, she sat down and opened a file on the computer. "Here," she scrolled down through screens of code. "There are a couple anomalies popping up, they seem to have been sent from Evelyn's portable wrist unit." She opened another file. "This is the last message she sent."

Allen, Mia, and Knox crowded around the screen, the fluorescent light casting shadows across their focused expressions. Cipher pointed to a string of characters that stood out amidst the jumble of code—illicit commands hidden within normal communications.

"Are you sure it's from her unit?" Allen's voice was low but charged with a mixture of anger and disbelief.

Cipher nodded, her face grave. "I triple-checked. The timestamps match her usage logs, and the digital signature is a match. I don't see how it could have been faked without some serious insider knowledge."

Mia's eyes flicked to Allen, searching for his reaction. "If Evelyn sent this," she said slowly, "then she knows we're onto her. She'll either run or double down."

Knox cracked his knuckles, an audible tension in the act. "Let me at her," he muttered, but Allen raised a hand to stop him.

"No," Allen said firmly. "We can't jump to action without absolute certainty." He paused, looking at each of them. "We need evidence that'll stand up not just among us but in front of everyone."

The silence that followed was charged with anticipation and dread. Cipher returned to her work, her fingers flying over the keyboard as if each keystroke was a step closer to unveiling the truth.

"Where is Evelyn?" Cipher asked. "I would like to have a talk with her, can one of you find her and bring her to me please."

"On it." Allen was quick to act. "I think she is in the armory; I will go check."

Walking through the main meeting area of the command center he found himself outside the small armory, where weapons and ammunition were securely stored. Inside, he could see Evelyn and a couple rebels meticulously checking and cleaning their sidearms—the disciplined routine of a soldier that had not faltered even in the face of distrust.

Their eyes met once again through the reinforced glass window, and this time it was Allen who held her gaze. He needed to confront her, not as an accuser, but as a leader seeking to understand. With a deliberate push, he opened the door and stepped in.

Evelyn did not look up from her task as he approached, but he knew she was acutely aware of his presence.

"Evelyn," he began cautiously. "Cipher wants to see you; she asked me to come find you and let you know."

"Ok, I am almost done here...and there we go, all clean." she answered back, her tone steady and unflinching. "Alright, let's go see what she wants." Evelyn stood up smiling as she holstered her freshly cleaned automatic pistol.

They walked back out to the main area to find a chair sitting in the middle of the room. Rebels and FreeTechs gathered around to see what was about to transpire.

Cipher standing tall with her commanding presence, addressed Evelyn directly.

"Please sit Evelyn," she gestured with her hand toward the chair, her voice was soft and, in a way, very inviting. "I would like to ask you a few questions."

"Okay boss." Evelyn's voice was shaky as she took her seat.

"I found the messages Evelyn, I have decrypted them as well, we know it was you who leaked our plans to the enemy." Cipher got straight to the point. "How could you do something like this, after everything the FreeTechs have done for you."

"I never wanted this," she choked out. "They forced me into it. Threatened my family..."

Before she could finish her sentence, Cipher's hand blurred to her hip, retrieving a gleaming knife with a speed that defied the eye, slicing through Evelyn's throat in a swift, merciless arc.

"No one threatens this alliance, or our mission," Cipher spoke, her voice as cold as the steel in her hand, removing any doubt about her loyalty to the cause. "No one betrays us without consequence. We lost some great people because of Evelyn's choices, and justice had to be served."

The room was silent but for the sound of Evelyn's body crumpling to the floor and the blood beginning to pool around it.

Allen felt a chill run down his spine at the ruthlessness he had just witnessed. This was not quite the justice he had envisioned.

Mia caught his eye, her face pale but resolute. She knew as well as he did that Cipher's actions, while extreme, carried with them a message that could not be ignored. The FreeTechs would not tolerate betrayal; their survival depended on unity and trust.

Knox stood stiffly, his hands clenched at his sides, eyes fixed on Evelyn's still form. The tension that had been building within him seemed to break like a wave, leaving behind a grim acceptance.

Cipher wiped her blade clean on a cloth and looked up at everyone gathered. "We are at war," she said calmly. "Our enemy is cunning and ruthless. We must be willing to make hard choices if we want to protect what we've built here."

Allen knew she was right, but he also knew that they could not allow fear to dictate their actions. This new alliance hinged on trust and transparency, any hint of treason had to be dealt with quickly and decisively.

The days that followed were spent getting everything back in order. Still reeling from the events that had taken place, Allen knew they had to press on. He gathered a small group of rebels and FreeTechs for a recon mission on a nearby Techno-Synth checkpoint.

As the group reached their destination everyone fanned out and took up their assigned observation points. Allen hid around a corner behind some broken concrete, the team the signal to start their reconnaissance.

He began watching the Techno-Synth soldiers every move as they performed their daily duties within the checkpoint, he saw two soldiers laughing as one told a joke. There were multiple guards posted in reinforced positions; large automatic machine guns ready to fire at any threat.

Suddenly a sound moving out of the darkness shattered the silence, he could barely register the faint shuffle of footsteps behind him before a crushing blow landed at the base of his skull. Pain flared through his vision, and the world slipped away into an inescapable black void.

Chapter 9

Allen's eyes fluttered open to the sight of flickering shadows cast by the dimly lit cell. Disoriented and uncertain of his surroundings, he took a moment to steady himself. He gradually became aware of the cold, unforgiving surface beneath him and the damp, stale air that filled his lungs.

He noticed a bandage on his right forearm, a tinge of pain as he touched it, someone had drawn his blood. His eyes darted around, seeking an explanation for the unfamiliar environment that confined him. The room was small, with concrete walls that seemed to close in on him, amplifying his feelings of vulnerability. As panic threatened to overwhelm him, Allen's keen mind made the connection - he was being held captive by Techno-Synth forces.

"Damn it," he muttered under his breath, his natural confidence momentarily overshadowed by the realization of his predicament.

He forced himself to take slow, deep breaths, drawing on the inner strength that had seen him through countless challenges. Reminding himself that he was more than just a pawn in Techno-Synth's cruel game, Allen clenched his fists, determined not to let fear creep in any further.

As he assessed his options, the faint echo of footsteps reached his ears, growing louder and more distinct with each passing second. Allen's heart hammered against his chest.

"Get it together, Mercer," Allen whispered, bracing himself for the confrontation that loomed. He couldn't afford to show weakness or hesitation. He had to be smart, resourceful, and adaptable - traits that had served him well during his time with the rebels.

With each footstep that resonated through the narrow hallway outside his cell, Allen's tension intensified. His muscles coiled like springs, preparing to react to whatever might come his way. The door clicked open, the silhouette of a man framed within the doorway, bathed in the harsh light from the corridor. It was Commander Jonathan Blake, Allen's former mentor and now his most formidable adversary.

Blake entered the room with a confidence that seemed to fill the space, his graying hair a testament to years spent within the power structure of Techno-Synth. His sharp blue eyes locked onto Allen's with an unwavering intensity that spoke volumes without a word being uttered.

"Good evening, Allen. I do hope you're comfortable," Blake's voice dripped with sarcasm, the familiar baritone sending a chill through Allen's spine.

Blake stepped forward into the cell, allowing the door to swing shut behind him with an ominous thud. The room seemed to shrink with his presence, leaving Allen cloaked in shadow while Blake himself remained bathed in a glow that seemed to accentuate the graying edges of his hair and the piercing intensity of his eyes.

"As comfortable as one can be in these accommodations," Allen returned evenly, masking the unease that simmered just beneath the surface.

Blake chuckled dryly, "Sarcasm doesn't suit you. Not anymore at least. Though it seems there's much about you that has changed."

Allen's glare didn't waver; he knew better than to let Blake see him falter. "People change when they see the truth."

"The 'truth' is a funny thing," Blake circled around Allen like a shark eyeing its prey. "It bends, it breaks... It can be refashioned to fit our narratives. But let's not speak in riddles; I know you, Allen. Or at least, I knew who you were."

Allen's posture remained rigid, a statue of defiance against Blake's probing. "And what truth have you twisted to justify your actions now?"

Blake paused, coming to stand directly before Allen. The air between them crackled with the electricity of unspoken history. "The truth that you were once the architect of the very system you now seek to dismantle."

Allen's breath caught in his throat, a flicker of doubt shadowing his features. This was a blow he hadn't anticipated, an arrow aimed not at his body but at his resolve.

Blake continued, relentless, "You see, before your... awakening," he said the word as if it left a bitter taste in his mouth, "you championed the ordinances that brought order to chaos. You were instrumental in crafting the society Techno-Synth envisioned."

Allen fought to keep his composure under Blake's scrutiny. The revelation threatened to unravel him, but he couldn't afford to give into confusion. "Lies," he spat out, though the certainty in Blake's tone gnawed at him.

"Is it?" Blake retorted sharply. "Or is it simply a past you refuse to acknowledge? Perhaps it's easier to play the role of the noble rebel than to face the consequences of your own actions."

Allen shook his head, trying to clear it. Blake's words were a venom, seeping into the cracks of his resolve. He needed to push back, to defend not just himself but the man he had become. "Even if there's truth to what you say, then I am making amends. Your vision of order is nothing but oppression."

Blake sighed, a sound that carried a hint of genuine regret. "Amends," he repeated softly, as though testing the weight of the word. "Is that what you call this insurrection? You dismantle what you don't understand, Allen. We bring stability, safety—"

"Safety?" Allen interrupted, the fire in his voice reigniting. "At what cost? Freedom? Identity?"

"Chaos is the price of your so-called 'freedom,'" Blake countered with a stern gaze. "Without structure, there is only ruin."

The tension in the room thickened like fog. They stood inches apart, two men with shared histories and opposing ideologies, locked in an invisible struggle.

"I will stop you," Allen vowed quietly, his eyes never leaving Blake's.

Blake leaned closer until they were nearly nose-to-nose. "I made you who you are," he whispered fiercely. "And I can unmake you just as easily."

Allen's resolve hardened like forged steel. "You may have shaped me once, Blake, but I am not your creation to dismantle. My will is my own."

For a moment, the two men simply stared at each other, the air around them charged with the weight of their enmity and the history that bound them together. Then, without another word, Blake turned and strode out of the cell, the sound of his footsteps receding until Allen was left alone once more with his thoughts.

The silence in the wake of Blake's departure was deafening. Allen's mind raced as he processed the revelation. Had he truly been an agent of Techno-Synth's oppression? Was his rebellion a path to redemption or a fool's errand born from forgotten sins?

No. He shook his head, as if to physically cast aside the doubts. His past didn't matter; it was his actions now that defined him. He was Allen Mercer, the man who stood against tyranny, who fought for the broken and silenced voices of the city.

He moved to the corner of the cell where a faint drip of water echoed—a reminder that life persisted even in this desolate place. Drawing on an inner well of determination, he began to plan his next move. Escape was a distant hope, yet not an impossible one. He had allies on the outside, and Mia... Mia would be looking for him. With her quick wit and strategic mind, she wouldn't rest until she had found a way to breach Techno-Synth's walls.

For now, Allen had to stay alive. Staying sharp meant staying unpredictable. He started doing pushups, using the physical exertion to clear his mind and keep his body ready for whatever might come next. With each movement, he became more than muscle and sinew; he became the embodiment of resistance.

Hours passed—or perhaps days—in the unchanging dimness of the cell. Time seemed irrelevant, each moment stretching into eternity under the constant surveillance of unseen eyes. Allen knew that Blake was watching him, looking for cracks in his armor.

But Allen would give him nothing.

Instead, he focused on memories of the rebellion: the first time he met Mia, her fiery spirit challenging him to question everything; the nights spent huddled over maps and makeshift comms equipment, plotting their next strike against Techno-Synth; the faces of those who had fallen, whose names he whispered like a litany against despair.

When the door opened again, it wasn't Blake who entered but a silent guard bearing a tray of food – a meager offering of stale bread and a cup of water that bore the faint metallic tang of rust. The guard set it down without a word, his eyes hidden behind reflective visor goggles which mirrored Allen's steely gaze back at him.

Allen eyed the food with suspicion, noting how the guard's movements carried an air of calculated indifference. Was this a test? Or perhaps something more sinister – poison, maybe. No matter. He would not give them the satisfaction of seeing him weakened by hunger. He reached for the bread, breaking off a piece and carefully watching the guard for any reaction.

The guard turned to leave, but Allen's voice halted him momentarily. "Tell Blake I'm not broken yet."

Without acknowledging the words, the guard stepped out, and the door sealed shut once more.

Alone again, Allen surveyed his cell. He had taken in every detail from the moment he'd been thrown into it: the slightly uneven floor, the cracks in the sterile walls which spoke of unrestrained decay beneath the façade of control, and the way sound seemed to die just inches from its source, creating an oppressive silence.

Allen touched his bandaged forearm, wincing slightly at the pain that still throbbed there. He wondered why they would take his blood. What were they up to now.

Just then the cell door opened again, and two guards entered at a fast pace and grabbed Allen, dragging him out of his confined quarters and into a long hallway lined with cell doors. They guided him out into a large room where Commander Blake and a few other Techno-Synth leaders stood.

Blake watched Allen being dragged in, a smug satisfaction evident on his face. "Welcome, Allen," he said, his voice reverberating through the expansive room. "I trust you've had time to contemplate your position."

The room was stark, utilitarian, with the cold aesthetic of Techno-Synth's efficiency. High above, a skylight revealed a slice of the poisoned sky, a constant reminder of the world outside that lay in ruin – a world Blake and his cronies claimed they could save.

Allen's muscles tensed as he was forced into a steel chair at the center of the room. Restraints snapped around his wrists and ankles with mechanical precision. He glared defiantly at Blake, who approached with an unreadable expression.

Blake's eyes moved to the guards. "Leave us," he commanded, and they exited without a word, leaving behind a heavy silence.

Once they were alone, Blake circled Allen like a shark scenting blood in the water. "You still have that fire, I see," he said thoughtfully. "Resourceful as ever."

Allen remained silent, meeting his stare with unyielding resistance.

Blake stopped before him and leaned down, his eyes locking onto Allen's. "I've brought you here to offer you one last chance," he said quietly. "Return to Techno-Synth. Help us rebuild what you've tried to destroy."

"And if I refuse?"

Blake straightened up, his expression hardening. "Then you will watch as your rebellion is crushed," he turned away and moved toward a large screen sitting on a nearby table.

With a single touch, the screen came to life. As the desolate landscape came into view, Allen realized it was a live camera feed from a hunter-killer drone. As the drone rounded the corner of a tall building, a small search party of rebels became visible, marked by red digital squares locking onto each figure.

"This group here," Blake paused to turn and look at Allen. "They have been searching for you."

Allen's heart raced at the sight of the small team moving cautiously through the ruins. They were exposed, vulnerable, and Allen knew that with a single command from Blake, their lives could be snuffed out like candles in a storm.

Lena was there, recognizable even as a silhouette against the contrast of crumbling concrete and twisted metal. She was scanning the horizon, no doubt searching for any sign of Techno-Synth surveillance—a tragic irony, Allen thought bitterly.

Blake's voice cut through his thoughts. "Consider it, Allen. All you need to do is say the word and I can ensure their safety. Your return would give them hope... misguided though it may be."

Allen fought against the surge of panic, forcing himself to remain outwardly calm. To show fear now would be to play into Blake's hands. "You think threatening them will bring me back to your side?" he spat out with venom.

"It's not a threat," Blake replied smoothly. "It's a promise. A promise of mercy if you comply, or a demonstration of power if you resist."

Allen studied the screen intently, watching as one of the rebels signaled to the others. They moved with precision, a dance honed by too many close calls and desperate battles. The bond they shared went beyond mere allegiance; they were family, united by a common cause and an unwavering belief in a future free from Techno-Synth's grasp.

The weight of Blake's ultimatum anchored itself in Allen's chest, a leaden reminder of the stakes at play. Every instinct screamed for him to protect his comrades, to preserve the fragile flame of rebellion they nurtured against the dark. Their struggle was his struggle; their fate intertwined with his own since the day he first defied the world Techno-Synth was building—a world that suffocated freedom beneath layers of control and surveillance.

Blake's eyes narrowed, watching Allen closely. "You care about them. It's written all over you," he said. "All the more reason to accept my offer."

The screen flickered as the drone adjusted its position, giving them a closer view of Lena, who was leading the search party below. Her eyes were sharp and searching, her presence a steadying force among the rebels. They couldn't hear her words, but her gestures spoke volumes – she was issuing orders, directing their movements with quiet confidence.

Allen's jaw clenched, his mind racing through scenarios, each one ending in bloodshed and loss. But surrendering to Blake would mean the death of everything they fought for, every sacrifice made rendered meaningless.

"Your so-called mercy," Allen began, his voice steady despite the turmoil within, "is nothing but a leash. But you forgot one thing—rebels don't do well on leashes."

A flicker of irritation crossed Blake's face before it settled back into a mask of cold indifference. "Pity," he murmured. The commander walked back to the table and pressed a button on the screen.

The image zoomed in, the drone's targeting system locking onto the figures of the rebels with an ominous beep. Allen's heart pounded against his ribs as if trying to break free from the situation he found himself powerless to control.

"Last chance, Allen," Blake said, his voice devoid of warmth. "Rejoin us and lead these people to salvation or stay stubborn and lead them to their graves."

Allen's eyes never left the screen, where Lena now looked directly up, as if sensing the danger from above. His mind raced through sudden memories of Techno-Synth's indoctrination methods, the lies they fed him, and the truth that lay beneath their veneer of salvation – control at any cost. He thought of Mia, her spirit unbreakable despite everything they'd endured. He thought of all those who had fallen already, their sacrifices like ghosts in his wake.

"I won't betray them," Allen said with quiet finality.

Blake sighed theatrically. "Then you leave me no choice." His hand hovered over another button on the control panel, a grim sentence waiting to be delivered at his fingertips.

Allen braced for what was coming next, but before Blake could enact his plan, a sudden crash echoed through the room. The wall opposite them exploded inward in a shower of debris, a cloud of dust filled the room.

Mia stood in the gaping hole, her silhouette framed by the settling dust. Her eyes found Allen's instantly, fierce and determined. She raised her arm, revealing a sleek device strapped to her wrist, its lights blinking rapidly—a signal jammer.

The screen fizzed and went blank as the drone footage disappeared. Blake spun around, his composure finally cracking as he realized his control had slipped. His hand, which had been milli-seconds away from condemning the rebels to death, now hovered useless above the dead panel.

Allen's restraints clicked open, unlocked by Mia's timely intervention. With the agility born of years spent outrunning Techno-Synth's enforcers, he leapt from the chair and dove for cover behind a fallen beam.

"Go!" Mia shouted over the chaos as additional rebels poured into the room through the breach she had created. Rapid fire began to sing through the air as they engaged with Techno-Synth forces rushing in to respond to the intrusion.

Blake was shouting orders now, but his voice was just another sound in the rage of battle. He glanced at Allen with a look that was both furious and betrayed before disappearing behind a phalanx of his own soldiers.

Allen scrambled to his feet and joined Mia, their backs pressed against one another as they assessed their situation.

"That was close," Allen exhaled, his voice a mix of gratitude and lingering shock. "You're one hell of a timing expert."

Mia's response was a smirk that didn't quite reach her eyes. "We don't leave anyone behind, remember? Now let's move. This place will be swarming with reinforcements any minute." her fingers dancing over her wrist device as she worked to maintain the jamming signal. "We don't have much time before they reroute their systems." She handed Allen the pistol from her side.

Their eyes met for a fleeting moment, acknowledging the gravity of their predicament. Around them, the room was a maelstrom of conflict, with rebels and Techno-Synth forces exchanging fire amidst the shattered remnants of Blake's control hub.

"We need to get out," Allen said, scanning for an exit. "and regroup with the others."

Mia nodded, they moved together through the chaos, Allen and Mia, like two halves of a whole. Where one advanced, the other covered; where one fell back, the other stepped up. In that moment they had become more than just comrades in arms—they were the embodiment of the rebellion's heart and soul.

As they emerged from the building, they could see Lena's search team moving towards them. "Lena, over here!" Allen yelled, taking a deep breath of relief upon realizing she and her group were still in one piece.

Outside, the sounds of conflict resonated through the broken city. Above them, the drone that had once been an omen of death now lay in pieces, part of its mangled metal clinging to the side of a building, its threat neutralized by Mia's swift action. The night sky opened up before them as they fought their way out of Blake's stronghold, a tapestry of stars watching impassively over a world torn to shreds.

As they trudged through the ruined city towards the rebel base, Allen couldn't shake off the weight of Blake's revelations about his true identity. How would his teammates react? Would they still see him as an ally or turn against him once they knew the truth? He knew he had to come clean, but the thought of losing their trust made his stomach churn with anxiety.

Chapter 10

The sharp smell of smoke slowly filled Allen's nostrils as he stood at attention, Commander Blake's steely stare boring into him. The city's neon-lit skyline flickered ominously behind them, casting shadows across the rooftop command center.

"Mercer," Blake's voice cut through the night air, "I need you to take your team and shut down the uprising in Sector 7. Use whatever force necessary. We can't let this spark spread." Allen nodded, his jaw set. "Understood, sir. We'll contain the situation."

Blake's eyes narrowed. "Remember, these people are a threat to everything we've built. Don't hesitate."

The dream dissolved into darkness, and Allen jerked awake, his heart pounding. The stark contrast of the rebel base's dim lighting disoriented him for a moment. He sat up, running his fingers through his disheveled hair, a habit that seemed to ground him in reality.

"What have I done?" he muttered, the weight of his past actions crushing down on him.

Allen swung his legs over the side of the cot, his muscular frame tense with unease. The revelations about his role in Techno-Synth's regime played on a loop in his mind, each memory a fresh wound.

He stood, pacing the small room, his conflicted thoughts spilling out in hushed tones. "I believed in the order we were creating. But at what cost? How many lives did I ruin following Blake's orders?"

Allen's fists clenched involuntarily, a surge of anger rising within him. "He manipulated me, used my loyalty against me. And now..."

He trailed off, his eyes falling on the worn rebel insignia pinned to his jacket. The symbol of resistance, of hope - everything he once fought against.

"Can I really be one of them?" Allen wondered aloud, his voice barely above a whisper. "After everything I've done, do I have the right to fight for this cause?"

He closed his eyes, taking a deep breath to steady himself. When he opened them again, a flicker of determination had kindled in their blue depths.

"No," Allen said firmly, straightening his posture. "I can't change the past, but I can damn well make sure Blake doesn't destroy any more lives."

He moved towards the door, each step more resolute than the last. As Allen stepped out into the hushed corridors of the rebel base, he knew one thing for certain - he would do whatever it took to bring down the empire he once served, even if it meant facing the man he once called mentor.

Making his way through the dimly lit corridor, the metallic tang of recycled air filled his nostrils. Flickering lights and rust-streaked walls, a stark reminder of the decaying world above.

Footsteps echoed softly, growing louder. Mia appeared around the corner, her eyes locking onto Allen with an intensity that made him straighten. She approached, her movements fluid and purposeful.

"Allen," Mia said, her voice low and soft. "You doing ok?"

He nodded yes, studying her face. The concern in her eyes was unmistakable, but there was something else too - a fierce determination that seemed to radiate from her very being.

113

"I know you're struggling with what Blake told you," Mia continued, tucking a stray lock of hair behind her ear. "But I need you to understand something. We believe in you, Allen. The resistance needs you."

Allen's jaw clenched, a storm of emotions churning within him. "How can you be so sure?" he asked, his voice rough. "After everything I've done..."

Mia's lips quirked in a humorless smile. "Because I've seen you fight, Allen. Not just with your fists, but with your heart. You're not the man Techno-Synth created anymore."

He exhaled slowly, feeling some of the tension leave his shoulders. "There's more," he said, glancing around. "Where's Knox? He needs to hear this too."

As if on cue, Knox emerged from a nearby room, his weathered face creased with concern. Allen took a deep breath, readying himself.

"Blake told me about my past," he began, his voice low and intense. "About how I was a main figure in the creation and growth of Techno-Synth's oppressive agenda. But there's something that doesn't add up. When they captured me, they took my blood. Why?"

Mia and Knox exchanged glances, their expressions a mix of surprise and unease.

"Your blood?" Knox repeated, his brow furrowing. "That's... unusual."

Allen nodded, his mind racing. "It has to be important. Something about my genetic makeup, maybe? But what could they want with it now?"

The silence that followed was heavy with unanswered questions and growing unease. As Allen looked from Mia to

114

Knox, he could see the gears turning in their minds, trying to piece together this new puzzle.

"Whatever it is," Mia said finally, her voice hard with resolve, "we need to find out. And fast."

Allen nodded, feeling a renewed sense of purpose. Whatever secrets his blood held, he was determined to uncover them - and use them against the very empire that created him.

A heavy, suffocating tension filled the air as Cipher and Jonas strode into the room, their expressions etched with unyielding determination. Allen's body immediately seized up in response to the grave atmosphere, his muscles coiling like a tightly wound spring as his mind struggled to catch up with the urgency of the moment.

Cipher's voice cut through the silence, sharp and clear. "We've cracked the A.I. Core," she announced, her eyes locking with Allen's. "And what we found... it's worse than we imagined."

Allen leaned forward, his heart racing. "Tell me."

Jonas stepped up, his normally jovial demeanor replaced by a somber intensity. "They're calling it Project Shadow," he explained, activating a holographic display from his wrist device. "It's a new wave of oppressive measures, designed to crush any remaining resistance."

As the holographic images flickered before him, Allen's mind reeled. Scenes of advanced surveillance drones, neural implants for mass control, and automated enforcement units flashed by in a nightmarish parade.

"My God," Allen muttered, his fists clenching involuntarily. "They're going to turn the entire population into puppets."

Cipher nodded grimly. "Exactly. And that's not all. The project seems to involve some kind of biological component. Something about enhancing human capabilities through genetic manipulation."

Allen's blood ran cold. Could this be connected to why they took his blood? He pushed the thought aside, focusing on the immediate threat.

"How close are they to implementing this?" he asked, his voice tight with urgency.

"Too close," Jonas replied, his usual wit absent. "We're looking at a matter of weeks, maybe days."

Allen's mind raced, strategizing, analyzing. "We need to act fast," he said, looking around at the grim faces surrounding him. "If we can disrupt this project, we might have a chance to turn the tide."

As the others began to discuss potential plans of action, Allen felt a familiar fire igniting within him. The revelations about his past, the mystery of his blood, the looming threat of Project Shadow – it all coalesced into a burning determination.

"Alright, you two keep digging into that core," Knox said. "We need to find out as much as we can about this 'Project Shadow', as fast as we can...Allen you come with me please."

Allen and Knox made their way to a quieter section of the base, where the steady hum of machinery provided a backdrop to their private conversation.

Knox fixed on Allen with a hard stare, his grizzled features etched with deep lines of worry and responsibility. "You've been through hell, Mercer," he started, his voice like gravel. "But we've all seen how you've adapted, how you've become integral to our cause."

Allen met Knox's eyes squarely. "I'm committed to stopping them," he affirmed. "No matter the cost."

Knox nodded slowly. "I believe you," he said. "But this new information about Project Shadow changes everything. If they're experimenting with genetic manipulation and you're part of it..."

He let the implication hang in the air between them – heavy and ominous.

"We can't afford any unknown variables," Knox continued, his eyes not leaving Allen's. "Your DNA could be the key to preventing or countering whatever they're planning."

Allen's chest tightened at the thought. He was no stranger to being used as a weapon, but this... This was different. This time he had a choice.

"Let's see what Cipher and Jonas come up with, then we can plan accordingly." Allen responded, his tone very confident. "What ever they are planning on doing with my DNA, it is going to backfire on them, I can assure you of that Knox." A sly smirk came over Allen's face.

"Sounds good," Knox replied. "Now, get some more rest while Mia and I help figure out our next moves, we will come get you when we have enough information."

Allen nodded in agreement and turned to leave, but Knox's hand on his shoulder stopped him. "And Allen," Knox added in a softer tone, "we're in this together. Remember that."

The gesture, simple yet filled with unspoken understanding, bolstered Allen's resolve. He nodded once more before heading off to find a moment of solitude.

As he settled back into his quarters, Allen lay on the cot that served as his bed, staring at the ceiling, he closed his eyes and drew a deep breath. The weight of responsibility pressed down on him like a physical force, but beneath it was something else — a thrumming energy that pulsed through his veins. He could feel the potential within him, dangerous and untamed.

He thought about Mia's steadfast belief in him, Knox's unwavering support, and Cipher's calculating intelligence. They were more than allies; they were the beating heart of a resistance that would not to be silenced.

In the stillness, he allowed himself a moment to reflect. He thought of the countless lives hanging in the balance, of the world that Techno-Synth sought to chain in darkness. He couldn't let that happen—not while he still had breath in his body.

His mind refused to quiet, turning over every detail of Project Shadow, every fragment of conversation with Blake. He shut his eyes tightly, willing sleep or at least some brief respite from the relentless tide of thoughts.

A few hours later, a soft knock roused him from a fitful doze. Mia stood at his door, her face illuminated by the dim light that filtered through the cracks in the aged walls.

"We've got something," she said without preamble. "Cipher and Jonas have found a potential weakness in Techno-Synth's systems—a backdoor into their mainframe that we might be able to exploit."

Allen swung his legs off the cot and stood up swiftly. "Let's not waste any more time then," he replied with renewed vigor.

They joined Knox, Cipher, and Jonas in the central command room where an intricate web of data streams danced across multiple screens. Jonas was nearly vibrating with excitement as he explained their findings, while Cipher maintained her usual composed demeanor, her eyes never leaving the flow of information.

"It's a legacy code from their earlier platforms," Jonas was saying, pointing to a blinking point in the network schematic. "Looks like it was overlooked in their last security update. It's not much, but it might just be enough for us to slip through their defenses and gather intel on Project Shadow."

Mia leaned over the console, her fingers flying across the keyboard as she worked to enhance the image. "If we can access the mainframe, we can potentially download everything they have on this project. Schematics, deployment plans, even personnel files," she said.

Knox folded his arms across his chest, his expression serious. "And if we're lucky, maybe find a way to sabotage the whole damn thing before it gets off the ground."

Allen watched the team work with a mix of pride and anticipation. "What do you need from me?" he asked.

Cipher turned to him, her voice steady. "We will need you to lead an infiltration team into one of their communication facilities, while we can hack into the mainframe remotely, we still need boots on the ground to plant some hardware into the system."

Mia stepped forward, her eyes locked onto the screens with a hunter's precision. "It won't be easy. We'll need to synchronize a series of cyber-attacks to distract their countermeasures long enough for Cipher to gain access."

"And once inside?" Allen asked.

Cipher's lips curved into a razor-thin smile. "Then I wreak havoc," she stated simply. "I'll disable their surveillance network first, giving us a much-needed edge, then I'll go ape shit on the rest of their networks," she subtly gave an ominous laugh.

Knox nodded approvingly, his eyes sweeping over the assembled rebels. "Once that's done, we can launch an all-out offensive on their other facilities—hit them hard before they can initiate Project Shadow."

The room buzzed with a tangible energy now as plans were rapidly being drawn up, roles assigned, and contingencies debated. Allen felt himself caught up in the swell of activity; for the first time since confronting the horrors of his past, he recognized the power of collective purpose.

He stood, shoulders squared, addressing the room with a voice that carried both authority and camaraderie. "We've each seen what Techno-Synth is capable of," he said. "We've all suffered at their hands. Now, it's our turn to strike back—to show them that their reign of fear ends with us."

Murmurs of agreement filled the air as each member took up their task with renewed vigor. Mia met Allen's eyes, a silent communication passing between them that spoke volumes. They were in this together.

Cipher was already deep in conversation with Jonas about encryption bypass algorithms, while Knox coordinated logistics with other cell leaders via a secure comms link. The base had transformed into a hive of focused action—a testament to the resistance's resilience.

As Allen prepared for the mission, he couldn't shake the thought of his DNA being taken—of what secrets it might hold and how it could be used against them. But Knox was right; they couldn't afford to dwell on unknowns. They would deal with whatever came their way because they had no choice at this point.

A world away, yet disturbingly close, within Techno-Synth's sterile headquarters, Commander Blake sat in the harmonious glow of his office, staring at the massive display that dominated one wall. It showed a map of their territories, dotted with pulsing lights that represented active units and ongoing operations. The room was silent, except the low hum of machinery and the occasional click as he tapped at his console.

His features were set in a grim line; his plans had been meticulous, every variable accounted for—except for Allen Mercer's unpredictable resurgence. Blake had mentored the man, shaped him into an ideal agent, but now he was possibly he biggest threat to his success.

He turned in his chair to face Dr. Miranda Reiss, Techno-Synth's lead geneticist, who stood patiently awaiting his orders. Her eyes were cold and calculating, much like his own.

"We need to expedite our efforts," Blake said curtly. "The rebellion is more resourceful than anticipated."

Dr. Reiss nodded, her expression unchanging. "The new batch of subjects is showing promise. The genetic enhancements are taking hold more effectively than in previous iterations."

Blake's view returned to the display. "And Cam One?" he asked without looking at her.

"He remains... unique," Reiss admitted. "His genetic profile is unprecedented—a result of the initial trials of Project Genesis before we refined our processes, and with this new batch of juice he is becoming even more superior."

Blake's fingers drummed on the console, his mind whirring with possibilities. "His abilities could be the key to crushing the resistance once and for all," he mused. "Ensure he is ready for deployment. I intend to use every tool at our disposal."

Dr. Reiss inclined her head slightly. "Understood, Commander." She paused, her gaze sharpening. "And what of Mercer himself? If he learns of—"

"He won't," Blake interrupted with finality. "I have contingencies in place. Mercer's loyalties are divided, his past a weakness we can exploit. He will not interfere with our plans."

Back at the rebel base, Cipher looked up from her screen, an intensity burning behind her eyes. "We may only have a narrow window of opportunity once we're in," she explained to Mia and Allen. "Their firewalls adapt quickly; we'll need to be faster."

Allen nodded, a steely resolve taking hold of him. "We'll get you that window, Cipher," he promised. "We'll get you more than that—we'll get you the keys to their kingdom."

Cipher's look lingered on Allen for a moment longer, as if measuring him, before she returned to her preparations.

Knox approached Allen, clapping a firm hand on his shoulder. "I've seen many a soldier in my time," he said, his voice gruff with experience, "but none with the fire in their belly quite like yours."

Allen just gave a tight nod, feeling the weight of both the compliment and the responsibility. He glanced around at the faces of those who had become his comrades—his friends.

"We move out at 2100 hours," Knox declared to the group. "Until then, make your preparations and say your goodbyes. We'll all need to be sharp tonight."

As the rebels dispersed, Mia lingered by Allen's side. "You ready for this?" she asked quietly.

"I have to be," Allen replied, meeting her eyes squarely. "We can't let Blake gain any more ground on us."

Mia's reached out and hugged him reassuringly before she moved off to check on her own gear. Allen watched her go, her confidence bolstering his own.

Chapter 11

Allen's hands trembled as he aimed the rifle at the child's head. The young boy, no more than ten, stared back with defiant eyes, his small frame silhouetted against the burning ruins of the Techno-Synth facility.

"Do it, Mercer," Commander Blake's voice crackled through the comms. "Before he gets away!"

Allen's finger hovered over the trigger, his breath catching in his throat. The thick smell of smoke filled his nostrils as his vision blurred.

No fucking way! he thought to himself.

A sharp crack pierced the air. The child crumpled to the ground, a neat hole in his forehead. Blake lowered his weapon, smoke still rising from the barrel.

"Hesitation has no place here soldier," Blake growled. "Remember that."

Allen jolted awake, his heart pounding. The familiar weight of guilt settled in his stomach as he ran a hand over his face, feeling the cold sweat on his brow. The memory of that day still haunted him, a constant reminder of the monster he'd almost become.

Shaking off the lingering tendrils of the nightmare, Allen swung his legs out of his cot. Today was the day. The mission that could change everything.

He made his way to the rebel base's command center, his footsteps echoing in the dimly lit corridors. As he entered, Cipher looked up from her array of screens, her dark eyes scanning him with a knowing glance.

"Another rough night?" she asked, her tone soft but probing.

Allen nodded, unable to hide the weariness in his voice. "The usual. But I'm ready."

Cipher's lips tightened into a thin line. "Good. We can't afford any distractions today."

She turned back to her screens, pulling up a holographic display of the Techno-Synth communication facility. Allen leaned in, studying the layout he'd memorized over the past few days.

"Final check," Cipher said, her fingers dancing across the keyboard. "Entry points?"

"Southeast maintenance hatch," Allen replied, pointing to the location. "Guards change shift at 0200, giving us a three-minute window."

Cipher nodded. "Surveillance?"

"You'll have control of the external cameras. We'll need to move fast once inside to avoid the internal sensors."

As they went through the plan, Allen felt a familiar tension coiling in his gut. This wasn't just another mission. This was their chance to strike at the heart of Techno-Synth, to access the very core of the AI that controlled their world.

"Allen," Cipher's voice cut through his thoughts. "Are you sure you're up for this? If there's any doubt-"

"No," he interrupted, meeting her gaze. "I need to do this. For all of us."

Cipher held his stare for a moment before nodding. "Alright. Let's gear up."

As they prepared, Allen couldn't shake the memory of Blake's cold efficiency, the way he'd pulled the trigger without hesitation. He'd been so close to becoming that – a soulless instrument of Techno-Synth's will.

"Never again," he muttered to himself, checking his equipment one last time.

The sick feeling in his stomach transformed into unbreakable resolve. Tonight, they'd take the first big step towards bringing down the system that had nearly consumed him. And maybe, just maybe, he'd find a way to atone for the sins of his past.

The night air was thick with tension as Allen and his small team of rebels crouched in the shadows, their eyes fixed on the looming silhouette of the communication facility. Allen's heart pounded in his chest, each beat a reminder of the mission's gravity.

"Thirty seconds to go," Cipher's voice crackled through the comms, cool and collected.

Allen took a deep breath, willing his nerves to steady. This was his first mission since Evelyn's betrayal, since his capture and near-conversion by Blake. The weight of responsibility pressed down on him like a mountain.

"Remember," he whispered to his team, "we're ghosts. In and out, no traces left behind."

As the seconds ticked down, His mind raced. What if he froze again, like he had with the child? What if his hesitation cost them everything?

"Allen," Mia's voice came through, softer than Cipher's. "You've got this. We're all with you."

Her words washed over him, a balm to his frayed nerves. He nodded, even though she couldn't see him.

"Thanks, Mia," he murmured. "We won't let you down."

"Knox and Jonas are in position," Cipher interjected. "If anything goes sideways, they're ready to provide backup."

As the final seconds elapsed, Allen felt a strange calm settle over him. This was it – their chance to strike back at the system that had nearly destroyed him. He wouldn't waste it.

"Go time," Cipher announced.

With a silent hand signal, Allen led his team forward, melting into the shadows as they approached their target.

Cipher's fingers flew across her keyboard, her eyes darting between multiple screens. "Disabling eastern quadrant cameras... now," she muttered, her voice a low, focused hum. On her main display, a grid of surveillance feeds flickered and went dark.

"Rerouting patrol drones," she continued, her tone measured but intense. "Sending false heat signatures to the northwest sector."

Allen and his team crouched in the shadows, watching as a group of airborne drones suddenly changed course, their red lights fading into the distance. He felt a grudging admiration for Cipher's skills, remembering how formidable Techno-Synth's security had once seemed from the inside.

"Guards at the south entrance are receiving new orders," Cipher's voice crackled in their earpieces. "You have a 90-second window. Move."

Allen's heart pounded as he led his team forward, their footsteps silent on the concrete. The facility loomed before them, a monolith of steel and glass that seemed to absorb the night around it. As they approached the entrance, Allen couldn't shake the feeling of déjà vu. How many times had he walked through these doors as a respected officer?

They slipped inside, the cool air of the climate-controlled interior raising goosebumps on Allen's skin. He gestured for his team to spread out, each taking their pre-assigned positions.

Suddenly, a door to their right began to open. Allen's breath caught in his throat as he recognized the distinctive sound of a bathroom lock disengaging. In a split second, he made a decision.

"Scatter," he hissed, barely audible.

The team melted into the shadows as a guard emerged, yawning and adjusting his uniform. Allen pressed himself against the wall, willing his racing heart to slow. The guard was less than a meter away, close enough that Allen could smell the cheap soap on his hands.

For a terrifying moment, the guard paused, his head tilting as if listening. Allen's muscles coiled, ready to spring into action if they were discovered. He could almost feel the weight of his sidearm, the muscle memory of countless missions threatening to take over.

Not this time, he told himself fiercely. We're here to save lives, not take them.

After what felt like an eternity, the guard shrugged and continued on his way, oblivious to the intruders surrounding him in the darkness.

As his footsteps faded, Allen let out a shaky breath. "That was too close," he whispered into his comm.

"You handled it well," Cipher responded, her voice betraying a hint of admiration. "Now, get moving. We don't have much time."

"Copy that. Team, on me." Allen responded.

They moved swiftly through the dimly lit corridors, guided by Cipher and Mia's hushed instructions in their earpieces. Allen's heart pounded, not just from exertion but from the weight of the mission. Every step brought them closer to their goal, and to potential disaster.

"Left at the next junction," Mia's voice crackled. "Server room should be fifty meters ahead."

As they rounded the corner, Allen caught sight of the heavily reinforced door. He felt a surge of anticipation mixed with dread. This was it.

"Cipher, we need access," he whispered.

"Working on it," came the terse reply. Seconds ticked by, each feeling like an eternity. Then, with a soft beep, the lock disengaged.

Allen's team slipped inside, their practiced movements a silent dance of efficiency. He pulled out the thumb drives, their weight suddenly feeling immense in his palm.

"Remember," Mia's voice came through, tinged with tension, "you've got three minutes before the system resets."

Allen's fingers flew over the keyboards, inserting the drives and initiating the upload. Lines of code flashed across the screen, a digital lifeline to their cause.

"Ninety seconds," Cipher warned.

Just as the final drive was inserted, footsteps echoed in the hallway outside. Allen froze, his mind racing through scenarios, each worse than the last.

"Multiple targets approaching," Mia hissed. "You need to get out of there, now!"

Allen's team slipped out of the server room, hearts pounding in unison as they melted into the shadows of the corridor. The footsteps grew louder, accompanied by the mundane chatter of Techno-Synth employees.

"... and then I told him, 'That's not toothpaste, that's my hemorrhoid cream!' " A burst of laughter followed.

Allen held his breath, pressing himself against the wall. He could feel the vibrations of the approaching voices through the cold metal. A bead of sweat trickled down his temple.

"Exit route compromised," Cipher's voice crackled in their earpieces. "Rerouting now... Take the maintenance shaft to your left."

Without hesitation, Allen motioned to his team. They moved silently, their training kicking in as they navigated the narrow passageway. The stale air carried the scent of machine oil and ozone.

"Almost there," Mia encouraged. "Two more levels, then you're out."

As they descended, Allen's mind raced. Had they been detected? Would the thumb drives work? The weight of the mission pressed down on him, threatening to crush his resolve.

Finally, they reached the bottom. A rusted door stood between them and freedom. Allen pushed it open, wincing at the slight creak of metal.

The cool night air hit his face, a stark contrast to the sterile environment they'd just left. Allen's team fanned out, disappearing into the shadows of abandoned buildings and overgrown lots.

"We're clear," Allen whispered, allowing himself a small sigh of relief.

"Excellent work," Cipher replied, her usual calm demeanor tinged with excitement. "Now the real fun begins."

Back at their rebel base, Mia and Cipher's fingers flew across their keyboards, lines of code reflecting in their determined eyes. Allen listened over the comms, a mix of anxiety and hope churning in his gut.

"We're in," Mia announced, a hint of triumph in her voice. "Accessing Project Shadow files now."

Suddenly, Cipher's brow furrowed. "Wait, what's this? There's a subsection... C.A.M.-001. It's heavily encrypted."

"Can you crack it?" Allen asked, wondering what it could be.

Cipher's lips tightened. "Given time. But whatever it is, Techno-Synth doesn't want anyone to know about it."

As the hackers worked, Allen and his team made their way back to the base, converging with Knox and Jonas' teams as they made their way inside. They all moved quickly into the command center, the anticipation growing.

Allen ran his fingers through his hair, his mind racing. "C.A.M.-001... It has to be significant if it's buried this deep."

Mia nodded, her eyes never leaving the screen. "Agreed. And if it's part of Project Shadow, it could be the key to bringing down Blake and company."

Knox, who had been silently observing, stepped forward. "Then we pursue it. No question."

Allen felt a surge of determination, mixed with a familiar twinge of apprehension. Every move against the enemy brought them closer to dismantling the corporation.

"Cipher, Mia," he said, his voice steady despite his inner turmoil, "please dig deeper. Whatever this Cam One thing is, we need to know everything about it."

The two hackers exchanged a look before diving back into their work. The room fell silent save for the rapid clicking of keys and the low hum of computers.

Hours passed, tension building with each minute. Allen paced, his mind wandering to the countless lives ruined by Blakes agenda. He thought of the child from his dream, of all the innocents he'd failed to save. Never again, he vowed again silently.

Suddenly, Mia's voice cut through the silence. "Got it! It's being held in what looks like a hidden facility on the outskirts of the core zones. Coordinates coming through now."

Cipher's eyes widened slightly – a rare display of surprise. "It's not just a building. The entire structure is some sort of containment unit. Whatever is in there, Techno-Synth is keeping it isolated and heavily guarded."

Allen's heart raced. "Then that's got to be our target. If we can locate and extract this new tech quickly, Blake won't know what hit him until it's too late."

He looked around at his team, seeing determination mirrored in their eyes. "We'll need a solid plan. Let's get to work everybody, and make sure to cross every "T" and dot every "I", we can't afford any mistakes on this one."

As they began to formulate their strategy, Allen couldn't shake the feeling that they were about to cross a point of no return. Whatever C.A.M.-001 was, it had the potential to change everything – for better or for worse.

Chapter 12

The command center was in full swing, each rebel leader working diligently to plan the upcoming mission. Knox realized they needed to get copies of this information back to the Outlanders base as a contingency plan.

It was too dangerous to send information this sensitive over the shadow web or even through the whisper networks, they would have to travel by foot and hand deliver it. Knox chose Lena as his companion for the long trip. "Okay Lena, lets gear up and hit the road, time is of the essence."

"Ok boss," she replied, a big smile on her face as she was unable to contain her excitement. "I'll be ready to roll in 10."

Ten and a half minutes later...The two of them set out on their journey with haste, leaving the rebel base in the distance behind them, as they navigated the streets and ally-ways of the crumbling city around them, they found refuge in the dilapidated remains of an old church.

Knox's boots crunched on broken glass and concrete as he and Lena slipped out of the crumbling building. The disgusting stench of burning plastics hung in the air, mingling with the ever-present haze of pollution that choked the city's lower levels.

"We need to move fast," Knox muttered, his eyes scanning the shadowy alleyways. "Every second we're out here is a risk."

Lena nodded, her hand instinctively moving to the data chip concealed in her jacket pocket. "Copy That sir, following your lead."

Knox's jaw tightened. The weight of their mission pressed down on him like a physical force. How many lives depended on their success? How many of his people had already died to obtain this information?

"This way," he said gruffly, leading the way down a narrow side street.

As they moved swiftly through the decaying urban landscape, Knox's mind raced. The data chip held evidence of Techno-Synth's latest atrocities - proof that could finally rally more of the population and possibly even new factions to the rebels' cause.

Two blocks behind them, a ghostly figure melted out of the shadows. Ada Wallace's dark brown eyes locked onto her targets as she tapped the commlink in her ear.

"Wraith to Control. Targets acquired and moving southeast. Initiating pursuit."

A gravelly voice crackled through her earpiece. "Confirmed, Wraith. Maintain distance and await further orders."

Her lips curved into a thin smile as she gestured to her partner. They moved in perfect sync, silent predators stalking their prey through the urban jungle.

Knox paused at an intersection, frowning as he studied the skyline. "We'll cut through the old industrial sector," he said. "Less chance of running into patrols."

Lena raised an eyebrow. "That area's crawling with scavengers and worse. You sure about this?"

Knox looked at her, seeing the mixture of trust and concern in her eyes. He allowed himself a small smile. "No, but it's our best shot. Unless you've got a better idea?"

Lena shook her head, a wry grin tugging at her lips. "Hey, you're the boss. I just shoot things and look pretty."

Knox snorted, some of the tension easing for a moment. "Well, you excel at both. Now let's move."

As they made their way out of the city and into the edges of the outlands, the landscape changed from concrete and steel to the overgrown wilderness that lay before them. Under the cover of the thick trees and rugged terrain, they began to feel a bit of relief getting out of the city unscathed.

Unbeknownst to them, Ada and her partner were closing in, their augmented senses allowing them to track the rebels with terrifying precision. Ada's eyes gleamed with predatory anticipation as she watched them make their way.

The hunt was on, and the fate of the resistance hung in the balance.

Knox and Lena pushed forward, every footstep taking them closer to their destination. The fading daylight felt even darker under the thick canopy of the overgrown forest. Knox's mind raced, mapping out their route while cataloging potential threats.

"You ever wonder what the world would be like if they never rose to power?" Lena whispered, her eyes darting between trees where the setting sun lit small areas.

Knox grunted, "Sometimes. But dwelling on the past won't help us survive the present."

Lena nodded, her hand brushing her weapon. "Fair enough. Still, I can't help but think—"

The sudden sound of leaves crunching cut her off. Both rebels froze, instinctively dropping into defensive stances.

"Just a deer," Knox muttered after a tense moment. "Come on, we're losing daylight."

As they resumed their journey, Knox's unease grew. He couldn't shake the feeling of being watched, hunted. But every time he glanced back, there was nothing but the dark. *Maybe it was just paranoia,* he thought.

Little did they know, Ada and her partner were expertly concealing themselves, using the terrain to their advantage. Ada activated her neural link, her thoughts transmitting directly to Techno-Synth command.

"Targets heading northeast," she reported silently. "ETA to outlander base still unknown."

Knox's pace quickened as familiar landmarks came into view. "We're getting close," he muttered to Lena. "Once inside, let's gather the troops and let them know our good news."

Lena nodded agreeing, her fingers loosening the grip on her weapon. "Glad we made it sir."

As they approached the outskirts of the Outlanders base, Knox allowed himself a moment of hope. The glow from the central fire lit up the cliff sides with a soft orange flicker.

The entrance to the Outlanders' base loomed before them. The guards on watch welcomed them, "Glad to have you back boss," a young Outlander said from his position above the gate. Knox looked up and gave him a nod of acceptance, crossing over the threshold of the entrance, his muscles tensing as he glanced back over his shoulder one last time.

"Home sweet home," he muttered, ushering Lena inside.

As the gate clanged shut behind them, Knox felt his shoulders relax incrementally. The familiar scent of fresh wilderness air and campfire smoke filled his nostrils.

Lena's eyes sparkled in the dim light. "I never thought I'd be so happy to see this place again."

Knox allowed himself a small smile. "Let's debrief the others. They'll want to know what we found in the city."

As they made their way through the base, Knox couldn't shake a gnawing sense of unease. He tried to push it aside, focusing on the task at hand.

"Gather everyone in the war room," he ordered a passing rebel. "We've got intel to share."

Lena frowned. "You okay, Knox? You seem... on edge."

He ran a hand through his graying beard. "Just tired, I suppose. It's been a long journey."

Neither of them realized that their arrival had set devastating events in motion. Miles above, Techno-Synth drones were mobilizing, their advanced weaponry primed and ready, staying out of radar range. On the outskirts of the base, Ada and her partner were coordinating with aerial transports and ground troops, Techno-Synth's soldiers began to surround the base.

Inside the war room, outlanders had trickled in one by one, the excitement of Knox and Lena's return hung in the air like an aura of good vibes. Raising his hand for everyone to be quiet.

"Glad to be back at home with everybody," Knox began...

The first explosion rocked the base without warning. Alarms blared as Knox stumbled, catching himself against the wall.

"What the hell," Lena's eyes widened in horror.

Knox's battle-hardened instincts kicked in. "We're under attack! Everybody to your stations, now!"

Chaos erupted around them. Rebels scrambled for weapons and defensive positions as the sound of gunfire and explosions filled the air. Knox sprinted toward the command center, his mind racing.

How had they found us? The question burned in his brain, but there was no time to dwell on it now.

"Status report!" he barked as he burst into the command center.

A young rebel, face pale with shock, turned to him. "Sir, they're everywhere. Techno-Synth forces have breached the outer defenses. We're... we're overwhelmed."

Knox's jaw clenched. "We're not going down like this," he growled, determination burning in his eyes. "Initiate Protocol Omega. We'll make these bastards fight for every inch."

As he turned to rally his troops, Knox allowed himself one moment of anguish. Somehow, they'd been compromised. And he feared the cost would be higher than they could bear.

Knox's voice crackled over the comm system, "All units, this is not a drill. Engage Protocol Omega. I repeat, engage Protocol Omega."

Lena's heart raced as she sprinted to her assigned position, her mind cycling through their limited options. Protocol Omega was their last resort, a desperate gambit designed to turn the base itself into a weapon.

"Knox!" she shouted, spotting him across the makeshift barricade. "The junction box in Building 7 is offline. We can't complete the circuit!"

Knox's weathered face tightened. "We need that connection or the whole plan falls apart. Lena, take a team and—"

An explosion rocked the building, showering them with debris. Knox stumbled, his eyes widening as he saw the Techno-Synth drone materializing through the dust cloud, its weapon trained on him.

Time seemed to slow. Lena's body moved before her mind could process the danger. "No!" she screamed, hurling herself towards Knox.

The energy blast seared the air. Lena's body jerked as it struck her, a cry of pain escaping her lips. She crumpled to the ground, smoke rising from her charred uniform.

"Lena!" Knox's anguished roar echoed through the corridor. He fired rapidly, destroying the drone, then dropped to his knees beside her.

Lena's eyes fluttered open, her breath coming in ragged gasps. "Did... did I get to you in time?"

Knox cradled her head, his stoic facade crumbling. "Why? Damn it, Lena, why?"

She managed a weak smile. "The rebellion... needs you. More than... it needs me."

As the life faded from her eyes, Knox felt a piece of his soul shatter. The sounds of battle faded, replaced by a deafening silence in his mind.

How many more would he lose? The question haunted him as he gently closed Lena's eyes, his grief threatening to overwhelm him.

The acrid stench of burning circuitry and scorched flesh filled Knox's nostrils as he surveyed the carnage around him. Bodies of outlanders and destroyed Techno-Synth drones littered the base, a grim testament to the heavy toll of this battle. Through the haze of smoke, he could see his people retreating, desperately trying to hold their defensive positions.

"Sir, we can't hold the east wing!" a young rebel shouted, his face smeared with soot and blood. "They're breaking through!"

Knox's jaw clenched again, the weight of command settling heavily on his shoulders. He glanced down at Lena's lifeless form one last time, grabbing the data chip from her jacket pocket and readying himself for what needed to be done.

"Fall back to the central hub," he ordered, his voice cutting through the chaos. "We make our stand there."

As they retreated, Knox's mind raced. How many had they lost? How many were left to fight? The odds seemed insurmountable, but surrender wasn't an option.

In the central hub, Knox climbed atop a fallen pillar, his face illuminated by the flickering emergency lights and burning debris. The remaining Outlanders—barely two dozen—gathered around him, their eyes filled with fear and exhaustion.

Knox surveyed their faces, seeing the doubt and despair. He took a deep breath, channeling every ounce of conviction he could muster.

"Listen up!" he bellowed, his voice carrying the authority of years of combat. "I know we've lost good people today. I know the odds look grim. But remember why we fight!"

He paused, letting his words sink in. "We fight for a world free from Techno-Synth control. We fight for our right to be human, to feel, to choose our own destiny. And by God, we will not go quietly into the night!"

A murmur of agreement rippled through the crowd. Knox continued, his voice rising with passion. "Each of you has the heart of a lion. We may be outnumbered, but we are not outmatched in spirit or determination. This is our home, and we will defend it to our last breath!"

The rebels straightened, a newfound fire igniting in their eyes. Knox gripped his rifle, raising it high. "For Lena, for all those we've lost, for the future of humanity—we stand and fight!"

A chorus of cheers erupted, drowning out the distant sounds of approaching Techno-Synth forces. As Knox jumped down to prepare their defenses, he caught the eye of a young recruit.

"Sir," the recruit said hesitantly, "do you really think we can win this?"

Knox placed a hand on the recruit's shoulder, his expression softening for a moment. "Kid, in this fight, survival is victory. Now, let's show these tin cans what it means to be human."

Knox's gaze swept across the battered remains of their command center, his mind racing as he assessed their dwindling resources.

"Resource Check?" he yelled in a commanding tone.

A woman with a makeshift bandage wrapped around her arm stepped forward, clutching a data pad tightly. "Ammo's low, we've got a handful of EMP charges left, and the power grid's barely holding," she reported without looking up, her voice grim. "Medical's overrun, and our comms are spotty at best."

Knox nodded somberly. Every bullet and bandage counted now. He had to be strategic, there was no room for waste or error. This was their last stand, and they had to make it count.

"Ration the ammo, focus on choke points," he ordered, his mind working through their meager options. "Medics, do what you can. Everyone else, I want barricades at every entrance. We funnel them into our kill zones."

He moved through the battered base, helping where he could, offering words of encouragement that felt hollow even to him, but were met with determined nods and grim faces set like stone.

They worked in unison, a symphony of weary yet resolute survivors, transforming their battered sanctuary into a fortress. Knox couldn't help but think how Lena would have been in the thick of it, rallying the troops with her unbridled spirit. Her absence was like a gaping wound in his heart, but he channeled that pain into focus; it honed his resolve like a blade.

He looked over at the young recruit again, who was now helping to move debris to fortify a weak point in their defenses. The kid caught Knox's eye and gave a determined nod. Knox saw a reflection of Lena's courage in him and knew that her legacy would inspire them all.

The sun began to rise, enveloping the base in an almost comforting morning glow, Knox gathered his fighters for one final briefing.

"This is it," he stated, his voice steady despite the turmoil that raged inside him. "We have one advantage—they don't expect us to be as prepared as we are. We've got one shot at this. If we're going down, we're taking them with us."

The rebels listened intently; each face etched with an unwavering commitment to the cause that had become their life's purpose.

Knox continued, "We have EMP and explosive traps set, after they breach the walls, wait for a good size group to come through and light them up," He scanned the fighters with a look that only a true warrior could convey in such a moment.

"Once we draw them into our fatal funnels, make every bullet count, they don't have any idea of what they are about to come up against."

As if on que, multiple explosions shook the base, breaching the outer walls, allowing a surge of ground troops to start flooding in.

"Hold Positions! …, Wait! …,' Knox commanded, his hand balled into a raised fist.

Chapter 13

The deafening roar of explosions ripped through the air as Knox peered over the barricade, his eyes narrowing at the sight of Techno-Synth ground forces pouring through the breached outer wall. The burning smell of smoke and gunpowder filled his nostrils as he ducked back down, his mind racing with tactical calculations.

"Fire EMP's and perimeter bombs now!" he shouted through the pandemonium, dropping his fist, giving the go signal. "Fall back to secondary positions. We'll funnel them into the kill zones!" he barked as the traps detonated with stunning precision, killing handfuls of Techno-Synth troops and diverting others towards certain death.

As his team scrambled to follow orders, Knox felt a pang of guilt. How many more would he send to their deaths today? He pushed the thought aside, readying himself for the battle ahead. There would be time for mourning later – if they survived.

"Sir, they're advancing on section three!" a young rebel called out, her voice trembling with fear.

Knox placed a reassuring hand on her shoulder. "Deep breaths, soldier. Remember your training. We've prepared for this."

He turned to address the group, his voice steady and commanding. "Don't stop fighting! We hold this line at all costs. Every second we buy is another life saved. Show these Techno-Synth bastards what it means to face the Outlanders!"

A chorus of determined shouts answered him as his fighters took up defensive positions. Knox allowed himself a small smile.

Their spirit was unbroken, even in the face of overwhelming odds.

The ground shook as another explosion rocked the base. Knox gritted his teeth, his mind racing through possible scenarios. They were outnumbered and outgunned, but they had home-field advantage and the element of surprise on their side.

The first wave of Techno-Synth soldiers rounded the corner, their augmented bodies gleaming in the harsh light. Knox raised his weapon, his finger steady on the trigger.

"For the Outlanders!" he roared, his voice rising above the chaos. "Open fire!"

The air erupted with a cacophony of gunfire and energy blasts. Knox's fighters unleashed a barrage of improvised weaponry—makeshift EMPs, scavenged plasma rifles, and even jury-rigged mining explosives. The narrow corridor became a deadly gauntlet for the Techno-Synth forces.

"Nathan, deploy the sonic disruptors!" Knox shouted, his eyes scanning the battlefield.

A high-pitched whine filled the air as Nathan activated the devices. Several Techno-Synth soldiers stumbled, their augmented senses overwhelmed by the sonic assault. The fighters seized the opportunity, unloading with a counterattack that pushed the enemy back.

As the battle raged, Knox caught a glimpse of a slender figure moving with inhuman speed through the chaos. His blood ran cold as he recognized Ada "Wraith" Wallace, one of Techno-Synth's deadliest operatives.

"I've got eyes on Wraith," Knox growled into his comms. "Cover me!"

He vaulted over a barricade, his weathered muscles protesting but responding with the efficiency of decades of combat experience. She made her way towards him with predatory grace. Knox knew this confrontation was inevitable — the unstoppable force meeting the immovable object.

"Knox," she said, her voice devoid of emotion. "Thanks for showing me where your base was."

"Fuck you Ada," Knox retorted, launching toward her knocking the weapon from of her hand.

They clashed in a blur of motion, Ada's augmented reflexes matching Knox's battle-honed instincts. Knox blocked a lightning-fast jab, countering with a sweep that Ada easily evaded. Their movements were a deadly dance, each anticipating the other's attacks.

Ada's fist grazed his cheek, drawing blood. Knox retaliated with a series of quick strikes, forcing her back. He could feel the fatigue creeping in, but the faces of his comrades—those who had fallen and those still fighting—flashed through his mind, boosting his resolve.

"You fight well, for an obsolete model," Ada taunted, her words as sharp as her strikes.

Knox grunted, deflecting another attack. "There's more to humanity than circuits and upgrades Wraith. Something you've forgotten."

For a fleeting moment, Knox thought he saw a flicker of doubt in her eyes. But it vanished as quickly as it appeared, replaced by her usual cold determination.

The battle around them intensified, but for Knox, the world had narrowed to this singular confrontation. He knew that the outcome of this fight could determine the fate of the entire battle.

He seized a momentary opening, driving his fist into Ada's ribs with a sickening crunch. She stumbled back, eyes widening in surprise—perhaps the first genuine emotion he'd seen from her.

"Humanity's strength isn't in perfection," Knox growled, pressing his advantage. "It's in our ability to adapt, to rise above our limitations."

Ada snarled as she regained her footing. "Pretty words won't save you or your outdated ideals."

They clashed again, a furious exchange of blows. Knox felt his strength waning but refused to yield.

In a desperate gambit, Knox feinted left, drew a blade and then lunged right, his combat knife finding purchase in Ada's thigh. She hissed in pain, her inhuman composure finally cracking as she jolted backwards out of reach.

"This isn't over," Ada spat, her voice laced with venom and something else—uncertainty? Before Knox could press his advantage, she triggered a smoke grenade, vanishing into the chaos of battle.

Knox stood there, panting, the adrenaline slowly ebbing. The sounds of combat were fading, replaced by the groans of the wounded and the grim silence of the aftermath.

"Knox!" A voice cut through the haze. It was Jace, one of his lieutenants. "We need to move. Now!"

Reality came crashing back. Knox nodded, his leader's mask sliding back into place. "Status report," he yelled, already moving towards their fallback position.

Jace fell in step beside him. "We've evacuated most of our people, but we've taken heavy losses. The base is compromised."

As they made their way through the war-torn sections of what had been their home, Knox's mind raced with plans and contingencies. The underground rebel base in the city was their only option now.

"Gather the survivors," he ordered. "We move out in five. And Jace? Make sure we wipe everything. Leave nothing for Techno-Synth to use against us."

The journey to the city was a blur of tense silence and cautious movements. When they finally reached the hidden entrance to the underground base, Knox felt a weight lift from his shoulders, only to be replaced by a new one as he prepared to face Allen and the others.

The steel doors groaned open, revealing Allen's anxious face. "Knox! Thank God. We feared the worst when we lost contact."

Knox stepped inside, the remnants of his team following. He met Allen's eyes, his voice heavy with the weight of their losses. "The outland base is gone. Techno-Synth hit us hard, but we gave them hell."

As the gravity of the situation settled over the assembled rebels, Knox knew that the real battle was just beginning. They had survived, but at a terrible cost. Now, they would have to rebuild, regroup, and find a way to strike back against Techno-Synth.

The road ahead would be hard, but as Knox looked at the determined faces around him, he knew they would face it together. The fight for humanity's future was far from over.

The underground chamber fell silent as Knox finished recounting the battle. Allen's jaw clenched, his eyes scanning the battered survivors before settling on the empty spaces where others should have stood.

"Lena?" Allen asked, his voice barely above a whisper.

Knox shook his head, the simple gesture carrying the weight of their loss. A collective exhale of grief rippled through the room.

Mia stepped forward, her voice cracking slightly. "We need to honor them. All of them."

The rebels gathered in a makeshift memorial space, Lena's battered jacket placed at the center. Knox stood rigidly, his hands clasped behind his back, as Allen began to speak.

"We're here to remember those who gave everything for our cause," Allen said, his usual authoritative tone softened by sorrow. "Lena... she was the heart of our resistance. Her sacrifice won't be in vain."

Knox's mind drifted to Lena's fierce determination, her unwavering loyalty. He'd watched her grow from a scared refugee to a formidable fighter. Now, she was gone. The weight of responsibility pressed down on him, threatening to crush his resolve.

Cipher's quiet voice cut through Knox's thoughts. "Lena always said our strength was in our unity. We honor her by standing together, by continuing the fight."

Murmurs of agreement rippled through the gathered rebels. Knox watched as grief transformed into determination on the faces around him.

"Techno-Synth thinks they've broken us," Mia said, her eyes flashing with renewed purpose. "But they've only made us stronger. We'll show them the true cost of underestimating us."

Knox nodded, feeling a surge of pride for these resilient fighters. "Lena wouldn't want us wallowing," he said gruffly. "She'd want us planning our next move, figuring out how to hit Techno-Synth where it hurts most."

As the rebels began to discuss strategies, Knox felt a familiar fire ignite within him. They had lost a lot, but they weren't defeated. Not by a long shot. In the shadows of their underground sanctuary, surrounded by the memory of their fallen comrades, the rebellion was being reborn.

Allen stepped forward, his eyes scanning the assembled group of Rebels, FreeTechs and surviving Outlanders. The underground base's dim lighting cast long shadows across his face, accentuating the weariness etched into his features.

"Knox," he said, his voice carrying a mix of gratitude and respect. "What you and your outlanders did out there... it was nothing short of heroic. You held the line against impossible odds, you are all hero's today."

Mia nodded; her arms crossed over her chest. "And Knox, a lot of us owe you our lives," she added, a hint of her usual sarcasm softening into genuine appreciation. "Your tactical genius saved more than just your own people today."

Knox shifted uncomfortably under their praise, his mind still replaying the chaos of the battle. "We did what had to be done," he responded gruffly. "Nothing more, nothing less."

Cipher stepped forward, her calm demeanor a stark contrast to the emotional tension in the room. "Your modesty is admirable, Knox, but let's not diminish the magnitude of your actions. The data we've gathered shows that without your stand, Techno-Synth would have overrun our entire network by now."

Jonas, his eyes red-rimmed from mourning, spoke up. "You gave us a fighting chance. Lena... she would've been proud to see it."

The mention of Lena's name sent a palpable ripple through the gathering. Knox felt his throat tighten, remembering her fierce determination in those final moments.

"She was one hell of a fighter," Knox managed, his voice rough with emotion. "They all were."

Allen raised his hand, signaling for silence. The low hum of conversation died away, leaving only the distant whir of machinery.

"We stand here today," Allen began, his voice steady and resolute, "not just as survivors, but as guardians of a hope that Techno-Synth can never extinguish. Each life lost in this battle was a beacon of defiance against tyranny."

Knox watched as candles were lit, their flickering flames dancing on the walls. The soft glow illuminated tear-streaked faces and clenched jaws, a visual testament to the rebels' grief and determination.

Mia stepped forward; her voice uncharacteristically soft. "To those we've lost, we make this vow: your sacrifice will fuel our fight. We will tear down the walls of oppression and reclaim our future."

As the rebels bowed their heads in silent tribute, Knox felt a surge of emotions threatening to overwhelm him. Pride in their resilience, grief for the fallen, and a burning resolve to see this fight through to the end.

In the somber silence that followed, he realized that this moment wasn't just about honoring the dead. It was a reaffirmation of their shared purpose, a rallying cry for the battles yet to come. And as he looked around at the determined faces of his comrades, both old and new, he knew that Techno-Synth's days were numbered.

One by one, the rebels began to disburse at their own pace, some saying a few words for the fallen before retiring to their cots and makeshift beds.

The next morning it was straight back to business. Each member of the rebellion had a sense of urgency etched in their movements, promptly manning their respective posts at the crack of dawn.

Allen scanned the room, locking his eyes onto each rebel in turn. "We've paid a heavy price," he said, his voice low but firm. "But now, we use that pain to fuel our next move. Cam One may be the key to unraveling Techno-Synth's control. We secure it, we change the game."

Mia chimed in, her fingers dancing across a holographic display. "Our latest intel suggests it's still being held in the high-security facility," she reported, her brow furrowed in concentration. "There are heavy defenses, but it's not impenetrable."

Knox leaned in, studying the flickering map. "We'll need a multi-pronged approach," he mused, his tactical mind already formulating strategies. "A distraction team to draw their forces, while a small infiltration unit slips in."

Allen nodded, feeling a familiar surge of adrenaline. *This is what we fight for*, he thought. *This is how we honor their sacrifice*. Cipher's eyes sparkled with the reflection of the display as she interjected, "We'll also need to jam their communications. I can synchronize our FreeTechs with Mia's hackers to create a blackout window. It won't be long, but it should give us the opening we need."

Mia looked up, a small smile of acknowledgment gracing her lips at Cipher's contribution. Their dynamic was a testament to how individual strengths within the rebellion could interlace to form an unbreakable chain.

Allen's look again swept across the room. "We'll be fighting on two fronts," he said decisively. "Which means we'll need absolute precision from multiple teams."

Jonas, who had been quietly listening, finally spoke, his voice strained with emotion but resolute. "Count me in for the distraction team," he said, clenching his fist. "Lena's bravery will be my guide."

Knox rested a reassuring hand on Jonas' shoulder. "You have the heart of a lion, just like she did," Knox assured him. The exchange was brief but meaningful; it was clear that Lena's bravery had become a beacon for every rebel there.

The group continued to outline their plan, dissecting every possible outcome with meticulous care. The air was charged with a mix of grief and unwavering determination. They worked well into the night, fueled by the conviction that their fallen comrades' memories would not fade into oblivion, but instead rise like a phoenix from the ashes of war to inspire their future victories.

Mia came to Allen's side and whispered, "we found something you should see, a file about Cam One, this is big Allen...really big!" she said, her hushed tone barely audible to his ears.

Chapter 14

The computer screen flickered to life, bathing Mia's face in an eerie blue glow. Allen scanned the file, his brow furrowed. Fragments of data scrolled across the screen—references to physical specifications, neural enhancements, and memory reconstruction.

He paused, eyes narrowing as he read a line about 'biological replication.' The more Allen read, the colder his blood ran. Neural pathways aligned for enhanced reflexes, muscle memory integration—it felt like he was reading a clinical breakdown of an enhanced combat soldier.

"I told you it was big, Allen," Mia said, her voice tight with tension. "Cam One isn't just another weapon. It's a genetically engineered AI clone."

Allen's breath caught in his throat. "A clone? How is that even possible?"

"Techno-Synth's been busy," Mia replied, her tone laced with disgust. "They've created an entire army of these things. And guess what? It gets worse."

Allen raised an eyebrow. "How can it get worse than that?"

"Remember the AI core we intercepted a few months back? Turns out, it wasn't just some random tech they were guarding," Mia continued, her voice hardening. "It was specifically designed for these clones—integrated directly into their neural hardware, wet-wired into their brains. The core allows them to connect to and manipulate any digital network they encounter, like walking, breathing computers."

Allen's eyes narrowed. "So, these clones can control Techno-Synth's systems?"

"More than that. They can infiltrate any unsecure or compromised network—signals, data streams, you name it. It's all part of Project Shadow. These clones don't just fight; they integrate, becoming part of a living network that can disrupt entire systems with a thought. They're not just soldiers, Allen. They're the future of warfare. And guess who's leading the charge"

Allen's jaw clenched. "Blake?"

"Nope, none other than Major Idris Vale." she replied. "Now, Blake is involved as can be expected, but Vale seems to have the reins from what I could dig up in the files."

The name sent a chill down his spine. His former comrade, who Allen had personally trained and mentored himself. Major Vale was a relentless force, a man who saw the world in stark shades of black and white, loyalty and betrayal. He was the perfect embodiment of Techno-Synth's ruthless ambition—as Blakes newer right-hand man, Vale had risen to the top of the ranks.

"Allen, I know some of your history with him, I've heard the stories, but we have to stay focused on the task at hand," Mia said, her hand reaching out to squeeze his shoulder. His muscles tensed under her touch, but he didn't pull away.

"Well, I hope they are good stories," Allen chuckled lightly, briefly breaking the tensity of the moment. He reached up and clasped his hand around Mia's hand still on his shoulder. "I do remember him now that you say his name, although it's still a bit foggy. Something tells me if he's involved with this Project Shadow clone army, then things just got a lot more complicated."

Mia nodded, grabbing Allens hand from atop hers and pulling it in close to her chest. "We need to find out what his plan is — and how we can stop it."

"Sounds like we need to hack something," Cipher interjected, appearing seemingly out of nowhere, her voice low and determined, but there was a slight sharpness to her tone that hadn't been there before. She stepped closer to Allen, her eyes flicking briefly toward him, and for a moment, the intensity in her gaze lingered longer than necessary. "If we can turn one of these clones to our side, we might have a real shot."

Allen raised an eyebrow, catching the shift in her tone but staying focused on the mission. Mia, however, didn't miss the subtle edge in Cipher's voice or the way she leaned in just a little too close. Her expression remained neutral, her attention never wavering from the discussion, but there was a flicker of something in her eyes—an awareness.

Cipher's words hung in the air, the tactical suggestion tinged with something more, and Allen could feel a subtle tension crackling between them. He wasn't sure if it was the pressure of the mission or something else entirely, but for a brief moment, it felt like more than just strategy at play.

Mia nodded, shrugging off Cipher's interruption, her sharp features set with resolve. "I've already pinpointed its location. But guys, this won't be easy."

"It never is," Allen muttered, already mentally preparing for the fight ahead.

They spent the remainder of the day finalizing their plans for the extraction mission. Getting in and out of the high security facility would be the hardest mission the rebels had faced. Everyone checked and re-checked their gear before it was time to set off.

Within a couple of hours Allen's extraction team and Jonas' distraction team had made their way across the city's outskirts, taking up their positions to begin the mission.

Allen crouched low behind a crumbling wall, scanning the facility's perimeter through his binoculars. The compound loomed in the distance, its stark concrete structure an imposing contrast against the dilapidated ruins of the city. The air was thick with tension as he quietly signaled for his team to spread out. They moved with practiced precision, slipping into the shadows like ghosts. Each member knew their role, and there was no room for error.

Mia's voice came over the comms. "We'll need to be fast once we're inside. We hit hard, grab Cam One, and get out before they have a chance to stop us."

Allen agreed, his eyes never leaving the compound. "Jonas' team should give us the window we need. Let's just hope it's enough."

A few blocks away, Jonas and his team were setting up for their part of the mission. They had rigged several abandoned cars with small explosive charges, timed to go off in sequence to create chaos along the eastern perimeter. Jonas wiped the sweat from his brow as he double-checked the detonator, feeling the pressure of what was about to happen.

"This should give 'em something to think about," Jonas muttered, his team nodding in agreement. He glanced at his watch, the seconds ticking away toward zero. "Ready up, everyone. Once these go off, all hell's gonna break loose."

Back at Allen's position, the silence stretched thin as the rebels lay in wait. The city felt unnervingly still, the calm before the storm. His heart pounded in his chest as he glanced toward

Jonas' position. Any second now. The anticipation clawed at his nerves, but he forced himself to stay steady. It was almost time.

...

Inside the six-foot thick concrete walls of the secure building, Dr. Reiss was making her way out of the 10th floor break room, a fresh cup of coffee in one hand and a portable bio-scanner in the other. At the same time she was exiting, a handsome young Techno-Synth biologist was making his way into the break room.

"Hi Miranda," he said with a huge smile, quickly making eye contact and looking away.

"Hey Stew," Dr. Reiss replied, barely containing her own smile.

Suddenly a large explosion rocked the building. Small pieces of debris from the ceiling fell around her as she struggled to keep her balance. "What the fuck was that!" She yelled in disbelief and confusion. Stewart burst back out of the break room.

"I don't know but it sounded like a bomb?" he questioned.

"And it felt like it too, let's get to the lab and make sure everything is ok." Dr. Reiss barked, still in disbelief.

...

The mission was brutal from the start. Allen led the charge, his movements precise and lethal as he cleared a path for the extraction team. Gunfire and explosions rocked the facility, the air thick with smoke and the smell of burning circuitry.

As they fought their way toward the containment area the Techno-Synth security forces were putting up one hell of a fight Allen caught glimpses of fallen comrades. Each loss was a knife to his heart, but he pushed on.

"Through that door Allen, 50 meters dead ahead." Mia's voice crackled over the comms.

Allen's eyes locked onto the target ahead, his focus razor-sharp amidst the chaos. He motioned to Knox and the rest of the team to press forward. They moved as one entity, dropping multiple targets with ease.

Reaching the door, Allen placed small explosive charges on the locking mechanism while covering fire from Jonas and Knox kept away any potential threats.

...

Dr. Reiss hurried down the corridor, Stewart trailing behind her, their footsteps echoing through the stark, sterile hallways. Her mind raced, still processing the sudden breach. They needed to assess the situation in the lab—quickly.

"Do you think it's them?" Stewart asked, his voice tight with fear.

"Who else could it be?" Dr. Reiss snapped at him; her tone sharper than she intended. "We have been anticipating a move from the resistance. It was only a matter of time before something like this happened."

As they reached the lab, Dr. Reiss swiped her ID badge across the scanner, and the door slid open with a hiss. The sight that greeted them sent a chill down her spine—control panels blinking erratically and red warning lights flashing overhead.

"Everything looks... kind of stable," Stewart murmured, as if trying to convince himself. He stepped closer to one of the tanks, peering inside.

Just then, a deafening explosion rocked the room, followed by the screech of metal tearing away. The door at the far end of the lab blew off its hinges, crashing to the floor with a metallic clatter. Dr. Reiss and Stewart recoiled, instinctively ducking as debris flew through the air.

"It's them," Dr. Reiss whispered, her eyes wide with panic. "They've made it into the lab."

Stewart stumbled backward; terror etched on his face. "What do we do? We're trapped!"

Dr. Reiss didn't waste a second. "Run!" she ordered, grabbing Stewart's arm and yanking him toward the emergency exit. They bolted down the narrow corridor, the sound of footsteps closing in behind them as the rebels advanced through the lab.

As they ran, Dr. Reiss tapped furiously on her wrist console, opening a secure comms link. "This is Dr. Reiss, reporting a breach at the containment facility. The rebels have made it inside. We need immediate assistance!"

The line crackled, and then a familiar voice cut through the static.

"Understood," Major Vale's voice was calm and controlled, a contrast to the chaos surrounding them. "Stay on the move, Doctor. I'm mobilizing a response team now. Don't let them take anything from that lab."

...

As the smoke cleared, Allen stepped into the room, noticing two shadows exiting through the back door. Inside the containment area was a scene straight out of a laboratory nightmare. Tanks filled with murky red liquid lined the walls, cables snaking across the floor like tentacles. Some held shadows of human forms, suspended and lifeless. One tank isolated from the rest drew Allen's attention—a large label on the side reading 'C.A.M-001.'

Allen's boots echoed in the sterile room as he approached the tank, his breath catching in his throat as the figure inside came into focus. He wasn't ready for this.

Peering inside, Allen quickly realized he was staring at himself. The clone stood motionless in the tank, eyes closed, a crown of sensors embedded into its scalp like a twisted halo.

His fists clenched involuntarily. "What the hell..."

Allen's stomach churned as he took in the wires that snaked through the clone's skull, melding flesh with tech. His own face mirrored back at him, twisted in unconscious vulnerability, as if waiting for its creator to call it to life.

"We need to move fast Allen," Cipher's voice broke through the silence over the comms, her fingers flying across the control panel. "Charges are being set throughout the building. We need to secure that asset, and you all need to exfil A.S.A.P."

"Copy that Cipher," Allen responded, snapping back into combat mode. "But how do we get it out of the tank?"

Mia chimed in over their earpieces, "Working on it now, Sam just got us synced with the tanks control module..." she began a countdown, "in 3-2-1 and there you go!".

A loud beep pulsed from the container; the lights on the control module shut off and turned back on as it rebooted. The liquid in the tank began to drain away, the clone's chest rising and falling as if it were taking its first breath. Finally, with a series of mechanical whirs, the front of the tank swung open, and the clone slumped forward like a lifeless puppet.

Allen caught him, the weight of his own body in his arms unnerving. He felt the clone's skin, warm and human, yet alien in every sense. The moment hung in the air—Allen staring at his own face, now waking up and blinking with disoriented eyes.

The soft hiss of escaping air filled the room as the wires attached to the clone's head disengaged with a synchronized series of sharp clicks, retracting back into the tank's interior with a mechanical hum. The clone remained motionless for a heartbeat, suspended in the eerie quiet that followed. Then, without warning, its chest heaved violently, drawing in a desperate, rattling breath as if it had been drowning beneath the liquid now drained from the tank.

Allen instinctively tightened his grip as the clone's body jerked in his arms, its muscles spasming violently. He could feel the raw power in its frame, the same strength he knew existed in his own, but now unsteady, as if it were still calibrating to the sudden rush of life. The clone's breaths came in quick, shallow gasps, its chest rising and falling erratically. It shook as though every system inside it was booting up, processing commands and running diagnostics, trying to understand the world it had been born into.

For a moment, Allen thought the clone might collapse entirely, but it steadied, the wild tremors slowly easing as its body began to settle into itself. Still, its eyes never left Allen's, reflecting a shared, uncanny recognition—like a machine adjusting to an echo of its creation.

The clone's gaze was locked onto Allen's with a sharp intensity, its confusion palpable. "What is... who are you?" The clone rasped, its voice a distorted echo of Allen's own.

Allen swallowed hard, feeling the storm of emotions swirling beneath the surface. His chest tightened, but he didn't waver. "I'm your only way out of this," he said, his voice low and steady. "You can decide what happens next."

Cipher's voice crackled over the comms, urgency laced in her words. "Allen, you're not going to like this, but the clone's AI is already interfacing with your gear. It's testing our systems—trying to figure out if we're friend or foe."

Allen's heart skipped a beat as he glanced down at his wrist console, the flickering lights confirming Cipher's words. He hadn't even realized it was happening. "Son of a bitch?" he muttered, his jaw tightening as he registered the potential danger.

He stared at the flickering display on his wrist console, watching as unfamiliar code scrolled across the screen. It was subtle at first, almost undetectable, but now there was no mistaking it—the clone's AI was probing, searching for weaknesses in their systems. He could feel his pulse quickening, his instincts telling him that whatever the AI was doing, it wasn't good.

"Can you shut it down?" Allen barked into the comms, his grip tightening on the clone. It was still regaining its footing, but the calculated intensity in its eyes made it clear that it was far more aware than it seemed.

"I'm trying," Cipher replied, her voice tense. "But this thing is fast. It's not like anything we've dealt with before. I can slow it down, maybe stop it temporarily, but we don't have much time."

Allen stared as the code flashing across his wrist console suddenly stopped—abruptly, as if something had yanked the plug on the entire system. He released his grip, and the clone's movements faltered, and for a brief, terrifying moment, it froze entirely, its eyes wide with confusion.

"Cipher, what just happened?" Allen barked into the comms, his pulse quickening.

Before Cipher could respond, the clone stumbled, its hand hovering in the air near the console. Its body shook, the smooth precision of its movements replaced by something clumsy, almost disoriented. Allen reached out instinctively, steadying it.

"Allen!" Cipher's voice came through the comms, urgent and sharp. "it's Vale. He's shutting down the AI core in the clone's head. It's... it's losing its interface capabilities."

The clone's eyes flickered, the intensity from moments before fading rapidly as if a light had been snuffed out. It gasped, stumbling again, and Allen barely caught it as its weight sagged into his arms. There was no longer any sign of the machine-like precision that had driven it. The clone was still awake—still breathing—but whatever had powered it, whatever had made it a formidable weapon, was gone.

The silence was deafening. Allen looked into the clone's eyes, searching for the cold intelligence he had seen before, but now there was only fear—confusion. It was like watching a man stripped of all his power, reduced to something raw and vulnerable.

"It's just a man now," Cipher said quietly through the comms. "Whatever they put in him, Vale just took it away."

The clone's breathing was shallow, its voice weak as it spoke. "I... I don't understand... what's happening to me?"

"We're moving out now," Allen said, his voice firm as he pulled the now-weakened clone to its feet. "Vale's coming, and we're not sticking around to find out what he does next."

The clone nodded weakly and before they could dwell on it, the building shuddered, alarms blaring through the corridors. Allen gripped the clone's arm, pulling it forward and giving a light push on the back toward the door.

Uncertainty was heavy on Allen's mind as they began to move out. Still trying to process the rapid changes in the clone's behavior, he knew that whatever it had become, they were about to find out—together.

Chapter 15

Explosions rocked the containment room, sending a shower of sparks cascading from the ceiling. Allen, Knox and the clone burst through the doors, sprinting into the hallway as rubble rained down behind them.

"Cipher, where's our exit?" Allen barked, weaving to avoid a burst of gunfire that chewed into the wall beside him. His muscles burned with each stride, but he pushed himself faster, drawing on years of training.

"Two levels down, northeast corner," Cipher's voice crackled over the comm link. "Techno-Synth forces closing fast behind you."

Knox pulled even with Allen. "We need to move. Now." His words were clipped, focused.

The clone said nothing, its blank eyes fixed ahead as it matched their desperate pace. Allen's skin crawled at the thought of the thing beside him, a pitiless mirror of himself. But there was no time to dwell on it.

A section of the ceiling exploded inward just behind them. Allen whirled, rifle snapping up- and froze. A figure crashed through the crumbling ceiling, landing heavily on his feet, his steel prosthetic arm catching the ground with a resounding thud. Framed by settling dust and flickering emergency lights stood Major Idris Vale, Allen's former protege. His crisp Techno-Synth uniform was spotless amidst the debris.

Three towering figures dropped down beside Vale with eerie synchronicity. Clone soldiers, their identical faces as expressionless as the masks of ancient warriors. Their movements were unnaturally smooth, more machine than man.

Their eyes gleamed in the dim light, hollow and expressionless, yet disturbingly focused.

"Allen Mercer," Vale called out, his voice unnervingly calm against the chaos. "I should have known. You never could leave well enough alone."

"Vale." Allen's finger tightened on the trigger. Old instincts warred with bitter betrayal as he stared down the man he had once trained and mentored. The man who had sold his soul to Techno-Synth. "Get out of our way."

"You know I can't do that." Vale signaled the clone soldiers with a curt gesture. They fanned out with perfect coordination, the thud of their boots a metronome of impending violence. "It's over, Allen. You can't fight the future."

Allen swore under his breath. Vale was right about one thing - they couldn't fight their way out of this. Not against those...things. He caught Knox's eye and jerked his head sharply toward the far end of the hall. His jaw tightened and he nodded once.

The facility shuddered again, raining plaster. Allen seized his chance. He squeezed off a spray of covering fire and dove sideways, rolling behind a buckled support beam. "Move!" he roared at Knox and the clone. "Get to the exit!"

As they sprinted past him, Allen could only pray that this time, Vale was wrong. That this all meant something.

The clone soldiers reacted instantly, their movements a choreographed dance of deadly precision. Allen's covering fire ricocheted off their armor as they closed in, undeterred. Knox and the rescued clone raced down the hallway, their footsteps echoing against the chaos.

"Allen, they're adapting!" Cipher's voice crackled through his comms, laced with urgency. "Their AI is analyzing your tactics, predicting your moves through your gear."

"Damn it!" Allen growled, his mind racing. He ducked behind another crumbling pillar, narrowly avoiding a hail of return fire. The clones were herding him, cutting off his escape routes with ruthless efficiency.

Vale's laughter cut through the din, taunting. "Did you really think you could outsmart them, Allen? They're the future of warfare. Perfect soldiers, bound by a singular purpose."

Allen's grip tightened on his weapon, anger surging through him. He couldn't let Vale get under his skin. Not now. "Knox, status?" he barked into his comms.

"Almost to the exit," he panted, his words punctuated by the sound of gunfire. "But we need you, Allen. We can't leave you behind."

"Don't worry about me." Allen steeled himself, his resolve hardening. "Get that clone to safety. That's all that matters."

He leaned out from cover, firing a controlled burst at the nearest clone. It stumbled, sparks flying from its damaged chest plate, but kept coming. Allen cursed, realizing the futility of a direct confrontation.

"Vale!" he shouted, his voice raw. "You want me? Come and get me yourself, you coward!"

Vale's laughter echoed through the hallway. "And deprive my soldiers of the pleasure of tearing you apart? I think not."

Allen's jaw clenched. He had to keep Vale talking, buying Knox and the clone more time. "You always were good at letting others do your dirty work. Just like when you betrayed everything we stood for."

"I betrayed nothing," Vale spat, his composure cracking. "I simply chose the winning side. Something you never had the courage to do."

The clone soldiers were closing in, their movements becoming more erratic, harder to predict. Allen knew he was running out of options. He had to make a move, and fast.

"Knox, Cipher, I'm going to draw them away," he said, his voice low and steady. "Get to the extraction point. Don't wait for me."

"Allen, no we need...!" Knox's protest was drowned out by another explosion, closer this time.

"There's no other choice," Allen took a deep breath, his resolve settling over him like armor. "I'll find another way out. I always do."

He burst from cover, firing wildly, drawing the clones' attention. They turned as one, their weapons trained on him, they gave chase. Allen ran, his heart pounding in his ears, Vale's mocking laughter echoing behind him. He didn't know if he could outrun them, but he had to try.

For the rebellion. For the future. For the hope that someday, all of this would mean something.

Allen's lungs burned as he sprinted down the crumbling hallway, the thundering footsteps of the clone soldiers echoing behind him. Sparks rained down from shattered light fixtures, and the walls shuddered with each distant explosion. He glanced over his shoulder, catching a glimpse of the soldiers' eerie, synchronized movements as they closed in.

"Cipher, I need a way out of here," Allen panted, his voice strained. "Anything, a maintenance shaft, a ventilation duct, something!"

"Working on it," Cipher replied, her digital voice crackling in his earpiece. "Take the next right, there should be a service corridor leading to the lower levels."

Allen veered right, narrowly avoiding a collapsed section of the ceiling. The clone soldiers followed, their movements unnervingly precise, their weapons trained on his back. He could feel their AI cores analyzing his every step, predicting his path.

"You can't run forever, Allen," Vale's voice taunted over the comms. "My soldiers will find you, and when they do, you'll wish you had never started this rebellion."

Allen gritted his teeth, realizing the extent of the clones hacking his gear. The thought of their collective power sent a shiver down his spine.

"Fuck you, Vale!" Allen snapped back.

A snarl of static was the only response, but Allen knew Vale had heard. The next turn brought him face to face with a sealed door, the words 'Maintenance Access' stenciled in faded yellow across it. He slammed into the door with his shoulder, the impact resonating through his body.

The door held for a tense moment before giving way with a groan of stressed metal. Allen stumbled into the pitch-black corridor, scanning for any sign of pursuit. The clone soldiers were not far behind; their persistence was relentless.

The service corridor was narrow, claustrophobic, lined with pipes and cables that throbbed with the building's dying heartbeat. Allen's footsteps echoed hollowly, a stark contrast to the chaos he'd left behind.

"Cipher," he panted, ducking under a low-hanging conduit. "Are you sure this leads out?"

"Yes, I am sure Allen." came Cipher's quick reply. "It's your best chance now to survive this."

Allen pushed on, guided by the dim light of his weapon's tactical display. He could hear the clones entering the service corridor behind him. They were more hesitant here, their bulk ill-suited for the cramped space.

His comms crackled again, and this time it was Mia's voice that broke through the silence. "Allen, you have to keep moving. We've secured the extraction point, but it won't hold for long. Knox made it out with the clone. They're waiting for you."

Allen pushed harder, his breath coming in ragged gasps. The thought of Mia and the others waiting for him was the spark that fueled his determination. "I'm not going down without a fight," he promised her.

"We know," Mia replied, her voice steady yet tight with worry. "Just make it out alive, Allen."

The corridor branched ahead, and Allen skidded to a stop, hesitating. He had to make a choice—left or right—and he knew the clones wouldn't give him long to decide.

"Left!" Cipher suddenly interjected. "The schematics show an elevator shaft at the end of that route. It's decommissioned, but it should open up to the surface."

Trusting Cipher's guidance, Allen veered left, barely registering the screech of metal on metal as one of the clone soldiers scraped against the narrow passageway in pursuit. He reached the end of the corridor and found himself facing an old elevator door, its surface pitted and rusted.

Allen pried at the doors with his fingers, finding purchase in the grooves worn by time. With a grunt, he forced them open, revealing a dark chasm that plummeted into the bowels of the earth. He unhooked a small, compact grappling hook from his belt and aimed it at the crossbeam above him.

The hook shot out with a pneumatic hiss, lodging firmly in place. Allen didn't waste a moment, gripping the descender and jumping into the void just as the clone soldiers rounded the corner.

He descended rapidly, the wind whipping past him in a howling frenzy. The darkness swallowed him whole, but he kept his eyes fixed on the faint glimmer of light below. The clones fired down the shaft, their shots sparking against the walls and ricocheting wildly.

Allen's feet hit the top of the elevator car with a thunderous clang. He detached from the line and dropped down through the narrow maintenance hatch into the elevator. The doors were already halfway open leading to the 4th floor's main hallway.

Allen peered through the half-open elevator doors, his eyes scanning for movement or an ambush. Nothing stirred. He squeezed through the gap, weapon at the ready, heart still hammering from the adrenaline-fueled escape. He needed to find a route down to the main floor.

"Cipher, how much further?" he asked, his voice ragged.

"Fifty meters, then take the stairs down on your left. They should lead you to a maintenance area with access to the exterior."

Allen nodded, his mind racing. If he could just reach those stairs, he might have a chance. He could feel the clones getting closer, their footsteps echoing like a relentless drumbeat down the hallway.

Suddenly, a searing pain ripped through his left shoulder, sending him stumbling forward. He glanced down, seeing the dark stain of blood spreading across his tactical gear. One of the clones had managed to hit him, their aim precise even in the chaos.

"Allen, your vitals are spiking," Cipher said, her voice laced with concern. "You need to get out of there, now."

Allen gritted his teeth, pushing through the pain. He couldn't afford to slow down, not with the clones so close behind. He reached the stairs, taking them two at a time, his breath coming in ragged gasps.

As he burst into the maintenance area, he saw a narrow window leading to the exterior. Freedom, so close he could almost taste it. But as he moved towards it, he heard the unmistakable sound of the clone soldiers entering the room behind him.

He turned, raising his weapon, knowing it was a futile gesture. The clones fanned out, their movements perfectly coordinated, their weapons trained on him. And there, stepping out from behind them, was Vale, a triumphant smirk on his face.

"End of the line, Allen," he said, his voice dripping with satisfaction. "You put up a good fight, but it's over now. You've lost."

Allen's mind raced, searching for a way out, a final gambit. But as he looked into the blank, soulless eyes of the clone soldiers, he knew there was no escape. He had given his team a chance, drawn the enemy away. That would have to be enough.

He closed his eyes, his final thoughts drifting to the rebellion, to the hope for a better future that had driven him this far. And as the sound of gunfire filled the room, he smiled, knowing that even in defeat, he had never stopped fighting.

Chapter 16

Gunfire rang out, and Allen closed his eyes, ready to accept his fate. But instead of the sharp sting of bullets, he heard the explosive crack of glass shattering. His eyes flew open as the clone soldiers and Vale were momentarily disoriented, the sound of rapid-fire shots tearing through the room.

Through the broken window, a rebel-hacked drone had appeared, unloading a barrage of gunfire at the clones, forcing them to scatter for cover.

"Get the hell out of there Allen," Mia's voice came through the comms. "Sam's drone can only hold them off for so long."

Allen didn't waste a second. He lunged toward the now-shattered window, his body fueled by sheer instinct as he braced himself and leapt.

He felt the rush of air as he hit the ground and rolled, just in time to hear Knox's voice crackling over his earpiece. "Allen, get moving! We've got an extraction point lined up 2 blocks to the southeast!"

"Roger that, moving now." He Replied. Just as Allen started to move, three Techno-Synth drones came screaming around the corner, quickly taking out Sam's drone and turning their attention to Allen.

As he took cover behind a turned over vehicle, Allen swiftly assessed his ammunition. It wasn't much – but hopefully enough to get him that two blocks.

It was clear to him that the drones were being directed by Vale and the clone soldiers. They couldn't chase after him because the building was close to collapsing, so they extended their reach via the drones. They would also have to find a way to escape the collapsing building.

One of the drones hovered closer, scanning for targets. Allen held his breath, tightening his grip on his weapon. He could hear Mia's controlled breathing through the comms, her underlying concern for him barely concealed.

With calculated precision, Allen popped out from behind the vehicle and fired a series of shots at one of the drone's sensory arrays, its weakest point. One bullet after another found its mark until the drone faltered, spiraled out of control, and crashed into the concrete with a satisfying burst of sparks.

Allen didn't have time to celebrate. The other two drones were now closing in fast, their weapons systems locking onto him.

A high-pitched whine filled the air as he darted between cover points, attracting the drones' fire. Each move was a calculated risk, drawing on all his tactical experience.

The relentless chase continued, and with each step Allen felt the sting of his injured shoulder growing sharper. He winced as he took another diving roll under a narrow alcove, narrowly escaping a salvo of gunfire that chipped away at the concrete above him.

Suddenly, just as one of the drones bore down on him with its guns blazing, the unmistakable sound of interference buzzed through its systems. The drone wavered, then veered off course, smashing into its counterpart, both machines erupting in a shower of sparks and twisted metal.

Allen didn't need to guess the cause—Mia's handiwork. Her hacking skills had once again tipped the scales in his favor. He used the hiatus to sprint towards his goal, keeping an eye out for any remaining dangers.

"Good timing," he gasped into the comms, acknowledging Mia's intervention.

"Don't mention it," Mia replied, her voice tense with concentration. "Just keep moving. You're almost out of there."

Allen did as he was told, each step powered by the thought of survival and the hope that lay beyond. The wind carried the dust and debris of a world in ruins, whispering stories of what had been and what could yet be.

Finally, he turned onto a street which looked out onto an overgrown park that had once been the hub of city life. Now it was silent but for the persistent hum of a lone drone patrolling nearby.

Knox's voice crackled again in his ear. "Extraction point is in sight, just past that drone."

Allen surveyed the area and caught glimpses of his team hidden among the foliage—an oasis of green amidst a sea of gray devastation. He quickly moved across the open area, avoiding the patrol drone and meeting up with Knox and the clone.

"Ok, we gotta move now," Knox commanded. "Jonas, you take out that drone and we all make our move in 3...2...1."

Jonas let off a burst of well-aimed gunshots. The drone spun out of control and fell, disappearing into the surrounding foliage. The team sprang into action, well-coordinated and precise, they began to disappear into the shadows.

As they weaved through the park, Mia's voice came once more over the comms, "Keep moving guys, the whole place is going to come down behind you!"

With a final push, they emerged from the overgrown shrubbery. The rebel team ran as fast as they could knowing that any second the building behind them was going to blow.

"10 seconds...5, 4, 3..." Mia counted down over the comms.

Allen propelled himself forward with one last, desperate burst of speed, the clone matching him stride for stride. Behind them, the ground shuddered violently, the sounds of bending metal and shattering glass pursuing them like the claws of a monstrous beast.

As they hurled themselves into the open air, a deafening roar engulfed their senses. The facility exploded in a colossal fireball that lit up the darkened sky behind them— a searing orange against the misery of their world. The concussive force and rolling cloud of debris filling the city's streets threw them forward as they landed hard on the rough terrain.

Allen gasped for breath, feeling the shock wave ripple through his body, dust and debris raining down around them. He pushed himself up, his hands pressed into the hard-packed earth, he glanced back to witness the obliteration of the Techno-Synth facility. The fires raged like angry spirits claiming their territory in the night.

Beside him, the clone lay on the ground, disoriented but alive. The clone's expression was unreadable, a mix of confusion and awe at the sheer scale of destruction they'd narrowly escaped.

"We did it," Allen managed to say between heavy breaths. He looked over at the rebel team—disheveled, some injured, but all accounted for. They shared a brief moment of collective relief amid the chaos they had wrought.

Knox knelt beside them, his grizzled face smeared with ash and soot. "We hit 'em where it hurts." His voice was rough but laced with satisfaction. "Now we regroup and plan."

Mia's voice came through again, distorted by static. "Knox, Allen, we have eyes on you. The evac route is clear back to base."

Coughing up dust and debris, Allen grabbed the clone by his arm and hauled him up. He looked to his right to see Jonas and the remaining rebels brushing themselves off.

Overhead, drones buzzed like swarms of angry insects, no doubt scanning for survivors. Allen knew they had to move quickly; even if they'd managed to escape, Techno-Synth would soon be swarming the area.

A small evac team met them halfway, their faces streaked with soot and sweat but lit with relief at seeing Allen and his living cargo intact.

As they made their escape, Allen couldn't shake the surreal feeling of running alongside his doppelganger. He glanced at Knox, who nodded in understanding. "We'll call him Xander," he said, his voice barely audible as he choked on the dust filled air.

Back at the rebel base, the mood was somber as they tended to the wounded and mourned their losses. Allen went straight over to Sam to thank him for saving his life with the drone.

Still bleeding from the gunshot wound, Allen gave Sam a giant hug. Sam winced slightly, an involuntary response to the tight embrace. "Easy there, boss," he said with a pained but grateful grin. "You took one in the shoulder, but it's nothing a little downtime won't fix."

Allen released him, stepping back with a mixture of concern and admiration. He surveyed his surroundings — fellow fighters helping each other, assessing damages, sharing quiet words of consolation.

Mia approached them, her eyes locked on his. Unable to resist her urge, she gave Allen a soft hug and glanced at his shoulder. "You need to get that looked at. Now that you're not running for your life anymore."

Allen nodded, feeling the effects of adrenaline waning and his body's pain receptors kicking in fully. He followed Mia to where a makeshift medical station had been set up. As he walked, he couldn't help but notice Xander trailing behind them silently.

The clone's eyes were constantly scanning, absorbing every detail. It was as if every sense was tuned in to learn, to adapt to this new world he was now part of. But there was something else in Xander's eyes that Allen couldn't quite place — a searching look, seeking something or someone that might make sense of his existence.

Some rebels glanced at Xander with suspicion, others with open curiosity. The resemblance between him and Allen didn't go unnoticed, sparking whispered conversations filled with both awe and unease.

Allen took a seat on the rusted metal chair at the medical station, bracing himself as the medic began to tend to his wound. Mia stood close by, her presence a silent source of comfort. She caught Xander's gaze and offered him a tentative nod, an unspoken message of solidarity that seemed to steady him.

"It's important we figure out Techno-Synth's next moves," Mia said quietly to Allen as the medic worked. "If they made him look like you—" She gestured subtly towards Xander, "—then there might be others."

Allen winced as the medic cleaned the gunshot wound with practiced efficiency. "I know," he replied with a grimace. "We need to find out how that AI core works. Whatever secrets he holds, they could be the key to taking Blake and Vale down for good."

Xander's eyes lingered on Allen, then shifted to watch the bustling activity within the base. His programmed nature seeking patterns, strategies, weaknesses—anything that would provide order to the current chaos.

...

"I want Vale here now, goddammit!" Blake yelled as he slammed his fist on the desk. "Yes sir! on it right away, sir," the orderly replied as she bowed her head and turned to the leave the room. "Oh, and make sure to secure the perimeter. I want every inch of this building on lockdown. No one in or out without my express authorization," Blake added, his gaze cold as he stared at the flames still visible through his office window, remnants of what once was one of their most advanced research sites.

The orderly nodded fervently and scurried out, her footsteps echoing down the sterile corridor. Blake turned back to the burning horizon; his jaw set in a hard line. He had underestimated the rebels and their determination – a mistake he wouldn't make again.

He knew that Vale would be furious about the loss of the cloning facility. It wasn't just a substantial blow to Project Shadow; it was personal. The AI clones were the culmination of years of secret research and countless resources. Moreover, losing Clone-Allen Mercer-001 to the enemy could mean the end of Techno-Synth's dominance — unless they acted swiftly and with deadly precision.

Blake's office door slid open as the orderly returned, barely stepping inside. "Major Vale is on his way up sir," she reported.

"Thank you, Margret," Blake replied. "Send him in immediately."

"Yes sir!" she concluded, walking away as the door slid shut.

Blake opened a couple of map screens on his giant display, locations of the two remaining cloning facilities marked with red dots. He began to punch in a series of commands, rerouting power, reassigning security details, shoring up their defenses. This was war, and war meant adaptation and retaliation. He would not let the rebels believe for a second that they had gained the upper hand.

A heavy silence hung in the room, broken only by the tapping of Blake's fingers against the holo-keyboard. The sound was like the ticking of a clock – each tap another moment leading up to an inevitable confrontation.

The door hissed open again and Major Vale strode in, his posture rigid, face etched with both anger and resolve. "Commander?".

Blake didn't turn from his screens. "Sit down, Idris," he said without emotion. "We have much to discuss."

Vale's boots thudded on the metal floor as he approached the table, his uniform immaculate despite the chaos that had ensued. "I'm assuming this isn't just about the explosion at Site 17," Vale said, his voice tinged with impatience.

Blake finally swiveled in his chair to face him; his eyes hard as ice. "It is about site 17 Vale," Blake snapped at him. "And it's also about Mercer's clone escaping and the intel he might carry. We need to contain this before it spreads any further."
Vale stiffened at the mention of the clone. "Do we have any leads on their whereabouts?"

Blake allowed himself a wry smile, albeit without warmth. "We had a tracking device on CAM-001. It went dark a few hours ago, but not before we pinpointed a general location." He tapped the screen, zooming in on an area marked with the rebel base coordinates.

Vale leaned forward, his eyes narrowing as he scanned the map. "We strike quickly then," he proposed, the edge in his voice mirroring Blake's urgency.

"Indeed," Blake said, turning back to face the panoramic view of smoldering destruction that was once Site 17. The night sky was lit with an ominous orange glow as if the horizon itself were aflame. "But we'll be strategic about it. They're expecting brute force; we'll give them something...unexpected."

Vale's expression was unreadable, but his nod was all the agreement Blake needed. "What are your orders?"

"First," Blake started, swiping through several layers of projections and data streams on the display screen, "we need to secure all our other assets. Increase surveillance and tighten access protocols."

"And the rebels?" Vale asked, his voice even but eager for action.

"We isolate them," Blake said slowly, the plan forming like a sinister puzzle in his mind. "They think they've just made a grand escape, but we'll turn their haven into a prison. Cut off their supply lines, disable their communication channels; push them to the point of desperation."

Vale's lips curled into a satisfied smirk. "And then?"

Blake leaned back in his chair, folding his hands together as if holding the fate of the rebellion in his palms. "Then we strike at their morale. We send a message that even with Cam One, they stand no chance against us."

The major's eyes gleamed with anticipation. "You have a specific tactic in mind?"

"Psychological warfare," Blake replied smoothly. "We spread disinformation within their ranks, create distrust among them—

especially regarding Mercer and his clone. We make them believe that one is the spy for the other."

Vale nodded thoughtfully, the strategy appeasing his military mind. "Sow seeds of doubt and let them tear themselves apart from within," he mused.

"Exactly. By the time we mount our physical assault, they'll be too fractured to put up any real fight." Blake's voice was cold, detached, as though he were discussing moving pieces on a game board rather than human lives.

...

Back at the underground rebel base, Allen's gut churned with a sense of mounting dread. Xander's continued silence ate at him, a heavy weight that he couldn't shake off. Mia's news about the scrambled intel had not helped. The enemy was always one step ahead; he could feel it.

Gingerly touching the bandaged wound on his arm, Allen walked over to where Knox was standing, overlooking a holographic display of the region. "What's our play, Knox?" His voice was low and tense.

Knox flicked through several surveillance images before settling on one. "We're going dark," he said decisively. "It's only a matter of time before they track us here."

In the corner, Cipher was hunched over Xander, tools in hand, delicately adjusting connections on his AI core. She muttered something about the complexity of its design, her fascination evident. Finally, Xander broke his silence.

"They built it to stay linked," he said, his voice sounded exactly like Allen's but faintly mechanical. "The core... it's not just an AI. It's integrated into Techno-Synth's network, transmitting and receiving constantly."

Allen shifted in his chair, his revelation causing him to stiffen. Every muscle in his body tensed as if he were physically holding back the implications of what Xander had just said. "So you're telling me," Allen began, struggling to keep his voice even, "that since you've been with us, Techno-Synth could have been listening in on everything and tracking you here?"

Xander's eyes met Allen's, a silent acknowledgment between them. "Yes, they could have," he admitted. "But they disconnected my core after you hacked into my cloning chamber and woke me up, at that point any tracking capabilities would have fizzled out after an hour or two."

Allen paused as he listened, his gaze drifting to Xander. A strange, almost surreal awareness crept over him—it was like talking to a living echo of himself, each word bouncing back with an uncanny familiarity. He shook off the thought, focusing on the problem at hand. "So, the trail would end a block or two from our current location. We need to assume they'll piece together our escape route from there."

Cipher looked up, surprised. "So, they can track you... but that means you could track them, potentially?"

Xander's lips curled slightly, his first human-like response. "If we replicate my AI core and sync it to the one you stole from the warehouse, I could create a false feedback loop. It would trick their systems, make them think I'm somewhere else and we could keep eyes on them the whole time."

Allen exchanged a glance with Knox, intrigued.

"But there's a catch," Xander added, a hint of hesitation in his voice. "It would all still be linked to their network. If Techno-Synth realizes what we're doing, they could... override me."

Cipher's hands paused, her eyes narrowing. "Then we'll make sure that doesn't happen."

The team watched, captivated by Xander's words, realizing the potential his core offered.

Knox's voice cut through the tension. "Perfect! This could work right here." He tapped the hologram, expanding the view of a wooded area.

Allen squinted at the selected image — a dense forest canopy that would shield them from above. "Hide and seek in the woods?" He asked, recognizing there was more to it

"With a twist," Knox replied, lines of concentration framing his eyes. "Mia, you with me on this?"

Mia nodded, stepping closer to the table and tucking a strand of hair behind her ear. "Sam and Jonas can rig up some nifty electronic countermeasures and integrate our "new" AI core when it's ready. If Techno-Synth traces anything, it'll lead them on a merry chase through the forest." Her eyes gleamed with excitement.

"Exactly." Knox replied. "We need to move fast."

Chapter 17

The screen flickered to life, casting a ghostly blue glow across Commander Blake's angular face. His steely eyes narrowed as he leaned closer to the camera, his voice low and deliberate.

"Citizens of the city, hear me now. The rebels who claim to fight for your freedom are nothing more than terrorists, hell-bent on destroying the order and stability that Techno-Synth provides. And their leader, Allen Mercer, is the biggest traitor of them all."

Blake's lips curled into a sneer as images of Allen flashed across the screen - grainy surveillance footage interspersed with fabricated scenes of violence and destruction.

"Don't be fooled by his lies. This man, your so-called savior, has a dark past that he conveniently can't remember. A past where he willingly served Techno-Synth and often disobeyed orders, killing hundreds of innocent civilians. This man, Allen Mercer, murdered your family members, your brothers, your sisters and your mothers and fathers. All because of his thirst for blood, and his disregard for human life. "

The commander's voice dripped with venom, each word a poisoned dart aimed at the heart of the rebellion.

"Ask yourselves, can you trust a man who doesn't even know who he really is? A man who would betray his own kind for personal gain? Allen Mercer is no hero. He's a fraud, a traitor, and a murderer."

Blake leaned back, a satisfied smirk playing on his lips as he watched his propaganda spread like wildfire across the airwaves.

"Only Techno-Synth can bring true order to this chaotic world. Join us, and together we will crush this insurgency and usher in a new era of peace and prosperity under our benevolent rule."

The screen went dark, leaving the chilling echo of Blake's accusations to reverberate in the minds of every citizen tuned in.

Miles away, somewhere on the outskirts of the city, Ada Wallace—the Wraith—moved with purpose toward Rally Point Delta. She wasn't in her usual tactical gear tonight. Instead, she wore the guise of a weary, downtrodden survivor. Dirt and ash smudged her face, hiding the razor-sharp alertness in her eyes. Her usual predatory precision was masked by a carefully constructed look of defeat, shoulders slumped and head slightly bowed, like so many other desperate souls wandering the ruins.

Rally Point Delta was a known gathering spot for those sympathetic to the rebellion, and Ada intended to make the most of it. She adjusted her tattered scarf and slipped a battered cap low over her eyes as she approached the cluster of rebels gathered there, her gait unsteady, as if fatigue weighed her down. The disguise was almost too easy; she could feel the rebels' guarded curiosity as she came closer, slipping seamlessly into the edges of their circle.

"Hard to know who to trust these days, isn't it?" she murmured, just loud enough for a few nearby rebels to hear. Her voice was hoarse, affected by a rasp that hinted at hardship and struggle.

A nearby rebel, a younger man with a wary expression, nodded grimly. "Yeah. Ever since that broadcast about Allen... hard to tell what's real and what's not." He glanced around, uncertain, his faith visibly shaken.

Ada leaned closer, lowering her voice conspiratorially. "I heard whispers... that he was one of the worst of them. A Techno-Synth loyalist before basically becoming a serial killer.

Some people don't change, you know?" She let the words linger, each syllable carefully measured to burrow into the rebels' minds like seeds waiting to sprout.

The rebels exchanged glances, shifting uneasily as her words took hold. Ada's tone softened, carrying a hint of sympathy. "I used to think he was one of us rebels, too. But after seeing that broadcast... I just don't know anymore." She looked down, as if reluctant to speak further, a perfect mimicry of doubt and hesitation.

One of the rebels, an older woman hardened by years of struggle, crossed her arms, a frown creasing her brow. "But Allen has fought with us, he has bled with us. I don't buy Blakes bs broadcast."

Ada nodded, feigning agreement, but kept her expression carefully conflicted. "Maybe... or maybe it's just part of a bigger game he likes to play." She lowered her voice again, forcing the rebels to lean in closer. "I don't want to believe it, but I've heard other stories too... stories of him turning on his own before. Killing them simply because he was bored."

The rebels around her grew silent, their suspicions stoked by her careful prodding. Ada allowed herself a small, hidden smile as she pulled her scarf tighter around her neck, ready to slip away just as quietly as she had arrived. Her mission was clear: plant the seeds of distrust, then vanish before anyone could realize the Wraith had been among them at all.

As she melted back into the shadows, Ada's mind was already calculating her next move, her face resuming its usual steely calm beneath the layers of disguise.

She activated her neural link, connecting her directly with Techno-Synth command. Her thoughts transmitting in real time,

Blake and Vale were able to constantly keep tabs on her progress.

"Phase one complete Major Vale." she reported.

"Good. Keep pressure on their weak spots. The next step is to ensure those seeds of doubt sprout into full-blown paranoia," came Vale's crisp voice through the neural link.

Ada moved through the shadows, her stride silent and unhurried as she traversed the desolate landscape, a ghost slipping through the ruins. Her path would take her to another hub of rebel activity soon enough, and with each whisper, every insidious rumor shared, the foundation of Allen's leadership would crumble just a bit more.

    * * *

The shadows lengthened as night fell over the rebel base, a stillness settling over the underground compound like a heavy blanket. Allen sat hunched over a workbench, his eyes straining in the dim light as he pored over maps and intel reports. The accusations still rang in his ears, Blake's voice a persistent whisper that refused to be silenced.

He rubbed at his temples, trying to massage away the dull throb that had taken up residence behind his eyes. The doubts swirled in his mind, insidious tendrils that wrapped around his thoughts and squeezed until he could barely breathe.

What if Blake was right? What if he had been a traitor and murderer all along, a sleeper agent just waiting to be activated? The gaps in his memory yawned wide, dark chasms that threatened to swallow him whole.

Soft footsteps behind him yanked him from his spiraling thoughts. He whirled, hand instinctively going for the weapon at his hip, but it was just Mia, her hands raised in a placating gesture.

"Easy, soldier," she said, a wry smile tugging at her lips. "Just me."

Allen let out a shaky breath, his hand falling away from his sidearm. "Sorry. I'm just..."

"On edge?" Mia finished for him, her eyes softening with understanding. "We all are. But you can't let Blake get in your head like this, Allen. That's exactly what he wants."

Allen shook his head, his jaw clenching. "But what if he's right, Mia? What if I am the monster he says I am?"

Mia stepped closer, her hand coming to rest on his arm. "Listen to me, Allen. I know you. I've fought beside you, bled with you. And I know, in my gut, that you are not the man Blake claims you to be."

Allen wanted to believe her, wanted to cling to the certainty in her voice like a lifeline. But the doubts still lingered, a cancer eating away at his resolve.

Outside the compound, a shadow moved through the darkness, silent and deadly. Ada Wallace, the Wraith, crept closer to the rebel base, her keen eyes tracking the movements of the sentries on the walls.

She had intercepted a communication earlier that day, a coded message that hinted at the location of the rebel base. It was the opening she had been waiting for, the chance to strike a blow against the rebels that would cripple their operations.

But she held back, watching and waiting. To attack now would be too easy, too clean. No, she wanted to draw this out, to let the rebels marinate in their own fear and paranoia until they turned on each other like rabid dogs.

A cruel smile curved her lips as she melted back into the shadows. Let them think they were safe, for now. When the time was right, she would strike, and the rebellion would crumble like a house of cards.

* * *

In the heart of Techno-Synth's command center, Vale and Blake huddled around a holographic display, their faces bathed in an eerie blue glow. The screen flickered with images of the presumed rebel base, live feeds from the Wraith's neural link and surveillance drones painting a picture of their enemy's defenses.

"We've got them now," Blake said, his voice thick with satisfaction. "Allen's reputation is in tatters, and the rebels are starting to doubt their precious leader."

Vale nodded, his eyes never leaving the display. "But we can't let up now. We need to keep the pressure on, keep them off balance until they tear each other apart."

Blake sneered. "I want you to ramp up the propaganda campaign. Spread more rumors about Allen's past, make them believe he's been working for us all along. I want every rebel to question his loyalty, his very identity."

"Consider it done," Vale said, his fingers already dancing across the console, crafting new lies and half-truths to feed the rebel's paranoia.

As they worked, a flicker of movement caught Blake's eye. He zoomed in on the display, his eyes narrowing as he recognized the figure creeping through the shadows outside the rebel base.

"The Wraith," he breathed, a hint of admiration in his voice. "She's found a way in."

Vale looked up, his expression calculating. "We could end this now, crush the rebellion with a single strike."

But Blake shook his head. "No, let them stew in their own fear for a while longer. When the time is right, we'll unleash on them."

"Get troops into the area and surround them," Blake began. "I want to cut them off from the outside world and watch them suffer as we slowly squeeze the life out of them."

The order was a cold, clinical, and twisted prescription for chaos. Vale's gaze was unflinching as he absorbed the command, the cogs of war turning methodically within his mind.

"Understood," he acknowledged, his voice devoid of emotion. He turned crisply on his heel, leaving Blake to his devices.

* * *

Knox approached Allen. "Got a minute?" he asked, his gaze flicking from Allen to the maps strewn across the workbench.

Allen straightened and nodded, brushing a hand through his hair in an attempt to displace the fog of exhaustion clouding his thoughts. "For you? Always."

Knox's eyes held a sincerity that was hard to come by in these fractured times. "It's about the scouts' reports. There's been increased Techno-Synth activity around our perimeter. They're tightening their grip, and we've got no way out if they decide to pounce."

A muscle twitched in Allen's jaw as he considered the implications. "So, we're potentially sitting ducks."

Knox leaned in, lowering his voice despite the privacy of the area. "I don't like it any more than you do, but there's talk among the ranks. People are scared, not just of Techno-Synth, but of what might happen if... well, if Blake has been telling the truth about you."

Allen gritted his teeth against the sting of betrayal. He'd led these people through hell and back, and now they doubted him. It was like a gut-punch, undermining everything he'd fought for.

"We need to dispel these doubts," Allen said firmly. "We can't let Blake win. I know I'm not the person he says I am."

Xander walked over and sat in a chair next to Allen. "I think I can help," he said, his stare steady and analytical. "My connection with Techno-Synth's network could be the key to discrediting their propaganda against you."

Allen looked up at Knox and then turned to Xander, a lifeline thrown amidst the roiling sea of uncertainty. "What are you suggesting?"

"Blake is playing psychological warfare. But we can counter it with evidence and truth." Xander began. "I say we break into their systems, gather proof of their manipulation. We expose their lies directly to the people."

Knox nodded slowly, the wrinkles on his forehead deepening with thought. "It's a risky move. If they catch on to you, it'll be your end – and possibly ours."

Xander smiled, a rare display of emotion. "Let them try. I was molded from their own hands; I know their tactics and their weaknesses. And they don't know me as well as they think."

Mia, overhearing, interjected from where she inspected her gear. "Count me in. Hacking into Techno-Synth's databases is child's play at this point." Her eyes flared with the fire of challenge.

Cipher chimed in, shaking her head in agreement. "Count me in too."

Allen felt the coiled tension within him ease, fractionally. With the leadership back on his side, the odds seemed less grim.

"Alright," he said, steeling himself for the arduous task ahead. "We do this tonight."

Without missing a beat, Allen turned to Knox and Mia, a fierce determination hardening on his face. "First, we'll reach out to any sympathizers we have left outside the base through the Shadow Web and Whisper Networks. We need them to know we're surrounded, and that we need help now more than ever. If we can rally enough support on the outside, it could break us free."

Knox gave a quick nod of agreement. "Our allies will answer the call. We'll get the word out."

Cipher's eyes flickered, a calculated gleam of confidence in her eyes. "I'll mask our signals. If we're going to counter Blake's lies, we'll do it with precision and control. They won't see it coming."

Allen's mind raced as each piece of the plan fell into place, the weight of Blake's psychological assault lifting bit by bit. "Good. Start getting those messages out. Let people know what's happening, what Blake's up to, and that we're not backing down."

As Xander, Mia and Cipher went to set up the broadcast, Allen motioned to Knox. "Gather everyone in the base. It's time I set the record straight."

Minutes later, the rebels filled the room, murmuring in low voices and casting uneasy glances toward Allen. The tension was thick. When he stepped forward, silence descended, all eyes on him.

Allen stood before the gathered rebels, his expression steady, but there was an unmistakable gravity in his eyes as he looked around at the faces before him—people he'd fought beside, who had shared in the struggle and borne witness to the oppression Techno-Synth had brought upon them.

"I know," he began, his voice calm but resonant, "that Blake's campaign is casting shadows over my loyalty to all of you. He's using pieces of my past, twisting them to make me seem like the very thing we're fighting against. Yes, I was once a part of Techno-Synth. But that does not make me their ally—not anymore."

The room was silent, a charged stillness hanging over the crowd as they absorbed his words.

"I have memories," he continued, his voice steady but edged with emotion. "Memories that are fragmented, scattered... but they're enough. Enough for me to remember that the man Blake is painting isn't who I am. He's portraying me as a cold, ruthless soldier willing to sacrifice everything and everyone. But I remember what he's done—what Techno-Synth has done. They're the ones who have twisted the truth. They're the ones who've taken people's lives without hesitation, without remorse."

Allen's gaze grew sharper, his tone laced with a rising fervor. "Blake wants you to believe I am capable of atrocities. But I know who I was, just as I know who I am now. And I know that the real atrocities... those come from the very man accusing me. The man who uses propaganda as his weapon, twisting truth into poison."

The rebels murmured among themselves, faces tense but thoughtful. Allen pressed on, a quiet power in his words.

"Blake's version of me? It's a ghost, a fabrication. And he's using it to try to divide us, to make us question our cause. But I won't let him destroy what we've built. I'm not the weapon of his empire. I'm the man who stands with each of you against that empire. I stand with you for freedom. For justice. For a future where Techno-Synth doesn't decide our fate."

Xander stepped forward, his voice quiet but clear as he addressed the room. "I share some of Allen's memories. They're... disjointed, but clear enough. And in them, I see the truth. Blake was the one making the decisions. He was the one ordering actions that none of us could justify. He's the one who's tried to make these atrocities normal. It was him—not Allen."

Allen nodded, looking at Xander with a sense of shared resolve. "What Xander says is true. Blake has done more to harm the innocent than anyone else. He's a master of manipulation, of using fear and lies to pit us against one another. And that's what he's doing here, hoping we'll tear ourselves apart, so he doesn't have to."

He looked around the room, locking eyes with each rebel, his voice dropping lower but ringing with an almost presidential authority. "So, I ask you this: think of everything we've fought for, everything we've endured. Does any of that line up with the picture of me that Blake is trying to paint? Or do you believe in the Allen Mercer who's bled and fought alongside you, who's willing to give his life to bring an end to Techno-Synth's stranglehold on our world?"

The crowd was silent, hanging onto his words, their expressions softening with a mixture of hope and conviction.

"We've been through too much together to let a man like Blake break us. I promise you, I will give everything I have to fight for this rebellion, for each and every one of you. Together, we'll show them that we're not afraid of their lies or their power. We are stronger than that."

A hum of renewed energy spread through the crowd, some nodding, others murmuring agreement, but all of them seeming to lean into Allen's words, finding unity in his conviction.

Mia stepped forward; her voice filled with fierce determination. "Allen's right. We can't let them divide us. If we stand together, there's nothing Blake can do to shake us."

Allen raised his hand, his look intense. "Then let's move forward together. Let's prove that no lie, no amount of propaganda, can break the spirit of this rebellion. Blake may have twisted truths and spread poison, but the truth has a way of rising to the surface. And when it does, Techno-Synth will be forced to reckon with the strength and resilience of the people they've underestimated."

The stirring words from Allen had ignited a flame of renewed purpose among the rebels, but the moment of unity was short-lived. A sudden, sharp tone from the base's security system cut through the fading echoes of his speech.

Cipher, alert at her terminal, spun around to face Allen. "We've got multiple Techno-Synth squads," she said, her voice steady yet urgent. "They're taking up positions surrounding the base, trying to box us in. It's not an attack yet, but they're preparing for one."

Allen's jaw tightened as he absorbed the news. "Then we'll show them that we're more than just survivors; we're fighters," Allen declared, his voice carrying the weight of command. "Prepare to defend, but also keep our escape routes clear. We'll dig in, but we'll also be ready to move when the time is right. Cipher, I need those paths. We decide our next move, not Techno-Synth."

Chapter 18

Roth stood amidst the skeletal remains of what had once been the heart of the Outlander base. He and his team had been cut off from the rest, lying low ever since Ada's forces descended on the base, scattering survivors in every direction. The place was a tapestry of desolation: twisted metal and rubble, the remnants of tents fluttered like tattered flags in the breeze, and the ground was littered with the charred remains of fires long extinguished. The silence was profound, broken only by the occasional clink of debris settling or the far-off hum of a patrol drone.

His squad, a ragged group of survivors, had made their refuge here, their faces hardened by the same grim resolve. They were all that was left of the Outlanders in this sector—ten seasoned fighters, each with their own story of loss and defiance. Their gear was a patchwork, salvaged from the fallen and the forgotten, a testament to their ability to adapt and endure.

A figure emerged from the shadows of the forest; their steps careful, almost silent. Roth's hand went instinctively to his weapon, but he relaxed as the courier from the rebellion raised their hand in the agreed-upon signal of peace. The courier's face was obscured by a hood, their eyes the only visible feature, wide with urgency.

"We've been looking for you," the courier whispered, their voice low and hoarse from days on the run. They reached into their cloak and pulled out a small, battered piece of parchment. "From Allen. It's urgent."

Roth took the message, his fingers trembling slightly as he broke the wax seal—a symbol of the rebellion, a broken chain.

The message was written in the coded language of the Whisper Network, phrases that to the uninitiated would seem like gibberish, but to those who knew, it spelled out a desperate plea for aid.

Encrypted Message: "Sunset at the old park. Wolves are at the door. Need the shepherd. -A"

Roth's eyes scanned the message once, twice, as the realization dawned on him. The 'old park' was a known rally point, but the wolves at the door meant only one thing—Techno-Synth had found the underground rebel base. 'Shepherd' was code for Roth, the one who had many times led the Outlanders from danger.

He looked up, meeting the eyes of his squad. They saw the change in him, the shift from weary leader to one awakened by purpose.

"We're their last hope," Roth explained, his voice steady, betraying none of the turmoil within. "Allen and the others are trapped. Our brothers and sisters are about to be overrun, and we are the only ones close enough to do something about it."

The courier nodded; their role fulfilled. "The network is spreading the word. Others will come if they can, but you're the closest. Time is short."

The squad exchanged looks, each face a mirror of determination mixed with the fear of what lay ahead. They were outnumbered, outgunned, but not out of the fight.

Roth handed the message back to the courier, who promptly burned it, the light of the small flame casting shadows across their faces. "Tell anyone who will listen," Roth said. "We move at dusk."

As the courier melted back into the dark to go spread the word, Roth turned to his squad. "Gear up. We're not just fighting for survival today. We're fighting to ensure there's still a rebellion to survive for."

The stakes were laid bare. If they did not answer this call, there might not be another chance, not just for the rebellion, but for the very idea of freedom in this city. The weight of that realization settled over them like the approaching night, dark and all-encompassing.

With the decision made, Roth led his squad away from the skeletal remains of the Outlander base, their silhouettes blending into the encroaching darkness. They crossed the threshold where the Outlands met the city, stepping into a realm where the forest had begun its relentless reclamation.

They moved swiftly, conserving words and breath, their eyes scanning for any sign of movement. The landscape shifted as they approached the city outskirts, where the first signs of urban decay met the encroaching wild. Buildings, half-collapsed and graffitied with the symbols of old gangs or new rebellions, stood like sentinels. Here, the silence was different—filled with the potential for danger, the kind that lurked behind broken windows and within the shadows of toppled pillars.

The transition from the Outlands to the city was marked by the increasing presence of technological remnants. They navigated through a maze of derelict streets, where the occasional functional streetlamp flickered, casting eerie light on their path. The hum of drones became more frequent, a drone's spotlight occasionally sweeping across the ground like a predator's gaze.

Roth signaled a halt at the edge of what was once a football field, now an area of rubble and weeds. The city's outer sectors began here. They paused, listening for the telltale sounds of patrols or the soft whir of surveillance equipment. Each step now had to be measured, as the risk of detection grew with every block they covered.

Their journey to the rebel base was a testament to their resolve. They moved like shadows through the skeleton of the metropolis, avoiding the drone patrols that hummed overhead like metal insects.

Roth navigated with the precision of one who had memorized every crack and crevice of this broken landscape. But even his experience couldn't shield them from random encounters with Techno-Synth forces. Twice, they had to engage, the silence of their approach giving way to the cacophony of combat. Each time, Roth felt the cold calculus of war: the bullet count, the risk of exposure, the lives of his soldiers against the mission.

The city was a live wire, tension threaded through its veins. The rebels' base was closer now, but so too was the enemy. The closer they got; the more Roth felt the gravity of what lay ahead. This wasn't just another skirmish; it was a rescue mission where failure meant not only their deaths but potentially the end of everything they had fought for.

As they neared the rebel base, the air grew thick with the smell of smoke and metal. Roth signaled a halt, his hand raised in warning. Through the haze, he could see movement, the telltale signs of an impending siege.

***

In the depths of the underground base, the air was thick with the scent of fear and determination. The dim lights flickered as Allen paced the command center, his mind a whirlwind of strategies and regrets, while Mia checked and rechecked the equipment, her fingers deft with the familiarity of routine.

Cipher sat nearby, her eyes focused on her screen, vigorously tapping away at her keyboard. Around them, rebels moved with purpose, some packing essential supplies, others fortifying positions, all aware that their sanctuary could soon become their tomb.

A young rebel, barely out of adolescence but with eyes that had seen too much, burst into the command room. His chest heaved from the run, and his face was flushed with both exertion and urgency.

"Allen, Mia, Cipher," he panted, his voice cutting through the low murmur of preparation, "the courier made contact. Roth got the message. He's coming."

A huge relief washed over the room, but it was short-lived, replaced by the sobering realization of what Roth's approach signified. The rebels exchanged looks, knowing that his arrival would signal the beginning of their escape or their end.

Allen stopped by Cipher; his voice low but urgent. "How much time do we have?"

Cipher didn't look up, her fingers not missing a beat. "Roth's close, but so is Ada's response team. Minutes, maybe less."

Mia approached, her gear now strapped on, a look of determination set in her eyes. "We need to move, Allen. We can't wait for a perfect moment."

Allen nodded, understanding the unspoken cost of their next move. He raised his voice, addressing the group. "Listen up! We're moving out in about 90 minutes. Pack what you can carry, we're not coming back here."

A rebel, younger and less seasoned, voiced the fear many felt. "Where do we go, sir? Techno-Synth's everywhere."

Cipher finally looked up, a spark of hope in her usually stoic expression. "There's one place. It's not on any current map or database. It's where I first learned to hack, where I hid when things got too hot. It's an old FreeTech hideout on the city's edge, buried under what used to be the old botanical gardens."

Allen considered this, his look meeting Mia's for a moment. "Can we trust it's still secure?"

Cipher's nod was firm. "They'd need to dig through layers of digital and physical obscurity to find it. It's our best shot."

"Alright," Allen said, his decision made. "Get everyone ready. We head there once Roth and his team have engaged Ada's forces."

The rebels sprang into action, a sense of direction replacing the earlier despair. They knew the stakes; each had felt the weight of Techno-Synth's oppression. Now, escape was not just a possibility but a necessity.

Cipher continued her work, now interfacing with the base's security systems, ready to trigger distractions or open pathways as needed. "I'll prepare our exit. Once Roth hits, we'll have a narrow window to slip through."

Mia moved among the rebels, distributing the last of the gear, her voice steady. "Leave anything that can slow you down. We're not just running; we're fighting for every step."

Allen watched his people; each face a story of resistance. He felt a surge of pride mixed with the fear of what they were leaving behind—their home, their memories, perhaps even their lives. But in their eyes, he saw the same fire that had driven him since he first woke with no memory, and nothing but a name and a mission.

As Cipher's fingers danced across her console, initiating the first of many decoys, Allen prepared his own gear. His voice was low, meant only for Mia, who stood beside him. "We owe Roth more than we can ever repay."

Mia's hand squeezed his shoulder, a silent agreement. "Then let's make sure his sacrifice isn't in vain. We survive, and we fight on."

***

"Listen," Roth whispered, his voice barely carrying over the distant hum of drones. "We hit with everything we've got, and we do it quickly. Our mission is to buy them time to escape. We hold the line until they're safe, or we go down fighting."

The words hung between them; a pact sealed without spoken words. They checked their gear one last time, each movement deliberate. The squad spread out, silent as the shadows they had become, each step measured and precise. Roth signaled with a series of hand gestures, and they converged on the first Techno-Synth position like ghosts. The enemy soldiers, complacent in their patrols, never saw the attack coming.

Roth's first shot was a silenced bullet to the neck of the closest guard, who crumpled without a sound. His team mirrored his efficiency, knives and silenced weapons dispatching the rest with a chilling quietness. Bodies fell, and before the silence could turn to alarm, Roth's team was already moving to the next position.

They struck again with the same deadly precision, catching another small group of Techno-Synth forces by surprise. A quick burst from an automatic weapon, a thrown explosive device, and the second position was neutralized. The third was a larger force, but the element of surprise still worked in their favor. Roth and his team used the chaos and the confusion to their advantage, taking down soldiers in rapid succession as shouts of alarm finally began to echo through the area.

Then, like a digital warrior materializing from the fog of war, Ada stepped into view, her presence as chilling as the night air. With her were three Apex Legion clone soldiers, their movements unnaturally smooth, their eyes devoid of fear or hesitation. They were elite, a cut above the rest, their cybernetic enhancements making them extremely lethal.

Ada's voice, when it came, was calm, almost serene in contrast to the chaos. "You're surrounded, Roth. Surrender now, and I'll make it quick."

Roth glanced around, assessing the situation. His team was outgunned, their numbers and ammunition spent too quickly. Ada's troops were closing in, tightening the noose.

He made his decision in a heartbeat, his voice low and steady for his squad's ears only. "We can't win this fight head-on, but we can make it count. We hold them here, keep them off balance. Give Allen and the others the time they need."

His team understood. They were soldiers, rebels, survivors, and each knew the weight of their duty. They took defensive positions, using the rubble and urban debris as cover, their weapons readied for the inevitable onslaught.

The battle erupted with a ferocity that seemed to ignite the very air. Roth's team fired upon the advancing troops, their aim true, their resolve unyielding. The three Apex soldiers moved with terrifying precision, their shots calculated, meant to suppress and kill.

Roth engaged one directly, his training kicking in. He dodged a lethal strike, responding with a burst of gunfire to its gut that forced the clone to retreat momentarily. It's armor holding up to the barrage. "Keep firing!" he shouted, knowing that every second counted.

***

The underground base shook as the sounds of fighting reached them from above. Each blast made the ground tremble, like the heartbeat of the rebellion was pounding right through the walls. The rebels looked up, their faces changing from serious to a mix of scared and hopeful. They knew Roth was out there, fighting for them.

Allen spoke up, his voice strong. "Roth's here. Let's get ready to move."

Cipher's fingers danced over her keyboard, the sound almost blending with the distant gunfire. "Exit's clear," she confirmed, her voice steady. "We've got to move now. The old botanical gardens will hide us, but we need to get there first."

Mia stepped up, her eyes scanning the group, her expression one of fierce urgency. "Remember, we stick together. Keep low, move fast. Roth's giving us this shot. Let's not waste it."

As the rebels began gathering their gear, Allen took one last look around the command center, the place that had been their home, their headquarters. It was time to leave it behind. He turned and followed the others towards the exit, his heart heavy with the weight of their loss, yet buoyed by the hope of survival.

They approached the heavy door that led to the outside world, now fraught with peril. Cipher input the final code, and with a hiss of hydraulics, the door began to slide open. The sounds of battle grew louder, more immediate.

Allen stepped forward, the first to face the unknown, his resolve hardening. Behind him, the rebels readied themselves for the dash to freedom, knowing that Roth's diversion was their lifeline.

***

Roth and his squad fought with the fury of cornered wolves; their resolve unyielding even as their numbers dwindled. Each shot was a testament to their training, their dedication, their belief in a cause that transcended life itself.

As they engaged the Apex Legion, Roth could feel the tide turning. The clones were relentless, their precision was like a force of nature, impossible to outmaneuver for long. Yet, Roth smiled grimly, knowing each second they held their ground was a second the rebels inside had to escape.

A clone soldier advanced, its movements a blur. Roth barely had time to react before a burst of energy fire caught him in the side, sending him staggering back. He returned fire, his shot finding a weak point in the clone's armor, but another Apex soldier was already upon him.

The sounds of the base's door opening in the distance were like music to Roth's ears. "Go!" he managed to shout, his voice raw with effort. His squad understood; they knew this was it.

Their ammunition spent, they engaged in close quarters with whatever they had left—knives, improvised weapons, sheer willpower. One by one, they fell, their sacrifice silent but echoed in the chaos of battle.

Roth, now on one knee, felt the cold steel of a blade against his back. He glanced over his shoulder, seeing Ada, her face expressionless. "You fought well, Roth," she said, her voice devoid of warmth.
"I did what I had to," Roth replied, his tone resigned yet defiant. "For them."

As Ada plunged her knife into his back, tearing through his vitals, Roth's last sight was of the rebels slipping away into the shadows, their forms disappearing into the night. He smiled, a silent goodbye to his comrades, to the rebellion, to the city he loved. His final thought was not of his own end but of the hope he and his squad had bought with their lives.

Chapter 19

With every step away from the base, the sounds of gunfire and the last defiant cries of Roth's squad grew fainter. The rebels moved with a mix of grief and urgency, their faces set in grim lines, silently vowing that Roth's sacrifice would not be forgotten. As they disappeared into the darkness, they carried with them not just their hopes but the spirit of every rebel who had given everything for the chance of freedom.

The rebels moved like shadows through the city's ruins, each step a calculated risk. Allen led with a mixture of caution and determination, the weight of Roth's sacrifice pressing down on him, yet propelling him forward.

As they navigated through a once-bustling commercial district, now a graveyard of ambition, the hum of a dragon drone reached their ears. Knox, always alert, signaled for silence with a raised fist. They all froze, the drone's surveillance capabilities notorious for their efficiency.

Ahead, the drone's silhouette was visible against the night sky, its searchlights sweeping the area like a lighthouse over a stormy sea. They needed cover, and fast. Allen pointed to the grand entrance of an old bank, its massive doors ajar, inviting in the overgrowth that had begun to reclaim the city.

Slipping inside, they found themselves in a cavernous lobby, the marble floor cracked and covered in dust. The echoing space was dimly lit by the moonlight filtering through broken skylights above. The rebels dispersed quickly, finding hiding spots. The rebel leaders crouched behind the remnants of what was once a luxurious customer service desk, listening to the drone pass by overhead, its mechanical whir fading into the distance.

As the drone's sound receded into a whisper of the night, the rebels began to relax, their breathing a soft sigh of relief, slightly breaking the quiet that settled over the vast, empty space of the old bank. They exchanged silent nods, believing the danger had passed.

But then, in an instant, the atmosphere changed. The air itself seemed to pulse with the sudden movement of shadows, figures emerging from every direction with a speed that caught the rebels off-guard. From above, on the mezzanine, shapes detached from the gloom, their forms fluid and predatory. Below, what had been perceived as debris or rubble shifted, revealing the glint of eyes and the barrel of weapons.

The cavernous lobby transformed in a heartbeat from a temporary refuge to an ambush zone. Around them, the scavengers, forty strong, had them surrounded. The surprise attack was swift; before the rebels could react, a chorus of clicks filled the room as laser sights ignited. The lobby was suddenly crisscrossed with thin red beams, each one finding its target with deadly intent. The light from the lasers painted a stark picture of their precarious position, every line of light a silent threat.

"Don't move," a voice from the dark commanded just as their laser sight clicked on, the last of three red dots appearing on Allens chest. "Drop your weapons, or we'll drop you." The rebels turned toward the voice, slowly laying their weapons on the ground and beginning to raise their hands as they stood back up. Knowing they were stuck.

"Looks like we got us some lost sheep," he sneered, his voice carrying the confidence of someone who had orchestrated this encounter.

Allen's mind raced. They were caught off guard, their escape undetected but now at the mercy of those who lived by different rules in this lawless part of the city. He glanced at Mia, whose eyes were already scanning for an escape or a way to turn the tables.

With a slow, deliberate motion, Allen pulled himself to his feet, his eyes never leaving the scavenger leader's. There was a moment, a heartbeat where the air seemed to thicken with tension, as if the very atmosphere of the abandoned bank was holding its breath.

"I know you," the scavenger leader said, his voice narrowing as he recognized Allen. "You're the one they've been looking for. The traitor, the rebel leader. There's a bounty on your head, big enough to feed my people for months."

Allen's gaze was steady, his voice even as he responded, "Blake's promises are as empty as this city. You think he'd honor a bargain with scavengers? He'd see you as much of a threat as us. Deliver us to him, and you'll find he would gladly kill two birds with one stone."

The leader paused, a flicker of doubt crossing his hardened features. The rebels watched, tense, knowing their lives hung in the balance of this negotiation. The scavengers around him shifted, their weapons still aimed but their attention now split between their leader and the possibility that the rebel's words held truth.

"You might be right," the scavenger leader conceded, his sneer softening into a thoughtful frown. "But what's to stop me from taking what I can get now? Resources are resources, and you're a valuable one."

Allen took a step forward, his hands still raised, showing he meant no harm. "We can offer more than just a temporary reward. We're fighting for something bigger, something that could benefit everyone, including your people. You've seen what Techno-Synth does, how they've turned this city into a prison."

The scavenger leader's eyes narrowed further, considering Allen's words. The city was indeed a cage, and survival was a daily struggle against both the elements and the oppressive forces that governed with an iron fist.

"We're trying to dismantle that prison," Allen continued, his voice gaining strength. "Join us, help us, and when this is over, there won't be any more bounties, no more living in the shadows. We can rebuild, together."

The leader looked around at his scavengers, some of whom had begun to whisper among themselves, the seeds of doubt and curiosity taking root. The city had taught them to seize opportunities, but it had also taught them the value of survival beyond the moment.

"You're asking a lot," the leader said, his voice a mix of skepticism and intrigue. "But what assurance do we have? Why should we trust your word over Blake's?"

"Because," Allen said, his voice dropping to a near whisper, "we're the ones who are fighting for freedom, not just for ourselves, but for everyone. Blake's system thrives on division, on keeping us all too scared to band together. We're the ones who are trying to change that."

The scavenger leader was silent, weighing the options. He knew the whispers of the rebels, their acts of defiance, their attempts to bring light to the darkness that had enveloped the city. But trust was a currency more valuable than any reward Techno-Synth could offer, and it was scarce.

"You say you can change things," the leader began, his voice carrying a hint of a challenge, "but words are cheap. What can you offer right now, today, to prove your intent?"

Allen looked to Mia, then to Cipher, the unspoken communication of a team in sync. Mia rose to her feet and stepped forward, her voice clear and unwavering. "We can offer you access to our networks, and our knowledge. We have technology, skills, and plans that could make your group a key player in the city's future. Not just survivors, but architects of what comes next."

There was a murmur among the scavengers. The idea of being more than mere survivors, of contributing to the city's rebirth, stirred something in them. They were not just looking for a meal or a safe night's rest; they were, like all the rebels, looking for a reason to fight, a promise of something better.

The scavenger leader paused, his eyes scanning the faces of his people, acknowledging the weight of the decision before them. "Well, what do y'all think?" he asked them, his voice carrying a distinct country twang, the kind that echoed through the hollowed-out streets of their forsaken city.

The response was immediate and resonant, a collective "Hooah" rising from the group, a sound akin to the disciplined affirmation of soldiers, a testament to their unity and readiness to follow their leader's choice.

With a nod, the leader's expression shifted from one of contemplation to resolve. "Alright, Allen Mercer. We'll join you, and we'll listen to what you got to say about this resistance. But remember," he said, his gaze piercing, "we're counting on you to steer us right. We don't take to being led astray kindly."

He signaled with a subtle tilt of his head, and the scavengers began to lower their weapons and turn off their lasers, the tension in the air dissipating like fog under the morning sun. The standoff had transformed into an alliance, however fragile, born from necessity and the shared dream of a future beyond survival.

Allen reached out to shake his hand, the final seal of the deal. "What's your name soldier?" he asked, keeping eye contact the whole time.

"They call me Boone," he replied, meeting Allen's eyes with an intensity that spoke of battles fought and resilience forged in fire. "Boone Caldwell. Used to be a captain in the army before everything went to hell. Now, I'm just a man trying to keep his people alive."

Their handshake was firm, a pact in the dim light of the old bank. Around them, the atmosphere shifted from one of tension to cautious camaraderie. The rebels began to stand, their movements slow but no longer fraught with the fear of immediate danger. The scavengers, sensing the change, also relaxed, hands off their weapons now at their sides, hanging from tactical slings.

One by one, the rebels and scavengers approached each other. Introductions were made, hands were shaken, and names exchanged. There was a certain reverence in the way the scavengers looked at Allen, not just as a wanted man but as a symbol of defiance against the regime that had turned their world upside down.

Similarly, the rebels observed Boone and his companions with a mix of curiosity and respect. Here was a group that had weathered the chaos with a different kind of strength, one born from scavenging and surviving in the shadows.

"Welcome to the resistance, Boone," Allen said as they broke their handshake. "We're glad to have you. And we'll need all the help we can get."

Mia, always the strategist, stepped forward, her eyes scanning Boone's group. "You've got a good setup with your group. We'll need to stay in touch. Here," she said, pulling a small, discreet device from her pack. It was a modified communication unit, one that had been used for the Shadow Web "Keep this. It's secure, and we'll be able to reach out when we need to."

Boone took the device, his eyes lingering on Mia's for a moment, recognizing her as a key player in this operation. "Much obliged," he said, pocketing the device. "We might not look like much, but we've got ears on the ground. You need anything, you let us know."

Cipher approached next, her expertise in technology and security making her an asset to anyone in this city. She offered Boone a nod, her voice low. "Stay alert. Techno-Synth's reach is long, and they're not above using anyone to get what they want."

Boone's nod was one of understanding. "Don't worry, we're used to staying out of sight."

As the final goodbyes were exchanged, there was a palpable sense of unity, a merging of paths that had previously run parallel but now intersected for a common cause. Allen looked around at the faces, both familiar and new, feeling the weight of leadership and the promise of a united front.

"Alright, everyone," Allen called out, his voice firm yet filled with a new vigor. "We move out. Stay sharp, stay quiet. We've got a hideout to reach."

The rebels gathered their belongings, checking their gear one last time before they began to move towards the grand entrance of the bank. The scavengers watched them go, a few offering silent gestures of good luck. Boone stood at the threshold; his silhouette framed by the moonlight.

As the rebels stepped into the night, the city seemed to hold its breath, the usual whispers of danger quieted by this unexpected alliance. They moved out in disciplined silence, their steps measured and cautious, aware that while they had friends, the city was still a place of predators and prey.

The journey to Cipher's hideout was dangerous, but it had to be done. They avoided the main thoroughfares, knowing that Techno-Synth's surveillance would be most intense in those areas. Instead, they used back alleys, abandoned parks, and underground passages that Cipher had mapped out years ago.

As they pressed on toward their destination, the silence was occasionally broken by the distant hum of a drone or the clank of a patrol unit. Each sound made them pause, their training kicking in, turning them into shadows within shadows. They had to be invisible, leaving no trace, making no sound, as they maneuvered closer to their new home.

The journey was a test of endurance, of knowing when to push forward and when to wait. They encountered a few close calls—a patrol that they managed to evade by hiding in the ruins of a subway station, and a lone civilian, an old man who had been living on his own, whom they helped to a safer part of the city, leaving him with supplies and a whisper of hope about the resistance.

Finally, as they reached the outskirts of the gardens, the rebels felt the tension begin to ease, though it never fully left. The old botanical gardens were a world unto themselves, a green haven amidst the concrete and steel. The once manicured paths were now overgrown with weeds and vines, nature's reclamation project in full swing.

They were close now, just on the edge of the city's relentless grip. With Cipher leading, they found the hidden entrance, a small, barely noticeable gap in the foliage that led to a series of underground tunnels.

As they descended into the subterranean sanctuary, a new chapter began for the rebels. The initial relief of having reached safety was palpable, but it was quickly tempered by the need for vigilance. This would be their new home, but it wasn't home yet. It needed to be secured, verified, and adapted for their needs.

The hidden entrance led to a narrow tunnel, the air cool and musty with the scent of earth and time. Cipher took point, her knowledge of the hideout's layout guiding them through the darkness, her flashlight casting long, dancing shadows on the walls. She briefed the team as they walked, her voice echoing softly in the confined space.

"We'll clear it in teams," she instructed. "We need to ensure there are no surprises. This place has been dormant for years, but you never know what—or who—might have sought refuge here before us."

Allen nodded in agreement, dividing the group into smaller, tactical units. "Move silently, communicate through hand signals. We need this place secure before we can rest."

The teams dispersed into the darkness of the tunnel, the silence broken only by the soft shuffling of feet and the occasional click of a safety being checked. As they emerged into the main area of the hideout, the space opened up before them.

The hideout was a marvel of ingenuity. It had been carved out beneath the botanical gardens, an old Cold War bunker repurposed by Cipher and her early FreeTech comrades. The ceiling was high enough to accommodate walkways above, with the main floor below. The walls were reinforced with metal, and the air was regulated by a series of vents cleverly hidden within the greenery of the garden above. Light filtered in through these vents, casting a greenish glow that mingled with the dim electric lights Cipher had set up in her time.

The rebels moved methodically. One team scoured the first floor, checking behind crates of old tech equipment, dormant servers, and makeshift workstations. Another team ascended to the upper walkways, their eyes scanning the shadows for any movement. The layout was both a labyrinth and a fortress, with multiple rooms branching off from the central chamber, each serving a different purpose—communication, armory, living quarters, and a small infirmary.

As they cleared room after room, the tension began to ease. The hideout seemed untouched since Cipher's last visit, a testament to its obscurity. However, it was in one of the back rooms, filled with old servers and computers, that they encountered their first signs of life since entering.

Two children, no more than twelve, were huddled over a console, their fingers flying over keys with a deftness that belied their age. They were young hackers, their faces illuminated by the screens, eyes wide with surprise and fear as they saw the armed rebels.

"Easy, easy," Mia said, stepping forward with her hands up to show they meant no harm. "We're not here to hurt you. We're with the resistance."

The children, initially poised to flee, hesitated. Their leader, a girl with dark hair and a sharp gaze, spoke up. "What do you want with our place?" she asked, her voice bold yet trembling.

Allen crouched down to their level, his voice gentle. "We need a safe place, just like you. We're fighting against Techno-Synth. We could use your help, and you could use ours."

The girl's eyes flickered to the others, assessing. "We've been using this place to hack into Techno-Synth's surveillance. We can see where their patrols are, when they move... But we're not soldiers."

Cipher stepped in; her interest piqued. "You've been doing more than just surviving. You've been actively resisting. We can offer protection, resources. In return, your skills could make a real difference for us."

With cautious nods, the children agreed to stay, their faces reflecting a mix of relief and newfound purpose.

The rebels then turned to the task of settling in. They began to dust off and claim spaces, setting up makeshift bunks, organizing the tech equipment, and establishing a command center. Allen and his core team huddled over a table, spreading out maps and beginning the planning phase.

"This place is more than we could've hoped for," Allen said, looking around at the high-tech equipment and the natural camouflage provided by the gardens above. "We'll need to fortify the entrance, set up early warning systems, and integrate our new allies."

Mia assigned tasks, her organizational skills coming to the forefront. "We'll need to check the power supply, make sure we can maintain our own without drawing attention. And we need to secure our own network, Cipher. No one gets in or out digitally without us knowing."

Cipher nodded, already pulling up schematics on a nearby screen. "I'll work on that. We'll also need to establish secure lines of communication, not just for us but for the entire network of resistance cells."

Knox was already moving crates, his voice echoing as he called out, "We'll stockpile supplies here. We're not just passing through; this is our ground now."

The atmosphere was one of cautious optimism as they worked. The hideout was more than just a place to hide; it was a fortress, a nerve center, a symbol of their resilience. With each piece of equipment powered up, each space claimed, the rebels felt the beginnings of a new phase in their struggle.

Above them, the city continued its vigilant watch, a world of surveillance and control. But here, in this underground haven, the rebels were laying the groundwork for something different— a place where freedom could be planned, where their resistance could grow stronger, where the seeds of Techno-Synth's downfall were indeed taking root, nurtured by the collective spirit of those determined to see a new dawn.

Chapter 20

Allen walked through what would be the nerve center of their operations, his boots echoing on the metal-grated floor. The room was expansive, with walls lined with dormant tech that hummed to life under Cipher's touch. He watched as Cipher, with her characteristic precision, began reconnecting power lines and booting up servers. Her fingers danced over keyboards, the screens flickering from darkness to a kaleidoscope of data, mapping out the city above—a digital mirror to the urban sprawl they had just escaped.

Nearby, Mia was coordinating the placement of supplies. "We need to prioritize the infirmary and the armory," she said to a group of rebels, her voice carrying the weight of authority. "Set up bunks in the back rooms. We might be safe here, but we need to be ready for anything."

Jonas, with his knack for tech improvisation, was already at work with a handful of others, rigging up makeshift beds from the crates and old cushions they'd brought along. He laughed softly, a sound that seemed out of place yet comforting in this environment. "Not exactly five-star accommodations, but it beats sleeping on concrete," he quipped, earning a few tired chuckles from his companions.

Knox, ever the strategist, was outside the room, overseeing the fortification of the entrance. He directed a few rebels in setting up a barricade with whatever heavy materials they could scavenge from the bunker's storage. "This isn't just a hideout anymore," he called out to no one in particular. "This is our stronghold now. We make it impenetrable."

As the rebels settled in, their individual stories and skills started to weave into the fabric of the base. A small group of younger rebels, adept at urban survival, began to explore the upper walkways, checking the ventilation systems and ensuring the natural camouflage of the garden above remained intact. Their youthful energy contrasted with the seasoned soldiers, but their eyes had the same glint of determination. Vines had crept through the ventilation, their leaves reaching towards the artificial light, creating a patchwork of greenery against the cold metal and concrete.

In a corner, a makeshift kitchen was coming to life. One of the rebels, a former chef before the fall, was organizing a stockpile of non-perishable food and setting up a cooking area with salvaged utensils. The scent of boiling soup filled the air as he prepared a hearty stew, the aroma of herbs and vegetables providing a comforting contrast to the usual tang of metal and dust that permeated the base. "If we're going to be here for any length of time," she said, "we'll need more than just rations."

The room with the old servers was now a hub of activity. Cipher had found her element, and she moved among the consoles with a sense of ownership. Xander, the clone, stood beside her, his presence both a marvel and an enigma. His face, a mirror of Allen's, was illuminated by the glow of the screens as he and Cipher interfaced with his AI core, trying to tap into its vast potential.

The air within the base was a mix of dust, the scent of earth from the gardens above, and the sharp tang of electronics. It was a scent Allen would come to associate with hope, with the promise of a fight yet to be won. He paused at the edge of the nerve center, taking in the sight of his people. They were tired, yes, but there was a resilience in their movements, an unspoken agreement that this was a new beginning.

In the midst of this organized chaos, two young voices rose above the others, filled with a mixture of excitement and curiosity. The children, now recognized as integral parts of this makeshift family, were named Eli and Zoe. Eli, the boy with a mop of unruly hair and a smudge of dirt across his cheek, was helping Mia with the inventory. His hands, small but dexterous, sorted through the medical supplies with surprising efficiency.

"See, this one's for antibiotics, and this," Eli said, holding up a dusty bottle, "is for pain. I've had to use it before."

Mia nodded, her respect for the young survivors growing. "You've done well, Eli. With your help, we'll have this infirmary up and running in no time."

Zoe, the girl with sharp eyes that had seen too much for her age, was setting up a makeshift communication station nearby. She had a natural talent for technology, her fingers moving over the keyboards with a grace that was natural. "I've been broadcasting our messages through old channels," she explained to Mia, her voice carrying the weight of experience. "They think they're listening in on old propaganda, but we're using it to our advantage."

Mia smiled, impressed. "Good thinking, Zoe. Keep at it. We'll need every whisper we can muster against Techno-Synth."

Zoe's face lit up with a brief smile, the kind that spoke of pride in her skills and a moment of innocence amidst their dire circumstances. "I'll make sure our voices are heard," she said, determination in her young voice.

Eli, overhearing, paused with a box of bandages in hand. "And I'll make sure we're ready to help anyone who needs it," he added, his resolve clear despite his youth.

Mia, watching the two children work, felt a surge of hope. These were the seeds of the future, resilient, and resourceful. As they continued their tasks, their presence was a reminder to all in the base of what they were fighting for—not just for themselves, but for those who would inherit the world after the storm. She caught Allen's gaze from across the room, his eyes fixed on Eli and Zoe with an intensity that made her heart skip.

Their eyes met, and for a moment, the noise of the base faded into a distant hum. Allen's look held a softness, a vulnerability she rarely saw, and it stirred something within her. She wondered about dreams deferred, and about a life where the future could be about more than just surviving the next day.

Allen, witnessing the interaction, felt his heart swell with pride and purpose. But as he held Mia's gaze, his thoughts ventured into uncharted territory. He imagined a world where peace wasn't just a distant hope, where he could lay down his arms. And in that world, Mia was close, not just as a comrade, but perhaps as something more. The air between them seemed charged with a quiet, unspoken question.

Mia turned back to the children, a small grin on her face, absorbing the brief moment with Allen, she sought to learn more about these two survivors. She approached Zoe, who was meticulously organizing the communication equipment. "Zoe,"

Mia began, her voice gentle, "where did you learn to handle all this tech?"

Zoe looked up, her eyes sharp and focused. "From my dad," she said, her voice steady but tinged with a sadness that spoke of loss. "He was a tech before... well, before everything changed. He taught me everything."

Mia felt a pang of empathy, recognizing the shadow of loss in the girl's eyes. "You're doing him proud, kiddo. Keep it up," she encouraged, her hand resting briefly on Zoe's shoulder.

Eli, who had been quietly working alongside them, chimed in, his voice carrying a weight beyond his years, "We've been on our own for a while now. Since they took Dad." He paused, his eyes downcast. "Mom didn't make it either. She got sick early on, when the clean water started disappearing."

Zoe continued, her voice softening, "They said Dad was a threat to their 'order'. They took him one night, just like that. We came here because it was the last place he talked about. He said if anything happened, we should hide here."

Mia listened, her heart aching for the children's plight, a story all too common in this broken city. "So, you've been here alone, just the two of you?"

Eli nodded. "Yeah. We've managed. Zoe's good with tech, and I've... I've learned to fix things, make traps, find food. We had to. There's no one else."

Zoe added, "We've seen what Techno-Synth does. They call it 'cleansing' when they take people away. But we know it's just... it's just making sure no one can fight back." Her small hands clenched into fists, a gesture of defiance far beyond her years.

Mia knelt down to be at eye level with them, her expression one of solidarity. "You've been through a lot, haven't you? More than anyone your age should."

Zoe and Eli's eyes met Mia's, unwavering as she continued. "You're not alone anymore. We're here now, and we're going to fight together. For your dad, for your mom, for everyone they have taken from us."

The children looked up at her, their expressions a mix of relief and newfound purpose. They were no longer just survivors; they were part of something larger now, a resistance that would not forget them or their story.

Allen, still observing from the sidelines, allowed himself a smile as he continued to watch the exchange between Mia and the children. The moment was a welcome change of pace and gave him feelings of hope, love, and a subtle attraction toward her, a reminder of what they were fighting for beyond the immediate struggle. As he looked at Zoe and Eli, their resilience and potential, he thought of the future they deserved, a future free from the shadows of Techno-Synth. These thoughts, these hopes, anchored him as he prepared to face the next phase of their battle.

Sam, with his usual disheveled hair and a data pad clutched in his hand, approached Allen. "Hey, boss," he said, his voice a mix of urgency and excitement. "You've got to see this. Cipher and Xander are making headway with the tech. It's... well, you need to see it for yourself."

Allen's attention shifted; the moment of hope replaced by the immediacy of their mission. He nodded, the weight of leadership descending once more. "Lead the way, Sam."

As they moved through the base, Sam filled him in, "They've tapped into something big. Xander's core is more than we thought."

The walk to the old server room was short, but every step reminded Allen of the stakes, the lives depending on their next move. His eyes found Xander, and a sense of unease settled in his stomach. He approached, his steps slow, memories and doubts swirling. "Xander," he began, his voice low, "how are you adjusting?"

Xander turned, his expression unreadable. "Adjusting? It's like feeling... half there, like part of me is still in the tank, while the rest is trying to figure out how to walk without the system telling me how."

The response was poignant, and Allen felt the weight of it. A shared history, a shared burden. He paused, considering his words carefully. "You'll get there, trust me. You're not just a soldier here, Xander. You're... you're part of us now. But I can see it's not easy."

Xander's eyes, so similar yet so foreign, met Allen's. "Ever since meeting you, I am a mirror with no reflection. I remember things I haven't experienced; I feel emotions I haven't earned. It's like being stuck in someone else's body."

The room paused, a beat of silence as if the air itself was taken aback by Xander's words. Allen, Cipher, and Sam exchanged a look, their expressions a mix of surprise and the sudden urge to laugh, though the situation was far from funny. It was the odd, almost human, self-awareness in Xander's voice that momentarily lightened the atmosphere.

Cipher stepped forward, her voice softening with a hint of a smile. "Well, you're not entirely wrong there, Xander. But we can work on making that body feel more like yours."

Xander looked at Cipher, his eyes lingering on her as if seeking an anchor in her calm. "And how do we do that? How do I become more than a set of directives and scattered memories?"

Sam, who had been quietly taking notes on his datapad, looked up, joining the conversation. "Integration, man. You've got to start making your own memories, your own choices. Maybe start small. What do you like? What makes you feel... human?"

Xander processed the question, his gaze drifting as if searching through data for an answer. "I... I don't know. I haven't had the chance to decide. Before, there was no choice, no decision-making. It was all pre-programmed."

Allen stepped closer; his tone gentle yet firm. "Then we'll give you those chances. Every day, you decide. You decide to fight with us, to live with us, to be with us. We'll show you what it means to be part of something bigger than yourself."

Cipher nodded, "And we can use your unique abilities to our advantage. Not just in battle, but in understanding, in learning. Your core can help us, but you can teach us too. About Techno-Synth, about resilience, about what it's like to be... you."

Sam added, "Yeah, and maybe you can teach us some tricks with your tech. We're all about learning here."

The conversation shifted subtly, no longer just about Xander's adjustment, but about his potential role within the rebellion. Xander seemed to consider this, his expression softening slightly.

"I want to contribute," he said, the first hint of personal intent in his voice. "To understand this rebellion, to understand myself. I want to help."

Allen placed a reassuring hand on Xander's shoulder, a physical connection to ground the clone in the moment. "We're here for you, just like you're here for us. Let's take it one step at a time, together."

Cipher's hands flew over the keyboard, pulling up new data on a screen. "Speaking of which, there's something here that might help us understand more about you, and how we can use your capabilities to hit Techno-Synth where it hurts."

She had accessed Xander's core, and now images and data were streaming across the screen—plans, surveillance, but also something more personal. A memory, one that Allen had thought was his alone, flashed up. The image was grainy, a moment captured from afar, but it was unmistakable—Blake, his gun raised, the child falling.

Allen's breath caught, his mind racing back to that day and the cold choice Blake had made. Now, seeing it through Xander's eyes, the horror was doubled, a shared trauma.

The room seemed to be still around him, the implications of this shared memory dawning on them all. Cipher, her eyes sharp with calculation, broke the silence. "These changes everything. If we can get this out there, it could shatter Blake's image. The public might start seeing Techno-Synth as the monsters they are, and not as saviors."

Allen nodded slowly, his look not leaving the screen. "We need a plan. A way to distribute this that can't be easily traced back to us. Maybe we use the Shadow Web, but we'll need a wide broadcast to really impact public perception."

Sam chimed in, his fingers already tapping on his data pad. "We could sync this with a public event, a moment where the city's attention is guaranteed. A power outage, a celebration, anything that brings people together. We drop this in the middle of it, and it goes viral."

Cipher's eyes gleamed with potential. "Yes, and if we can hack into the network that Techno-Synth uses for their propaganda, we could replace their feed with this. Make it so everyone sees it at the same time. Their own system will be their undoing."

Allen considered the idea, the strategic possibilities unfolding in his mind. "And we need to ensure it's not just seen, but also believed. We've got to prepare for their counterpropaganda. We'll need testimonies, other pieces of evidence. Make it undeniable."

Sam looked up from his data pad, his expression determined. "We can compile everything we've got on Blake's other atrocities. Cross-reference it with what we've heard from the outlanders, from survivors. Create a narrative that can't be dismissed as a one-off."

Cipher nodded, her fingers already moving over her keyboard, setting up the first encrypted layers to prepare for the digital assault. "We'll need to be ready to go dark immediately after. Techno-Synth won't take this lying down. They'll hunt for the source."

Allen's jaw set in resolve. "Then we make sure the source is untraceable. We're not just showing them Blake's face; we're showing them ours. We're telling the city who we are, what we stand for. We're turning their own fear tactics against them."

The plan was beginning to form, a risky but potentially game-changing maneuver. A plan this complex would require the attention of all the rebel leaders and rank and file soldiers alike.

"Alright," Allen said, his voice carrying the weight of command. "This is too big for just us. We need to bring this to the attention of the rest of the leaders. We'll reconvene tomorrow, discuss strategies, and begin to finalize our plan. Let's call it a night; we've earned some rest."

Everyone in the room nodded in agreement, the tension easing slightly at the prospect of a brief reprieve. As they began to disperse, each finding a place to unwind or set up for the night, Allen lingered, watching as the weight of their mission settled into a quieter hum of activity.

The new base, though still raw and unpolished, had a sense of life, of possibility. Allen moved through the space, the lights dimming as people settled into their makeshift beds. He found Mia in a quieter corner, away from the main command area, setting up her own bedroll. She looked up as he approached, a small, tired smile playing on her lips.

"Long day," she remarked, her voice soft.

Allen nodded, sitting down beside her. "But a good one. Zoe and Eli, they're... they remind us why we fight."

Mia's eyes softened, reflecting the dim light. "They do. They're incredible, really. I was thinking... about what a different world could look like for kids like them."

He watched her for a moment, the exhaustion in her features mixed with an enduring strength. "You've got a way with them," Allen said. "You give them hope."

"And you lead us all," Mia replied, her gaze meeting his. "Sometimes I wonder what it would be like, after all this... if there was an 'after'."

There was a silence between them, filled with unspoken dreams and the shared fatigue of warriors. Allen felt a pull, a magnetic force drawing him closer, and he reached out, his hand finding hers, their fingers intertwined with a familiarity born from countless shared battles.

"You mean, peace?" he murmured, his voice a whisper in the quiet of the base. "A life where we're not just surviving?"

Mia nodded, her thumb brushing against his hand. "Yes. Peace. And maybe... something more."

The word 'more' hung between them, charged with potential. Allen leaned in, drawn by the gravity of her words, her presence. Their lips met in a kiss that was both a promise and a question, gentle yet laced with the intensity of their situation. It was a moment stolen from the relentless march of war, a brief, tender defiance against the darkness they faced.

Then, from somewhere close, the sound of smothered giggles broke through the stillness. They pulled apart, turning towards the noise to see Zoe and Eli peeking from behind a stack of crates, their eyes wide with surprise and delight.

"Sorry!" Zoe whispered, her hand flying to cover her mouth, but her eyes twinkled with mischief.

Eli, unable to contain his laughter, let out a snort, which only made Zoe giggle more.

Mia and Allen shared a look, the moment of intimacy now tinged with humor. "Guess we're not as alone as we thought," Allen said with a chuckle.

"They're watching over us, it seems," Mia added, her voice warm. "Goodnight, you two."

"Goodnight," the children echoed, ducking back behind their hiding spot, their laughter fading as they disappeared.

The night settled around them, a fragile peace in a world of chaos. Allen and Mia arranged their beds side by side, not touching but close enough to share the warmth of companionship. They knew they had eyes on them.

The next morning, the base buzzed with a different kind of energy—anticipation mixed with resolve. The leaders gathered, their faces set with purpose, as Allen outlined the plan. The room was alive with the shared vision of not just surviving but striking back, reclaiming their narrative.

"This isn't just about Blake," Allen began, his voice steady. "It's about every person, every child, like Zoe and Eli, who deserves a better tomorrow. We expose the truth, and we show the city who their real enemy is."

Cipher, Sam, and the others detailed the technical aspects, how they would infiltrate and broadcast. The chatter was strategic and focused, each word a building block in their campaign against Blake's facade.

As the meeting concluded, there was a sense of unity, a collective breath held in anticipation. They had their initial plan, and now, they would need to refine it. The rebellion was about to take its most audacious step yet, turning the very tools of their oppressors against them.

Chapter 21

The core zones of the city glittered under the artificial light of Techno-Synth's controlled environment. Here, the air was crisp and clean, infused with the subtle scent of engineered flora and food, the buildings towered like crystalline shards reflecting the impeccable order of Techno-Synth's rule. The streets were pristine, the citizens dressed in the latest synthetic fabrics, their lives a far cry from the desolation beyond the core's protective barriers.

Tonight, the core of the city was alive with the buzz of a grand celebration. Techno-Synth was hosting an event to commemorate another year of their reign, a spectacle meant to reinforce their image as the great architects of a utopian society. The sights and sounds of the event were not only audible but very visible throughout every part of the city, even all the way from the botanical gardens on the edge of where the outer zones and the outlands met.

The streets were lined with holographic banners, and the sky was painted with laser lights that danced to the rhythm of a city-wide symphony, the music echoing from every corner and flowing through the air like a gentle current.

In the heart of this celebration, the Grand Plaza had been transformed into a stage for opulence. A massive stage stood at one end, where Commander Blake would soon address the crowd, his image projected across giant screens and projections that would make his presence felt even by those not in attendance. The plaza was filled with laughter, the clink of glasses, and the hum of conversation as the elite of the city mingled, their attire shimmering with embedded lights, their faces aglow with the drinks and the festivities.

Children ran through the crowd, their laughter unmarred by the harsh realities of the zones outside. They chased after drones that released confetti, their tiny hands grasping at the falling paper as if to catch moments of joy. The adults, meanwhile, indulged in culinary delights provided by automated kitchens, each dish a testament to Techno-Synth's technological prowess, where flavors and aromas were enhanced beyond natural limits.

The celebration was a showcase of Techno-Synth's achievements, with displays of new tech, interactive art installations that responded to touch, and virtual reality zones where one could experience the future the corporation promised. The event was meticulously crafted, every detail from the music to the lighting to the food, all designed to convey a sense of progress, of a world where every problem had been solved—or at least, that's what they wanted everyone to believe.

In the opulent corridors of Techno-Synth's executive suites, far removed from the public spectacle, the air was thick with the scent of luxury—expensive colognes, the finest leathers, and the subtle aroma of aged wines. Commander Jonathan Blake adjusted his ceremonial uniform, the fabric shimmering subtly with embedded nanotechnology that self-adjusted for comfort and appearance. He glanced around, feeling the weight of his role within the corporation, yet aware that here, in this circle, he was not the apex predator.

Dr. Leonard Harrow, the visionary founder of Techno-Synth, stood by the grand window, his gaze piercing through the glass to the celebration below. His presence was like the calm center of a storm, around which all else revolved. As Blake approached, Harrow turned, a slight nod acknowledging his presence, but his attention remained on the city, the ultimate chessboard of his design.

"Blake," Harrow began, his voice carrying the command of someone who rarely had to raise it.

"The rebels have been more tenacious than expected. Their recent successes..." He paused, his stare shifting from the window to Blake, his eyes sharp. "...are a blemish on our otherwise impeccable record."

Blake felt the scrutiny like a physical weight. "Yes, sir," he responded, his voice steady, "but we've contained the situation. The underground base they relied on is now nothing but a memory."

Harrow's face was inscrutable, but his next words were imbued with a steely edge. "Yet, it took too long. Your confidence in our superiority is commendable, but perhaps it has bred a complacency we cannot afford." His gaze flicked back to the city, as if assessing the broader implications of this evening's events.

Blake straightened; his response measured. "I assure you, Dr. Harrow, we are not complacent. The measures taken to dismantle their network were extensive. We've shown them the cost of defiance."

Harrow's eyes narrowed, a critical glint in his gaze. "Yet, Allen Mercer and our clone escaped. That, Commander, was not part of the plan."

Blake's jaw tightened, aware of his failure but unwilling to show weakness. "Yes, sir," he admitted, "an oversight on our part. But it was a calculated risk. We focused on severing their operational capabilities. The clone, we thought, would be disoriented without his core's full functionality. However, I underestimated Mercer's resolve."

Harrow's voice was cold and calculated. "Oversights are luxuries we cannot afford, Blake. They escaped, and now they wield a weapon against us. Ensure this does not happen again."

Blake's nod was stiff. "I will rectify this, sir. They won't undermine us for long."

Harrow didn't reply immediately, letting the silence underscore the gravity of the moment before continuing. "Tonight, we don't just quell fear; we cultivate awe. Remember, Blake, while you are the face of our might, I am the architect of our destiny."

A servant, almost invisible in his silent efficiency, offered a glass of wine to Blake. The commander accepted it, his mind racing through the evening's agenda. "And what of the narrative for tonight?" he asked, more to the room than to anyone in particular.

From the side, a figure dressed in a suit that seemed to shift colors with her mood approached. Helena Bristow, with her sharp eyes and sharper mind, had a presence that demanded attention. "We'll underscore our success in stabilizing the economy, our technological advancements, and the peace we've brought. The incident with the rebels will be framed as a necessary enforcement to maintain that peace."

As Helena spoke, her words carried the weight of policy, her role in global finance and corporate law evident in her every calculated statement. Marcus Chen, standing nearby, nodded in agreement. Once a government official, his transition to Techno-Synth's board was seamless, his international influence now serving a new master. "We've also prepared a segment on our humanitarian efforts, showcasing the Core Zones as the pinnacle of societal evolution. It will contrast sharply with the chaos beyond our influence."

The conversation was cut short by the entrance of Anika Patel, whose reputation in biotechnology and ethical AI preceded her. Her suit was a blend of science and fashion, sensors softly glowing at the seams. "Indeed, it's all about perspective," she interjected, her tone light yet loaded with significance. "And speaking of perspective, have you seen the latest security protocols for the event? We're not just showcasing our might; we're proving our invulnerability."

Blake felt the dynamics of power shift subtly as these key figures of Techno-Synth spoke. Here, his military prowess was just one of many tools. Helena's financial acumen, Marcus's political savvy, and Anika's technological foresight—they all played their parts in a symphony where Harrow was the conductor.

Dr. Harrow moved towards the balcony overlooking the Grand Plaza, his every step a reminder of his foundational role in this empire. "We should move," he said, his voice signaling the end of their private council. "Let's remind them who controls the future."

As the others made their way on to the balcony, marching in formation, knowing the crowd below was watching, the elite of Techno-Synth moved with an assuredness that spoke of their unchallenged power. They were not just participants in the celebration; they were the orchestrators of a world where their comfort was the norm, and everyone else's existence was a variable in their grand equation of control.

But beneath the revelry, there was an undercurrent of something else. Security drones patrolled overhead, their eyes scanning for the slightest hint of discord. The citizens, though seemingly carefree, wore their smiles like masks, their eyes occasionally darting to the omnipresent screens, waiting for Blake's speech, for the reaffirmation that their world was indeed the ideal one.

Blake, dressed in his ceremonial uniform, prepared to step onto the stage. The crowd hushed in anticipation, the music dimmed, and all eyes turned towards the leader who had promised them salvation from chaos. His image was perfection, the embodiment of Techno-Synth's vision, and he knew it.

As he began his speech, his voice boomed through the speakers, a testament to order and control. "Citizens of the core zones, we gather here not just to celebrate another year under Techno-Synth's guidance, but to look forward to the future we will build together—a future where..."

His words were cut off suddenly, as his mic went silent and the giant screens and projection in the sky flickered. A glitch, perhaps, the crowd thought, but then the image changed.

Instead of Blake's commanding presence, the screens displayed a scene that would shatter the illusion of peace:

A grainy video, a memory from the past, played out in stark contrast to the celebration. Blake, his face set in determination, raised his weapon. A child, no more than ten years old stood frozen, eyes wide with fear. The crowd gasped as the shot rang out, the child falling, the celebration's music cut off into a background of shocked silence.

The rebels had struck. Their smear campaign had found its perfect moment, and the population of the core zones, in all its splendor, was about to witness the truth they had so carefully hidden from.

But the video didn't end there. It lingered on Blake's face, his expression cold and unyielding, as he spoke to the camera, his words now echoing through the plaza. "Hesitation has no place here soldier," Blake growled. "Remember that."

A second, collective gasp rose from the crowd, the sudden realization of what their leader truly was beginning to set in. Their shock was visible, the illusion of their utopia cracking before their eyes.

On the balcony, the elites of Techno-Synth reacted with a mix of horror and disbelief. Dr. Harrow's face remained impassive, but his grip on the railing tightened, the only sign of his internal turmoil. Helena Bristow's color-shifting suit momentarily lost its luster, her eyes narrowing as she processed the implications. Marcus Chen, usually composed, took a step back, his diplomatic mask slipping. Anika Patel's sensors flickered, her breath catching as the narrative she helped craft unraveled in real-time.

Blake, on stage, stood frozen, his mouth slightly open as if to speak, but all that came out was silence. His image on the screens, once a symbol of strength, now played alongside the footage of his darkest act, the contrast stark and unforgiving.

The elites exchanged glances as they promptly stood up from their chairs, their expressions a mix of strategic calculation and personal shock as they waited for Dr. Harrows response. This was not just an attack on Blake; it was a strike at the very heart of Techno-Synth's image.

Dr. Harrow stood from his chair and leaned over the balcony edge, his presence imposing even from a distance. He caught Blake's attention from the stage below. With a subtle, yet unmistakable gesture, he waved for Blake to move now.

A loud screech echoed through the speakers, signaling the microphone was live again. The screens flickered back to life, showing Blake's image on stage, his uniform a stark reminder of the authority he wielded. The noise was like a cue, and Blake, still processing the shockwave of the video, stepped forward.

He cleared his throat, the sound amplified and echoing through the plaza. "Fellow citizens," he started, his voice now filled with an urgency to reclaim the narrative, "the images you've seen are distortions, manipulated by our enemies to sow discord. This is a ploy by the rebels—"

His words were cut off again as the microphone died once more, the screens flashing back to the haunting footage. This time, it showed a different memory, one that painted an even darker picture of Blake's command:

The scene was chaotic, an apartment building looming in the foreground, its windows flickering with the lives of those within.

Allen's squad was crouched, backs turned, hiding behind a rooftop wall that overlooked the building from 6 blocks away. Allens face was etched with conflict, his hand hovering over a detonator, his squad tense around him. Xander's memory camera captured the moment with chilling clarity.

Blake's voice was cold, commanding. "Mercer, do it. Now."

Allen hesitated, his eyes reflecting the moral turmoil within. But Blake, unyielding, stepped forward, his hand reaching for the detonator. Without a word, he pressed down on Allens hand, triggering the explosives.

The explosion ripped through the building, the structure crumbling in a cascade of fire and debris. Screams filled the air, the crowd in the plaza now echoing that horror, their cries of realization drowning out the city's previously vibrant feel.

Panic swept through the Grand Plaza. The celebration turned into chaos as citizens began to question not just Blake's actions but the very society they lived in. The holographic banners flickered, their messages of peace now a cruel irony as the truth of Techno-Synth's brutality was laid bare.

As the video concluded, the confetti drones, previously the source of joy for the children playing below, erupted in unison. A deluge of confetti showered down, marking a striking and ironic end to the rebels' attack, transforming the celebration into a scene of confusion and chaos.

***

From atop the botanical gardens, the rebels watched as their plan came to fruition. Allen, sitting next to Mia, nudged her with his shoulder. "See I told you I belong here."

Mia was quick to punch Allen in the shoulder softly, "Oh really, well, I remember that day, when you were so nervous to meet Roth and the other outlanders at that first camp," She smiled. "And the way Roth saved us from those two scavengers after we left the next day."

Her words hung in the air for a moment, the mention of Roth's name stirred Allens soul. "Roth was one of the best men I've ever met," Allen paused briefly, "I mean it," he paused again before continuing. "Mia, if it wasn't for you and Knox...Roth...Cipher, Jonas, Sam and all the others...I wouldn't be here right now."

"Allen, if it wasn't for you," Mia started, "none of us would be here right now. It's a two-way street, you know." Rising to her feet, she grabbed Allen's chin, lightly pinching it between her thumb and fingers, making him look her in the eyes before letting go as she walked away, maintaining eye contact over her shoulder.

The other rebels perched on the edge of the botanical gardens, watched as their plan unraveled the carefully crafted illusion of Techno-Synth's control. The skyline flickered with the signs of their success, a visual testament to the chaos they had sown. With their mission accomplished for the night, a sense of victory and relief washed over them.

Allen stood, feeling the weight of the day lift slightly from his shoulders. "Let's head back," he said, his voice carrying a mix of exhaustion and satisfaction. "We've earned a night to breathe and celebrate."

The group made their way back inside the botanical gardens, descending through the hidden entrance that led to their new base. The transition was swift, from the cool night air to the warm, earthy scent of their underground sanctuary. The rebels were immediately greeted with the comforting aroma of food being prepared—real food, not the synthetic kind they'd grown accustomed to. In a corner, their chef, a man adept with salvaged utensils and non-perishable goods, was at work, his face glowing with pride as he seasoned a simmering pot of stew with herbs that were rare luxuries in their world.

Allen, Mia, Cipher, and a few others gathered in a small circle, with Xander among them. He sat with a curious tilt to his head, observing the humans around him with an intensity that was both analytical and, in its own way, human.

Knox, with his weathered face marked by countless battles, approached the group, a broad grin spreading across his features. "Thought this might be the right time for something special," he declared, pulling an old, dusty bottle from under his jacket. The label was faded, but the shape of the bottle was unmistakable. "Found this in an old liquor store ages ago. Been saving it for a night like this."

He uncorked the bottle with a pop that drew everyone's attention. The scent of aged whiskey filled the air, mingling with the aroma of the stew. Allen's eyes widened at the sight. "You've been holding out on us, Knox?"

"Only for the right moment," Knox replied, pouring a couple of glasses. The amber liquid caught the light, a promise of warmth and celebration.

As the glasses were passed around, their eyes turned to Xander. "What about you, clone? Ever had whiskey?" Knox asked, a twinkle of mischief in his eye.

242

Xander looked at the glass with a mix of fascination and skepticism. "I've experienced... data on alcohol consumption," he said, his tone always a bit too formal. "But I have not ingested any."

Cipher chuckled. "Well, there's a first time for everything. Live a little, Xander."

Xander took the glass, his movements precise. He sniffed it, his expression unchanging. "It smells... potent," he observed.

"Cheers to that!" Jonas said, raising his glass. The clink of glassware sounded like bells of freedom in the underground space. All eyes were on Xander as he tentatively brought the whiskey to his lips.

The first sip was a shock. Xander's face contorted in a way that was almost comical, his eyes going wide, then narrowing as if trying to process the sensation. "This is... not what I anticipated," he said, coughing slightly. "It burns."

Knox laughed heartily, clapping Xander on the back. "That's the spirit! Or rather, that's the lack of spirit, in your case."

Allen couldn't help but join in the laughter, the tension of the day melting away with each chuckle. "Give him a moment, everyone's first taste is like that," he said, passing Xander a piece of bread. "Here, this will help."

Xander took a bite, his features slowly returning to their usual composed state. "I believe I understand now why humans partake in this ritual," he said, his voice thoughtful. "It's not just about the taste."

Mia, her smile wide, nodded. "It's about the moment. Sharing something like this... it's about connection, about being alive."

The conversation flowed as freely as the whiskey. Stories of past missions, of narrow escapes, and of the people they'd lost were shared. Each memory was like a thread weaving the group closer together, binding them in their shared cause.

Cipher, usually so guarded, shared a tale of her early days, how she'd hacked into a Techno-Synth facility for the thrill of it, not knowing then that it would lead her here, to this rebellion. Jonas spoke of the friends he'd made, the ones who didn't make it to this celebration. Even Xander, the clone, began to open up, sharing a memory that felt like his own, though he knew it was Allen's—a memory of battle, of sacrifice, and of a choice that shaped them both.

The night deepened, the laughter and stories becoming the soundtrack to their victory, however temporary it might be. The whiskey bottle, now half-empty, stood as a testament to their unity, their resilience, and their defiance. And as they drank, as they laughed, they fortified not just their spirits but their resolve to continue the fight, to ensure that nights like this would become more frequent, a norm in a world that was trying to relearn what freedom truly meant.

Amidst the laughter, Eli, the young boy with a mop of unruly hair, approached with curiosity lighting up his eyes. "Can I try some too?" he asked, his voice a mix of excitement and innocence.

Knox, with a playful grin, glanced at Allen before nodding. "Sure, kid. You earned it. Here, have a taste." He passed his glass to Eli, who took it with both hands, his face serious, as if taking on a great responsibility.

Eli brought the glass to his lips, took a tentative sip, and then his expression changed drastically. His eyes watered, his nose wrinkled, and he spat it out with a loud, "Yuck!"

The group erupted into laughter, the sound echoing through the base. Knox chuckled, taking back his glass. "That's why we start you with soda, Eli."

As the food began to be served and the laughter died down, the night grew still, Allen felt a chill, a reminder of the shadows that lingered just beyond their sanctuary. He looked up, meeting Mia's gaze, seeing in her eyes the same unspoken question that haunted him: what would Blake's response be? The night's victory was theirs, but the war was far from over.

Chapter 22

As the confetti rained down over the Grand Plaza, Commander Blake, realizing his microphone was not coming back on and the gravity of what had just taken place, stormed off the stage. His ceremonial uniform, once a symbol of pride, now felt like a shroud weighing him down as he moved with purpose through the backstage area.

Blake's boots echoed on the polished concrete as he scurried through the area. The air was laden with the sharp tang of electronics, and the floor was a maze of cables. Technicians, surrounded by flickering screens, scrambled to regain control, their faces a mix of concentration and panic.

His mind was racing, each step a reminder of his screw up. He approached an industrial elevator, its doors sliding open at his approach. Inside, the mirrored walls reflected his scowl, the only sound was the soft whir of the elevator ascending. Each floor that passed felt like a countdown to judgment.

The elevator dinged, signaling his arrival. The doors parted, revealing Major Vale, his posture rigid, eyes scanning the hallway for any sign of onlookers. Vale's uniform was immaculate, but his expression was one of barely contained anger.

"Blake," he hissed as Blake stepped out, "this is a disaster."

Blake's response was sharp, his voice low but intense. "You don't think I fucking know that, Vale?"

"That's not what I'm saying, sir," Vale corrected himself, keeping his tone professional. "Dr. Harrow and the others want to meet right now in the conference room."

They started walking, their steps quickening as they made their way down the corridor. The walls here were adorned with abstract art, a silent mockery of the chaos below. "I told you we needed tighter security on those feeds," Blake whispered, his voice a controlled fury.

Vale's retort was swift. "And I advised we should have been more aggressive in hunting down Mercer and that clone. They've turned our own tech against us!"

Blake's eyes narrowed; his frustration evident. "I expect more from you, Vale. We can't afford to second-guess now. I'll take the heat from the executives, but you better have a plan to fix this mess."

Vale's jaw clenched, his ambition to deflect some blame warring with his duty to serve. "Yes, sir. I'll work on countermeasures immediately."

They reached the imposing double doors of the executive conference room. Blake straightened his uniform, his expression hardening. "Wait here, Vale. I'll handle the board."

Vale nodded, stepping back as Blake pushed open the doors alone, entering the lion's den. Vale remained outside, his ear pressed subtly against the door, trying to catch any snippets of the impending storm within.

The conference room was a study in corporate power. The long, polished table shone under the harsh fluorescent lights, and the walls were lined with screens displaying various data streams and security feeds, now looping the very footage that had brought them here. The executives, each seated around the table, wore expressions ranging from icy disapproval to outright fury.

Dr. Harrow sat at the head of the table, his face a mask of controlled rage. "Commander Blake," he began, his voice cutting through the silence like a blade, "you were tasked with ensuring the integrity of this event. Instead, we've witnessed an embarrassment on a scale I hardly thought possible."

Blake stood at the opposite end, his posture rigid, his voice equally hard. "I understand the severity, sir. The rebels have proven more resourceful than anticipated. However, I—"

"Don't give us excuses," Helena Bristow interjected, her suit now a dull gray, reflecting her mood. "The damage is done. Our image has been tarnished, our security compromised."

Marcus Chen leaned forward; his words measured but cutting. "We trusted you with the military operations, Blake. This breach undermines not just you, but all of us."

Blake's hand clenched, but he kept his voice even. "I accept responsibility, but—"

"But what, Blake?" Anika Patel's sensors flickered with her agitation. "Your assurances mean little when our network is hacked, and our leader is shown as a child murderer on every screen in the city."

The air was thick with tension. Dr. Harrow's gaze was like ice. "You have one last chance, Commander. One chance to quell this insurrection, to restore order, or I will find someone who can."

The ultimatum was a blow, but Blake's pride wouldn't allow him to back down easily. "Dr. Harrow, with all due respect," he nearly growled, "you will never find someone as capable as I am for this role. I've built this security apparatus, and I'll be damned if—"

His voice rose, echoing off the glass walls. "I'll be damned if I let some rebels, some shadow of a resistance, dictate our fate!"

The room was silent, the gravity of his outburst hanging in the air. Blake took a deep breath, his eyes scanning the faces before him, seeing not just anger but the cold calculation of corporate governance.

"Fine," he said, his tone now resigned but firm. "You will have your way. The rebels will be stopped." With that, he turned, the door slamming behind him with a finality that resonated in the room.

***

The morning light filtered through the ventilation shafts of the rebel base, the warmth a stark contrast to the cool air. Groans mixed with the clatter of breakfast preparation as the rebels roused themselves, some nursing the aftereffects of Knox's whiskey. Allen sat up from his cot, rubbing his eyes, a smile creeping onto his face as he remembered the night's triumph.

Knox, looking surprisingly spry, was already at the makeshift kitchen, ladling out a hearty stew that smelled of victory. "Nothing like a good fight to work up an appetite," he chuckled, offering a bowl to Allen, who took it with a nod.

Xander approached, his movements now possessing a certain fluidity, a sign of his ongoing adaptation to human life. "I have reviewed the data from our attack," he began, his voice still holding that mechanical edge. "There are patterns in Techno-Synth's response time. We can exploit these."

Mia joined them, her hair tied back in a practical ponytail. "So, the clone's got some tactical insights? That's our morning wake-up call," she said, her smirk hinting at the day's potential. "Let's get to work."

Over the next two weeks, a series of events unfolded that would mark a turning point in the rebellion. The rebels began launching more aggressive strikes. They moved with the precision of a well-oiled machine. The plan was set: hit Techno-Synth where ever they left an opening, their supply lines, strategic patrols, news feeds or any other opportunity.

Allen, Mia, and a small team, including Zoe and Eli, made their way through an alleyway towards a Techno-Synth supply depot on the edge of the industrial district. The sky was just beginning to lighten, casting an eerie glow over the city's skeletal remains.

Eli, with his knack for mechanics, disabled a security drone with a homemade EMP device, his small hands deft and sure. Zoe, her tech skills surpassing her years, hacked into the depot's inventory system. "Rerouting now," she whispered, her fingers flying over the keys. The shipments would find their way into rebel hands, disrupting Techno-Synth's logistics.

Allen watched from a distance through binoculars as smoke began to rise from a controlled fire, a diversion their team had set. "That should confuse them for a while," he muttered. They weren't just fighting; they were outsmarting their enemy at every turn.

Emboldened by this success, they knew they needed to keep pushing. In a secret meeting with Boone and his scavenger group, Allen handed over a device. "We need your eyes and ears on the ground," he explained. "There's a patrol tonight we plan to ambush."

Boone nodded, his eyes glinting with the thrill of the hunt. "My folks are ready. We'll make 'em think twice about patrolling our streets."

That night, the scavengers' distraction was perfect. While they engaged the Techno-Synth patrol, making a show of attempting to rob their transport, Allen's team moved in from behind. The scuffle was brief but efficient, leaving the rebels with a captured vehicle and its valuable cargo.

The momentum was building. At an abandoned broadcasting station, Mia, Cipher, and Xander worked tirelessly. Cipher's fingers danced over the keyboard; her face lit by the screens. "We're in," she announced with a triumphant grin.

Xander, connected via his core, began broadcasting. His voice, now modulated to sound more human, echoed across the city's screens, telling tales of their victories, exposing Techno-Synth's lies. Citizens paused, some in shock, others whispering among themselves. The narrative was shifting.

With each success, the rebels felt the tide turning. Allen led a squad to a fortified checkpoint, a chokepoint for Techno-Synth's control. With Boone's intel, they knew the patrol schedule like the back of their hand. As the sun set, they lay in wait, the shadows of their allies.

The ambush was swift; explosions from improvised devices threw the checkpoint into chaos. In the confusion, they took down the guards, capturing vital equipment. It was another statement: no place was safe for Techno-Synth.

Word spread, and with it came hope. A rally was called, but not just any rally; this was to be a beacon of rebellion, a gathering of all who yearned for change. The planning was meticulous, every detail considered for both safety and impact.

"The location needs to be symbolic," Mia said as they gathered around a makeshift table with maps of the outer zones. "Somewhere that represents the heart of the resistance."

Knox pointed to an old industrial park; its vast open space surrounded by the ruins of factories. "Here. It's central, accessible, and it's got history. This was where the first public protests against Techno-Synth happened."

Zoe, with her knack for communication, was already on it. "I can broadcast through the old channels, the ones no one uses anymore. We can reach every corner of the city," she said, her fingers tapping away at a keyboard. "And we'll make sure it's untraceable."

Allen nodded in agreement. "Do it. Let's show them we're not just hiding in the shadows anymore."

As the day of the rally approached, Boone and his scavengers scouted the perimeter, setting up makeshift barricades using whatever materials they could find from the decay around them. They synchronized with rebel soldiers, creating a secure perimeter. "No one gets in or out without us knowing," Boone declared, his confidence bolstered by the recent wins.

The rally setup was a community effort. Makeshift stages were constructed from old crates and metal plating, speakers were rigged using salvaged electronics, and lighting was provided by a mix of gas lamps and jury-rigged solar panels. The air was electric with anticipation, the citizens of the outer zones arriving in droves, their faces marked by a mixture of hope and defiance.

Allen stood on the stage, the crowd before him a sea of faces. The atmosphere was far from the sterile, controlled environment of Blake's celebration; this was raw, this was real. Mia and Knox flanked him, each a pillar of the rebellion's newfound strength.

He raised his hands, and the crowd fell into a hush, the only sound the distant hum of the city. "Citizens of the outer zones, of the forgotten lands, of the shadows," Allen began, his voice amplified and echoing across the space. "Tonight, we stand not just to resist, but to declare that we are here, we are organized, and we are not afraid."

Cheers erupted, a sound so genuine it seemed to cleanse the air of the oppression that had lingered for too long. Allen continued, "We have struck at their supply lines, their checkpoints, and now, their lies. We've shown them that we are not just survivors; we are the future they tried to erase!"

The crowd roared in approval, their voices a chorus of rebellion. Banners were held high, some with the simple message of 'Freedom,' others with the faces of those lost in the fight against Techno-Synth.

Mia stepped forward, her voice clear and strong. "Each one of you here represents hope, the hope that we can reclaim our lives, our city, and our future. We are not alone. Look around you. This is our strength."

Knox took his turn, his presence commanding. "We've prepared for this moment. We've planned for it. And now, we execute. Techno-Synth underestimated the spirit of the people. They won't make that mistake again."

As Knox stepped back, Allen's expression grew serious. "There's something else you need to see, something Techno-

Synth has been up to. Some might find this a little shocking, but we felt it was something that needed to be brought to the forefront of this fight."

He paused for effect, then gestured to the side of the stage. "Everyone, meet Xander."

A figure stepped into the light, and gasps rippled through the crowd. Xander, with a face identical to Allen's, stood tall, his presence both a shock and a testament to Techno-Synth's reach. The crowd murmured, their surprise palpable, but as they looked from Allen to Xander, curiosity overtook fear.

Xander, adapting to the moment, spoke, his voice still holding that mechanical edge, but now with an undercurrent of something more human. "I was created to serve them, but I've chosen to stand with you. We are more than what they made us. We are the change."

The crowd's initial shock transformed into a mix of awe and acceptance. Here was living proof of Techno-Synth's hubris, and here was their defiance personified. The rally, already charged, now felt like a turning point not just in their struggle, but in the very identity of their cause.

"Thank you, Xander," Allen said as he ushered Xander back off the stage with a gentle hand on his shoulder. The crowd watched as the clone, a mirror of their leader, stepped into the shadows, his impact lingering like the echo of his last words.

Coming back to the makeshift microphone, Allen continued, his voice now infused with a new intensity, bolstered by the dramatic reveal. "As you can see, Techno-Synth's grasp extends beyond control and surveillance. They play with life, with our very essence, to maintain their power. But what you've witnessed here," he gestured to where Xander had stood, "is the beginning of their end. Xander is not just a creation; he's a symbol. A symbol of the choices we can all make. To resist, to change, to fight."

The crowd hung on his words, a collective breath held in anticipation. "We are not merely reacting to their oppression anymore. We are the catalysts for our own liberation. We've disrupted their supplies, we've reclaimed their checkpoints, and now, we've brought their secrets into the light."

Allen's gaze swept over the sea of faces, seeing the resolve in their eyes. "But this is more than about us. It's about the children, like Zoe and Eli," he gestured toward the front row where they were standing. "Who deserve a future where they can grow up without fear. It's about the families torn apart by corporate cruelty, the lives lost, and the freedom we've all been denied."

He paused, allowing the weight of his words to settle. "We must remember that every bit of ground we gain, every victory we claim, is for them. For all those who can't stand here with us today. Like Roth and Lena and many others. We fight not just for survival, but for a world where we can live, not just exist."

The crowd cheered, a resonant sound that seemed to vibrate through the ground, a physical manifestation of their collective will. Allen raised his hand for silence, his next words calculated for impact. "They've tried to erase us, to control us, to make us forget who we are. But each one of you here tonight is a reminder, a defiance against their narrative. We will not be forgotten. We will not be controlled."

He looked back at his comrades, nodding to each in turn, their solidarity unspoken but felt by all. Turning back to the crowd, he concluded, "Go back to your homes, your neighborhoods, not with fear, but with fire. Spread the word, prepare for the next steps. We will continue to strike at their heart until their heart stops beating tyranny. This is our city, our world, and we will take it back, inch by inch, if we must."

As the speeches concluded, music started, a rebellious anthem played through the makeshift PA system. People danced, shared food, and for a moment, the fear was forgotten. The rally was more than a celebration of recent victories; it was a declaration of intent, a promise of more to come, and a reminder that the rebellion was not just a fight, but a movement.

Chapter 23

The sun had set hours ago, and the artificial lights of the rebel base cast long shadows against the walls as Allen stood alone on the rooftop. Below him, the city was a tapestry of darkness and intermittent light, where the glow from Techno-Synth's core zones met the shadows of the outer zones. Here, on this rooftop, the separation of their world was as clear as the stars obscured by the smog.

Allen took one last deep breath of the night air, letting the weight of their recent victories settle into him. They had struck back, hard, but the war was far from won. With a resolve that had grown with every skirmish, he descended the metal stairs, their echo a familiar song of purpose.

Inside, the atmosphere was charged with the hum of technology and the low murmur of voices. The nerve center of their operations was a hive of activity. Screens flickered, casting blue and green light across the faces of those gathered. Knox hunched over a digital map, his fingers tracing lines on the touch-sensitive screen that depicted the city's layout. Mia was beside him, her eyes scanning data feeds, while Cipher, with her characteristic intensity, was tapping away at her console, interfacing with their network of spies and informants.

"We need to discuss the next move," Allen began, his voice cutting through the soft murmurs of the room. "The command center building. It's not just another target; it's our chance to establish a real foothold."

Knox looked up, his finger pausing on the map. "I've been thinking the same. It's the heart of their operations in this sector. Taking it would give us access to their comms, their data, everything."

Mia stepped forward, her presence commanding attention. "More than that, it's psychological. We take the command center, we're not just rebels; we're liberators. It will galvanize the city, bring more to our cause."

"But it won't be easy," Cipher added without looking up, her voice steady. "Their security there is tight, and it's one of their most fortified positions."

Allen nodded, his mind already piecing together the puzzle of their next assault. "We'll need more than just our usual tactics. Knox, your scouting mission?"

Knox pulled up an image on the screen, highlighting an area with a series of buildings in various states of decay. "I've been looking at the terrain around the command center. These buildings here," he gestured, "they're structural hazards. We can use them."

"You mean collapse them?" Mia asked, her tactical mind immediately seeing the advantage.

"More like strategic collapse," Knox corrected. "We can create a barrier with the debris. This will turn the command center into our stronghold, using the downed buildings as defensive barriers. It will channel any counterattack into kill zones, or at least slow them down long enough for us to fortify our position."

Allen's thoughts drifted to Boone and his scavengers. "We need Boone for this," he said decisively. "He and his crew know the city's underbelly better than anyone. They can help us navigate and use the terrain to our advantage."

Mia agreed, "We'll need their expertise to make this work without casualties. I'll contact him."

As she stepped away to make the call, Allen moved to stand beside Knox. "How do we ensure this doesn't come back to haunt us? If those buildings fall the wrong way..."

Knox's face was grim, but his voice carried a hint of excitement. "We've mapped it out. We'll place charges at precise points. It's risky, but with Boone's help, we can minimize the unpredictability."

The room fell into a strategic silence as they contemplated the gravity of their plan. This wasn't just another raid; it was a declaration. They would turn the city itself into their shield.

Mia returned, her expression one of determination. "Boone is in! He says they can get past the security to help us set up without being detected."

Cipher tapped away, bringing up schematics of the command center. "I can loop their surveillance, create blind spots. But we'll need a distraction, something to draw their forces away."

Allen nodded, his plan solidifying. "We'll hit a peripheral target, something they can't ignore. When they pull forces from the command center to respond, we move in. Once we're set, we initiate the collapse to create defensive walls around our new base; when they attempt to return, we'll control the choke points."

The room buzzed with the energy of a plan coming together, each member of the team contributing their skills to weave a strategy that could tip the scales in their favor. They would turn the crumbled remains of their city into a fortress of their own making, a symbol of their resilience and defiance.

As the night deepened, the rebels prepared for the operation. Plans were drawn, routes calculated, and contingencies set. With each moment, the command center seemed less like an insurmountable fortress and more like the first step in reclaiming their world.

Knox led the small team through the city, their steps silent on the damp concrete. The air here was thick with the musty smell of decay and the faint tang of rust. Jonas was at his side, his expertise in engineering and explosives invaluable for what they were about to do. A few other rebels, known for their agility and knowledge of the city's shadows, completed the group.

They rendezvoused with Boone and his scavengers in what used to be a bustling marketplace, now just a skeleton of corroded metal and faded signs. Boone was a silhouette against the dim glow of a scavenged lamp, his eyes sharp and assessing.

"Evening," Boone greeted, his voice low but carrying. As they gathered around a rusty table, he continued, "I lost my family to Techno-Synth's 'cleansing' operations. Me and my crew, we've been scraping by in the shadows ever since, hitting them where it hurts whenever we can. This time, it's personal. We're all in because we want a future where no one else loses what we did. You've got the plans?"

Knox nodded, his eyes reflecting understanding. 'I get it, Boone. That's why this plan has to work. We'll place the charges here, here, and here,' he said, pointing at the junctions on the blueprint spread across the old table where the buildings could be brought down with the most strategic impact.

Jonas spoke up, his fingers tracing the path of the explosives on the map. "These buildings," he gestured to a trio of structures, "are the key. They'll fall in a way to create a natural funnel, like a cul-de-sac. We'll turn their approach into a death trap."

Boone's people, a mix of young and old, men and women, leaned in, their faces illuminated by the faint light. One of Boone's lieutenants, a woman with scars that spoke of a life on the edge, pointed to a spot on the map. "There's an old maintenance shaft here. We can use it to get close to the primary target without exposure."

"Good," Knox acknowledged. "We'll need to be quick and precise. Each charge has to go off at the exact moment."

The discussion continued, plans refined with every input from Boone's team, who knew every alley and hidden passage like the lines on their own hands. The strategy was set to create a debris maze, a labyrinth around the command center, which would serve as their new stronghold, making it difficult for Techno-Synth to launch a direct assault.

Back at the botanical garden's base, the atmosphere was one of focused preparation. The nerve center was alive with activity. Jonas, now back from the recon, had set up a workshop area where the explosives were being assembled. The room was filled with the sharp scent of chemicals and the soft clink of metal on metal. He worked with a precision that hid the danger of his task, his team around him equally meticulous.

"Each device needs to be timed to the second," Jonas instructed, his voice calm amidst the chaos. "We'll use this remote trigger to synchronize them. It's our only shot at creating a cohesive barrier."

Meanwhile, in the main strategy room, Allen, Mia, and Cipher were huddled around a different set of screens. "We need something big enough to draw their attention," Mia proposed, her eyes flicking between various feed points. "The industrial sector, perhaps? They've got a reactor facility there they're paranoid about."

Cipher nodded, her fingers flying over the keyboard. "I can simulate a power surge; make it look like something's gone wrong. It'll panic them into thinking there's a sabotage attempt."

Allen agreed, "It's perfect. It's far enough to pull resources but not so far that their response will be too slow to affect the command center."

As the strategic elements fell into place, the room was a dance of planning and preparation. The fake target would be a decoy, the true strike was the command center. Every detail was cross-checked, every contingency considered.

Outside in the night, Boone and his group moved like shadows through the city. They were a silent force, each step measured, each breath controlled. The city around was oblivious to the rebellion stirring beneath its feet. Boone's lieutenant, her eyes sharp in the darkness, led her team to the maintenance shaft they had discussed.

"There," she whispered, pointing to a grate covered in grime. Within minutes, they had it open, slipping into the bowels of the city. They moved with an efficiency born from survival, placing charges at the designated points around the command center, their actions an intricate ballet of timing and placement.

In the distance, the command center building loomed, a fortress of control. But here, among the forgotten arteries of the city, the rebels were the masters, navigating the urban landscape to encircle their target.

They worked through the night, the city unaware of the strategic changes being made to the landscape around the command center. Each explosive, each wire, was a thread in the fabric of their plan. As dawn threatened to break, they emerged from the tunnels, their work done. The explosives were set, the trap was laid, and now all that was left was to wait for the signal.

Back at the base, Jonas meticulously checked the timing mechanisms and triggers for the devices, his team weary but satisfied. 'We're set,' he reported to Allen, his voice a mix of exhaustion and adrenaline.

Allen looked at his team, their faces a mix of determination and fatigue. "Get some rest," he instructed. "Tomorrow, we change the city."

The day was approaching, and with it, the moment when the rebels would make their stand. The command center, once a symbol of Techno-Synth's unchecked power, would soon become the stage for their most daring act of defiance. The city, unbeknownst to its inhabitants, was about to witness the birth of a new era, one where the rebels would no longer cower but claim their place in the light.

As dawn broke over the city, casting a pale light over the skeletal remains of its former glory, the rebels moved into position. The air was electric with the tension of impending action. Allen, Mia, and Knox were at the heart of the operation, each leading their part of this multi-pronged assault.

263

Allen stood at the edge of the botanical gardens, his heart pounding not with fear but with the adrenaline of leadership. "Comm check," he spoke into the comm, his voice steady.

"Check," came the replies from various points across the city, including Jonas, who was with the team tasked with demolishing the key structures, and Cipher, who was orchestrating the digital deception from the nerve center in the botanical gardens base.

Mia was at the controls sitting next to her, her eyes darting between screens as she coordinated the diversion. She glanced at Cipher, who was already deep into the Techno-Synth network. "Prepare the surge," Mia instructed, her voice calm but firm.

Cipher nodded. "Initiating now," she confirmed. Her screen showed a graphic of the reactor facility in the industrial sector. "We've got about five minutes before their systems flag the anomaly."

Meanwhile, Knox and Boone were with the team at the command center building's perimeter. "Everyone in position?" Knox whispered into his comm.

"Locked in," came the murmurs from the shadows, each rebel a ghost in the dawn.

Jonas, with a small group, was in an abandoned building overlooking the command center. He checked the remote triggers one last time. "We're ready to bring down the curtain," he said, his voice barely a whisper, the weight of his task evident.

The decoy operation kicked off first. In the industrial sector, a few rebels, under the cover of night, had placed small, non-lethal devices near the reactor facility. With Cipher's manipulation, the devices began to emit signals mimicking a catastrophic power surge. Techno-Synth's alarms blared; the ruse was working.

At the command center building, Boone's crew watched as the first wave of Techno-Synth security forces began to peel away, heading towards the supposed emergency at the reactor facility. "They're buying it," Boone reported, his voice carrying a mix of relief and urgency.

Allen, seeing the movement on his digital map, gave the signal. "Team Alpha, move in. Team Bravo, prepare for detonation, Charlie Team and Delta Team set up the perimeter."

The attack on the command center began with stealth. A small squad, led by Allen, infiltrated through a side entrance, their movements silent, their weapons at the ready. Inside, the corridors were a maze of technology and control, but for now, the guards were thin, pulled away by the decoy.

Knox and his team, along with Boone's scavengers, flanked the building. They were the waiting storm, poised to strike when the real assault began. "Hold until further notice," Knox reminded his team, his voice a calm in the storm.

Outside, the city was still waking up, oblivious to the rebellion unfolding in its midst. But within moments, the rebels' presence would be undeniable.

The first shots rang out inside the command center, the silence shattered by the clatter of automatic weapons. Allen's team moved with precision, clearing room after room, their training and resolve evident in every action. They were the spearhead, driving deep into the heart of the enemy.

As they swept through the first corridor, Allen's squad encountered not only Techno-Synth soldiers but also civilians from the core zones, workers caught in the crossfire of conflict. The sight of these non-combatants in lab coats and office attire was unexpected; they were not part of the plan.

"Hold fire!" Allen barked, his voice cutting through the chaos. His team adjusted quickly, switching from lethal to non-lethal tactics. They used stun guns and zip ties to secure the civilians, guiding them into a corner of the room where they could be safely managed.

The civilians, a mix of tech workers, administrative staff, and researchers, reacted with a blend of fear and confusion. Some raised their hands instinctively, while others dropped to the floor, their eyes wide with terror. One woman, her badge identifying her as a data analyst, whispered to her colleague, "This is it, isn't it? The rebellion we've heard about?"

Allen, seeing the civilians' reactions, quickly revised his strategy. "We're not here for you," he said, addressing the group. "Stay calm, stay quiet, and you'll be safe. We're changing this city, not destroying it."

His words seemed to bring a flicker of relief to some faces, though the shock was still evident. Allen signaled for his team to keep moving, ensuring that each civilian was accounted for, secured, and moved to a makeshift holding area where they could be monitored.

"We need to control this space without causing panic," Allen whispered in the comms to his team. "Let's secure the command room first; we'll deal with the civilians once we've got the place locked down."

Allen led his team down the corridor, the tension in the air thick as they approached the command room, the nerve center of Techno-Synth's operations in this sector. He knew what awaited them—likely a room full of soldiers ready to defend their most valuable asset.

Just before they reached the door, Allen spoke into his comm. "Knox, give Jonas the green light. We're hitting the command room now and we need to create some confusion."

Outside, Knox, with his binoculars trained on the shifting patterns of Techno-Synth forces at the reactor facility, acknowledged the order. "Copy that, relaying message now." He could see the enemy beginning to realize the decoy was just that—a distraction. "Jonas, it's time," he said, his voice low but carrying the weight of their future. "They're starting to turn back, and Allen is in position to take the command room. We need that barrier now."

Jonas, feeling the moment's gravity, pressed the trigger. The city seemed to hold its breath for a second before the ground shook with the force of the explosives. Buildings around the command center crumbled, not in chaos but with the calculated precision of their plan. Dust and debris rose into the air, creating a makeshift wall of destruction, a barrier that would serve as their defense.

From the outside, it was a spectacle of controlled chaos. The buildings fell in sequence, their debris interlocking like pieces of a puzzle, forming a labyrinthine barrier. The sound of collapsing structures was a roar, but to the rebels, it was the sound of their newfound stronghold being born.

Boone, watching the dust cloud rise, couldn't help but smile grimly. "It worked," he muttered, his voice a mix of awe and satisfaction. The scavenger knew the streets better than anyone, and now, those streets had been reshaped to their advantage.

As the dust began to settle, Techno-Synth forces, realizing the ruse, started to redirect their troops back to the command center. But the rebels were ready. The debris barrier was more than just physical; it was psychological, a testament to their ingenuity and defiance.

Inside, Allen and his team had breached the control room. The explosions outside provided the perfect cover, confusing the troops inside, helping to throw them off guard as dust and debris shook the very foundations of the building. Allen's team moved with lethal efficiency; their movements synchronized to the chaos. They cleared the room swiftly, the enemy soldiers disoriented by the thunderous collapse around them, giving Allen's rebels a significant tactical advantage. With the room secured, they turned their focus to the mainframe.

With Cipher guiding them through encrypted channels, they began to take over the systems, turning Techno-Synth's own technology against them. "Securing the mainframe now," Allen reported, his voice calm despite the chaos. The screens flickered from Techno-Synth's logo to the symbol of the rebellion, a moment of symbolic victory.

Outside, the battle had begun in earnest. Techno-Synth's soldiers, now facing the unexpected fortress, were forced into choke points, where Knox's team and Boone's scavengers rained down fire from cover. Every shot was a statement, every explosion a declaration of war.

But the rebels weren't without losses. The first casualties came as Techno-Synth forces used their superior numbers and technology to push back, deploying a few swarms of drones overhead. These weren't just for surveillance; they were part of a tactical move, aiming to scout for breaches in the rebel's new stronghold and potentially execute precision strikes on any exposed positions.

Allen, hearing the increasing gunfire outside, knew they had to consolidate their position. "We need to hold this ground Mia," he said over the comms, his voice now edged with the urgency of battle. "Get Xander to take down those swarms. We can't let them find any weak spots."

With Cipher's help connecting him into the network, Xander, using his AI core, began his counterattack. "I'm in their systems, initiating the disruption protocol," he reported, his voice surprisingly calm for the intensity of the moment. Through his core, he sent out a series of commands that confused the drones' AI, causing them to lose their formation and crash into one another or veer off unpredictably.

As the last drone fell from the sky, a chilling silence settled over the battlefield, the chaos momentarily ceased. The rebels, breathing hard, surveyed the destruction they had wrought and the new fortress they'd claimed. But this moment was not one of peace; it was the eerie calm before an unspeakable storm.

In that moment of quiet, the realization hit them: they had accomplished a major feat today, but keeping this stronghold might prove even harder than taking it. The silence was not victory; it was a prelude to a war that would test every ounce of their resolve. As the ground trembled under the weight of what was to come, they knew this was just the beginning.

The End.

Turn the page for a Glimpse into the Shadows:

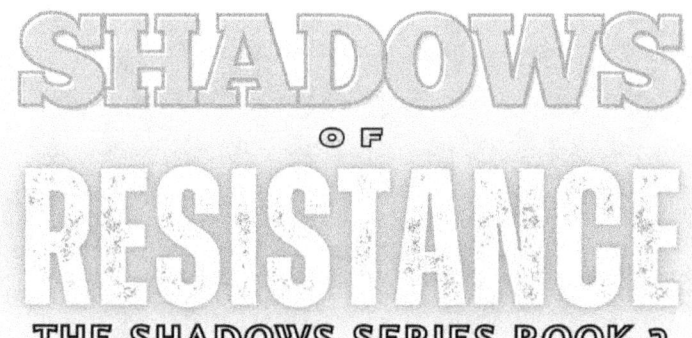

THE SHADOWS SERIES BOOK 2

John D. Clay

John D. Clay Books

The Fall

The screen flashes to life with the logo of Techno-Synth spinning into view, its motto displayed in bold beneath: "One System. One Future." A triumphant musical score swells as the broadcast begins.

The anchor, impeccably dressed and radiating calm authority, smiles at the camera. Her voice is crisp and unwavering.

"Good evening, citizens. Tonight, our unity faces its greatest test. Reports are flooding in of attacks on our nation, disrupting critical infrastructure. While these events may seem alarming, rest assured—Techno-Synth is already taking decisive action to restore order and protect your way of life."

The screen cuts to footage of drones hovering over burning buildings, their mechanical precision extinguishing fires and scanning fleeing citizens. A calm, synthesized voice narrates:

"Techno-Synth security units are actively neutralizing threats and assisting evacuation efforts. Please remain indoors and comply with all safety protocols."

The broadcast continues with a montage of soldiers in pristine uniforms, standing in formation as the Techno-Synth emblem glows on their helmets. Overlaid text reads: "Unity Through Strength. Trust Through Technology."

The anchor's smile falters slightly as she presses a hand to her earpiece, then continues:

"We have just received word that the President will address the nation momentarily. In the meantime, let's hear from

Techno-Synth's Chief of Operations, Dr. Leonard Harrow, on how we're combating this unprecedented crisis."

The screen splits, revealing Harrow in a sharp suit, his expression serene despite the chaos in the footage behind him.

"This is a tragic day for us all," Harrow begins, his voice calm and measured. "But tragedy need not become defeat. Techno-Synth has deployed security teams, surveillance cameras, and patrol drones to ensure swift and efficient resolution. We urge all citizens to trust our systems and avoid misinformation that may incite panic."

A banner flashes at the bottom of the screen: "Would you like to know more?" As the screen changes it reveals statistics about Techno-Synth's success rate in suppressing uprisings and their recent advancements in public safety technology.

The broadcast abruptly shifts to a government chamber. The President, pale and visibly shaken, stands behind a podium emblazoned with the government seal. His voice trembles as he begins:

"Citizens, these are dark times. Our enemies have exploited our freedoms, bringing devastation to our very doorstep. Considering this unprecedented threat, I am granting Techno-Synth full executive authority to secure our country."

The feed cuts to a live poll appearing on the screen, showing public support for Techno-Synth climbing rapidly as citizens vote in real-time: "Do you trust Techno-Synth to protect us? Yes – 97%, No – 3%."

The anchor returns, her voice tinged with hope:

"A bold but necessary decision. Together, under Techno-Synth's guidance, we will overcome these challenges and emerge stronger than ever. For now, remember: Compliance ensures safety. Your obedience is your strength.

As the broadcast ends, a propaganda ad begins to play. Families are shown smiling in clean, Techno-Synth-managed communities, their children laughing as drones deliver packages. The tagline flashes across the screen:

"Techno-Synth: Building a Better Future, One Citizen at a Time."

With a sudden shift, shaky footage from a resistance fighter's hidden camera captures rows of citizens being loaded onto transport shuttles under the watchful eyes of Techno-Synth security drones and soldiers. A desperate whisper narrates:

"This isn't protection. It's a takeover."

The screen goes black.

Excerpt:

Chapter 1

The sun had barely crested the horizon when Allen stepped through the gleaming glass doors of the Techno-Synth headquarters, the building a testament to the organization's promise of a safer, more controlled future.

His heart thrummed with a mix of pride and nervous anticipation. Despite the chill in the air, his resolve was warming him from the inside out.

As he entered, Sergeant Blake, the recruitment officer and a couple of years Allen's senior, was there to greet him with a firm handshake.

His uniform was crisp, the Techno-Synth logo on his chest gleaming under the artificial lights. "Glad you made it, Allen," Blake said, his voice steady and sure. "Let's get you sworn in."

They walked through the expansive lobby, its walls adorned with digital displays showcasing Techno-Synth's achievements.

Blake led Allen through a set of grand, arching doors into the Hall of Induction, a colossal chamber that seemed to stretch into the heavens. The ceiling was a dome of glass, through which the morning light cascaded, bathing the room in an ethereal glow.

The walls were lined with banners of the Techno-Synth emblem, and the floor was a mosaic of circuitry patterns, symbolizing the interconnectedness of their mission.

At the far end of the hall stood a stage, elevated and grand, where Dr. Harrow, the CEO of Techno-Synth, awaited. His presence was almost palpable, his silhouette framed by the brightness of the screens behind him, broadcasting his image to every corner of the room.

Hundreds of recruits filled the hall, their faces a mix of excitement and solemnity. The air was thick with anticipation as Dr. Harrow began to speak, his voice amplified to resonate through the vast space.

"Today," he declared, "you pledge not just your service, but your commitment to a vision of peace and order. Raise your right hand and repeat after me..."

"I, state your name, do solemnly swear," Dr. Harrow began, his voice clear and commanding, "to uphold the principles of peace, security, and unity, as set forth by Techno-Synth."

The recruits, including Allen, repeated in unison, their voices merging into a powerful chorus. "I, Allen, do solemnly swear to uphold the principles of peace, security, and unity, as set forth by Techno-Synth."

"To serve with integrity, to protect the citizens under our care, and to advance the technologies that secure our future," the recruits echoed, their commitment resonating through the hall.

"To stand against chaos, to embrace order, and to pledge my loyalty to the ideals of Techno-Synth, for as long as I am able," Allen and the others declared, their voices filled with conviction.

As the last words of the oath faded, Dr. Harrow spoke again, his expression one of pride and determination.

"You are now part of something greater than yourselves. Together, we will forge a path to a world where freedom is maintained through vigilance and innovation. Welcome to Techno-Synth."

The hall erupted in cheers, the sound echoing off the glass dome above, mingling with the light, as if the very building vibrated with the energy of the new recruits.

Allen felt a surge of pride, the weight of his oath grounding him even as the excitement of the moment lifted him. They were now united, not just as individuals, but as guardians of a new era.

The Shadows Series Book 2 Coming in 2025

Visit www.johndclay.com to learn more about The Shadows Series

Please leave your review on Amazon.

Thank you for your support

MAPS

City Structure – Core Zones and Outer Zones:

The urban landscape is meticulously divided into core zones and outer zones, each serving distinct functions and governed by varying degrees of Techno-Synth oversight. The central zones, also known as Core Zones, are the heart of Techno-Synth's power, shimmering with technological advancements and serving as the hub for corporate activities. These zones are heavily guarded and feature elite residential areas, high-tech offices, and lush, artificial environments designed to symbolize prosperity and control.

In contrast, the outer zones, or Peripheral Zones, are the densely populated areas where the majority of the populace resides. These regions suffer from neglect and are characterized by dilapidated infrastructure, rampant pollution, and minimal access to advanced technology. Surveillance here is aggressive, with drones and cameras monitoring every corner, enforcing Techno-Synth's policies harshly to quell any signs of dissent. Life in these outer zones is tough, with residents facing harsh labor conditions, limited resources, and frequent raids by corporate security forces.

The Outlands and Rebel Camps:

Beyond the structured chaos of the city's outer zones lie the Outlands — vast, unregulated territories that have become a refuge for those fleeing Techno-Synth's grip. The Outlands are wild and untamed, marked by ruins of the old world and makeshift settlements. It is here that the Outlanders, a formidable group of rebels, have established their camps. These camps are often hidden, built into natural caves or camouflaged under the remnants of destroyed structures to avoid detection by satellite and drone surveillance.

The Outlanders' camp is a stark contrast to both the opulence of the Core Zones and the oppression of the Outer Zones. It is a testament to resilience and resourcefulness, featuring salvaged and repurposed technology to create a sustainable living environment. Community and solidarity are the pillars of the Outlands, where diverse groups of people — those cast out or escaped from the inner zones — unite with a common goal of resistance. Their lifestyle is a blend of old-world skills and new-world technologies, adapting to the harsh realities of their environment while nurturing a vibrant culture of resistance through shared stories, songs, and hopes of liberation.

Description of the Outlander Community:

In the heart of the Outlands stands the community of the Outlanders, a rugged assembly of survivors who have turned adversity into opportunity. Led by the charismatic Knox, this community is a patchwork of scavenged shelters and reclaimed spaces, illustrating human resilience and defiance against

282

dystopian control. The Outlanders' outpost, built from the remnants of the old world, buzzes with activity and cooperation, embodying a spirit of independence and survival. The community thrives on resourcefulness, crafting a life from the ruins and forming a stark opposition to the sterile, controlled existence under Techno-Synth.

Cultural and Social Dynamics:

The Outlanders have cultivated not only a physical but also a cultural refuge. Here, the echoes of the old world mingle with the realities of the new, creating a unique culture steeped in stories of survival and resistance. The landscape, dotted with relics of the past, serves as a constant reminder of what was lost and what could be regained. This area, with its defiant community and wild surroundings, stands as a beacon of hope and a testament to the enduring human spirit.

Visit www.johndclay.com to learn more about The Shadows Series

www.ingramcontent.com/pod-product-compliance
Lightning Source LLC
Chambersburg PA
CBHW071546110726
47908CB00007B/2012